CORPSE IN THE COOKERY
(A Glory Girls Mystery)

by

Susan Spencer-Smith

For information, email **Cozy Cat Press**,
cozycatpress@aol.com or visit our website at:
www.cozycatpress.com

COZY CAT
P R E S S

ISBN: 978-1-939816-71-9

Printed in the United States of America

Cover design by Paula Ellenberger
http://www.paulaellenberger.com/

1 2 3 4 5 6 7 8 9 10

This book is for Edith Stealey Smith and her daughters, granddaughters and great-granddaughters.

Glory Girls Rule No. 1—A member of the Glory Girls service organization of Glory Hallelujah Church, Biddlebourne, West Virginia, must be a woman more than forty (40) years of age on January 1 of the year in which membership begins. *Glory Girls Book of Bylaws,* adopted May 1958, amended May 1976

THURSDAY, JUNE 14

CHAPTER ONE

Death gave Gudrun Wince a serenity unknown to her in life.

Her eyes and knees were closed. Mercifully, so was her mouth.

If her murder hadn't been so messy, most of Biddlebourne would have thanked God for it.

Matter of fact, Buddy Lee Delbert blasphemed when he stumbled on the body and got blood and broccoli on his steel-toed boots. So roundly did he swear that the eight surviving contestants looked up from their measuring.

The mess on Buddy Lee's brogans, which cost a week's wages for a job that lasted two months, reminded him of the oozing crimson patch on his privates and backside. The rash had appeared after a midnight romp with Lizzie Etta Edge in a pine glade lined with poison ivy. He had not regretted that day until now.

While Buddy Lee puked his breakfast grits into a colander and scratched his behind, the Glory Girls of Glory Hallelujah Church strode to Cooking Audition Station Nine, at which Gudrun Wince, desirous herself of becoming a Glory Girl, had lately been mixing Mammy's Marvelous Biscuit Casserole.

Those who remained in the contest murmured in mock concern, for they dared not approach the place where Gudrun lay or voice their unanimous hope that the field of competitors for the single Glory Girls opening had just decreased by one.

To their credit, however, neither did the women mention Gudrun's chronic sin of having proclaimed herself the uncrowned queen of culinary arts in Biddlebourne, West Virginia.

Edith Fay Smith, the wisest, but at forty-five far from the oldest of the Glory Girls, arrived last at Station Nine, her highlighted blond hair unmussed, her steps firm but quiet and her visage calm behind rimless spectacles. She wore a white apron, starched and pristine, over slim dark jeans and a pearly gray blouse. A fresh yellow rosebud sprang from a tiny silver reservoir pinned to her collar.

She faced Buddy Lee, put a hand on his shoulder and said, "Talk to me, young man."

All movement ceased in the kitchen of Glory Hallelujah Church. No one adjusted a burner, rinsed a spoon, shook seasoning into a pan or stole a glance at another contestant's ingredients.

Buddy Lee, a scrawny twenty-something with big ears and a wannabe beard who had cried for seven solid days when his pet rabbit Winky died, replied, "Oh, geez, oh, geez, oh, geez."

Edith Fay patted his shoulder and waited. The ten other Glory Girls and eight other Glory Girl hopefuls waited, each rooted to the floor like an early tomato plant to spring tillage. Even the building bided its time as the kitchen's three-ton air conditioner cycled off.

Buddy Lee hawked a final glob of vomit onto the floor and tried to grab Edith Fay's apron for a wipe rag. But she whipped a dish towel from her waistband and transferred it to his shoulder. With her other hand, she guided Buddy Lee to the chair beside the worktable where Gudrun had been assigned.

Edith Fay turned to the body of Gudrun Wince. All eyes widened as she knelt and touched Gudrun's neck and then her wrist—careful not to make contact with the white slacks and bloodied orange pullover that hugged the dead woman's gaunt form.

Then the top Glory Girl slowly straightened to her full five feet ten inches and surveyed the body, the congealing blood, the spilled food and the busted crockery.

She looked straight ahead at no one in particular and shook her head. Once. After a minor eternity she spoke.

"Gone."

The assemblage took a collective breath. Loosed a concerted babble. Until Edith Fay raised a hand.

"Jo Claire."

"Yes." Jo Claire Carsey, vice president of Biddle Banking & Trust Company, stepped forward, stylish in black-rimmed eyeglasses and a charcoal gray linen pantsuit protected by a smock bought at Zabar's in New York City.

"Please go tell Pastor Annie what happened. She'll be at the mayor's office. Interrupt her if you have to, but tell her I'm sorry.

Say that I need to meet her in my office—no, make that her office—in half an hour. At one o'clock."

The women remained silent, but with great difficulty and only because Edith Fay's hand was still raised.

Each contestant had met a rigorous, unbendable, sweat-inducing and soul-searching set of standards just to become a candidate for the Glory Girls. To speak out of turn now would be tantamount to disrobing in a front pew on Sunday morning.

Edith Fay lowered her hand and used it to extract a cell phone from a hidden pocket. Everyone waited for permission to speak or leave.

But Edith Fay had more instructions. "Alwildia Louise and Fonda Renee, don't let anyone come within twenty feet of the body. Ladies, please do not move anything in this kitchen. This is a crime scene."

"I find that I cannot agree," said Mayor Jass Pinbiddie.

His Honor pecked the desk five times with his right forefinger, an action that always silenced the Biddlebourne Town Council but which, unfathomably, made no impression on the Reverend Annie Ido Scovill.

Could it be? Yes, the preacher woman was still talking. Still berating him and his little suggestion. Still waving her arms. Still rapping her notebook with that darned blue pencil. Still pointing out the window, perhaps at the needy masses aided by those busybodies at Glory Hallelujah Church.

Jasper Eugene Pinbiddie, a mountain of man at six-five and 320 pounds, swigged Mountain Dew. He groaned. He stopped tapping the desk and began tapping his watch. The timepiece seemed frozen at 12:36 p.m.

He looked out to see what had so excited the preacher woman. But the only movement on the square came from a family of five picnicking in the shade of the old stone courthouse.

But wait. What was in that yellow box? He squinted. Yes, the family was busy with a Big Papa container of juicy, spicy pork ribs from the Mug, where Jass himself should be this very minute, fortifying his body for the pleasure of his woman.

Annie Scovill observed Jass' clockwatching but did not desist from her discourse. The town council, pressured behind the scenes by Mayor Pinbiddie, proposed to levy a "restaurant tax" on the church for every meal served at its many fundraisers. The notion was preposterous, of course, but the mayor had a way of pushing preposterous notions past Biddlebourne's compliant council and complacent citizenry.

"Cannot agree? You cannot agree!?" she bawled. Jass could see the veins in her throat. "One public dinner," she went on, "just one public dinner—let's say a Thursday night chicken barbecue—generates enough funds to sponsor a youth baseball team for an entire summer."

"That may or may not be so," Mayor Jass Pinbiddie returned. "But the town budget benefits everyone, young and old, boys and girls, men and women."

Jass had paid dearly for that comment, written by an underpaid English instructor at Skyler County Community College whom Jass secretly employed. Annie Scovill had heard it the first time Jass uttered it on Memorial Day.

No matter what Jass said, it was a fact that the Biddlebourne budget benefited whomever the town council chose—as prompted, paid or pushed by Jass Pinbiddie. And those beneficiaries did not include all the people living in or near poverty, who numbered nearly one-third of the populace.

Annie knew this because many Biddlebourne special interest groups, whose members were forced to talk with their pastor upon attending worship at Christmas or Easter, grew fat from Pinbiddie amendments, as Jass' "little suggestions" were known.

Jass rechecked the time and smiled. He had a date in one hour and twenty-three minutes with his hot little Cassie, his willing and uninhibited Cassie. He was happy enough with the prospect to ignore his rumbling stomach.

"If you disagree with me, Jasper, why do you decline to appear with me before Judge Lincoln so that we may obtain a court ruling on the legality of your, your unique attempt to charge a tax on food served at a church, which is a nonprofit, nontaxable entity?"

Annie's voice rose toward the end of her challenge, and she clenched her hands as if she wished to strangle Jass.

The mayor mused. *Did the preacher woman never eat? How had her edges become so nicely rounded if she never ate?* Jass marveled at the irony of it.

The problem was that if he did not have lunch before meeting Cassie, he might lack the strength to please her. And he would not waste their precious time together trying to scrimp a meal from her puny pantry.

"So you will appear before the judge then?" the preacher woman coaxed.

Mayor Pinbiddie licked his lips and adjusted his shirtsleeves. Sweat squirmed down his wide back, but he did not scratch in front of Pastor Annie Ido Scovill. The church had the upper hand as it was.

"My dear girl," the mayor said, "surely you—and all the good folks at the great Glory Hallelujah Church—would support the town that has built that very church, that has, why, that has seen it grow from a little bitty building to a magnificent structure that this town must now help secure and protect."

"Again, Jasper, please do not call me *girl*. And, again, I remind you that no public funds were used in the construction of Glory Hallelujah Church. And, indeed, the church is magnificent, but not because of the building. The church is so because its members are committed to God's work."

The big chrome clock over the door, which only Jasper could see, ticked with maddening languor.

Tick. Tick. Tick. Tick. Tick. One hour and twenty-two minutes to go.

"But surely you realize that some of those members let their water and sanitation bills go in favor of paying their church pledges," the mayor rejoined.

"You do not know that for a fact," the pastor said, "and it is beside the major point in this case anyway." Annie tugged the hem of her blue suit skirt, remembering that she needed to lose fifteen pounds.

"That major point being?"

Pastor Annie slumped in the chair. Circular discourse exhausted her. "The point being that Glory Hallelujah Church is, by law, a nonprofit and tax-exempt religious organization. By law, Jasper, by law."

An hour and twenty-one minutes now until Cassie. They would meet at her place, a particularly risky choice that excited him even before he climbed into a side window and crept upstairs to the bedroom.

"Oh, what did you say, Reverend Scovill? I was pondering tonight's council session and missed a word or two of your learned comments."

Maybe Cassie would wear the silky red panties and bra with the black lace that outlined her sweet breasts. Though Jass wore his usual work clothes, a faded sport shirt and baggy overalls secured by stained suspenders, he had taken the trouble that morning to change his own underwear.

"Really, Mayor, neither of us has time to repeat ourselves endlessly while. . ." Two knocks sounded at the door and it creaked open. Jo Claire Carsey stood in the opening, breathless and rubbing the knuckles of her right hand.

"Good afternoon, Mayor. Please excuse the interruption. Pastor Annie, there has been an incident at the church," Jo Claire said. "Edith Fay apologizes for breaking into your meeting but asks that you come at once."

"What kind of incident?" Mayor Pinbiddie demanded.

Jo Claire shot Annie a look of fierce urgency. The pastor scooped up her materials and stepped to the door.

"What's going on over there at that church?" Jass yawped.

Pastor Annie turned. "Jasper, this is not over. I assure you that the church will not back down on the tax issue. My own 'little suggestion' is that you reconsider the legality—and the morality—of what you have proposed."

But the mayor wasn't listening to the preacher woman. He had already wiped his palms on his shirt and had begun to punch in the phone number of Gudrun Cassandra Wince, his little Cassie. Maybe she could get away early.

There being no official men's group in Biddlebourne, its members met routinely at the American Legion Hall for the purpose, they told their wives and girlfriends, of allotting donations to charity.

Stuck in the midsummer blahs and all having jobs with limited time off, the men were relaxing in the storeroom behind the bar, beers in hand, when Arnie Coker said, "All in favor of sending a hundred to the Flight 93 Memorial?"

"Righteous, Dude," said Bucky Feinmeister. Several others added their assent by belching.

"Opposed?" The question was pure formality. "Motion passed. Old business?"

"We goin' fishin' on the Fourth o' July or not?" It was Creed Fedderman, who arranged his work around the comings and goings of muskies in Biddle Island Creek.

A few of the men, including one firefighter who set off the town fireworks and three guys who took their grandkids to see the fireworks, mentioned those obligations. Melvin Bishop wanted to go but said, "I've took a backset from that flu and better not be leavin' the terlit."

However, Bucky, Rymer Neff and Harley Baker, figuring they could remember "four on the Fourth," agreed to meet Creed in the parking lot of Larry's Drinkin' Depot at 4 a.m. on Independence Day to get supplies before heading to the kudzu blind where Rymer kept his drift boat.

"New business," said Arnie. "And hurry up 'cause I gotta cover for Bert."

"Ain't any," said Bucky. "Ain't nothin' happenin' in this backwater town. What'd Bert go and do?"

"Stayed out all night. Sleepin' it off."

The men nodded and lifted their longnecks to a fallen comrade, then subsided into wistful silence recalling their own tomcatting days.

The hush was so solemn that Arnie nearly dropped his Bud when his cell phone blatted the opening bars of *Leave That Junk Alone*.

"Deputy Coker."

He lifted his feet off a keg of Old Milwaukee and stood. "Yeah," he said. "Sounds like she's a goner."

The backroom boys perked up. Maybe the day held some promise after all.

Glory Girls Rule No. 2—Membership in the Glory Girls service organization of Glory Hallelujah Church, Biddlebourne, West Virginia, shall not exceed twelve (12) women, each of publicly proven and excellent character and competence. *Glory Girls Book of Bylaws,* adopted May 1958, amended May 1976

CHAPTER TWO

Outrage flowed from the contestants like water from Biddle Island Creek in April.

Who'd had the gall to kill Gudrun Wince? In the church kitchen? Under their noses? While important food was being fixed? And when the woman who made the best food would become the next Glory Girl?

Naturally, they did not ask *why* someone would kill the woman. *Good* Gudrun had educated half the kids in Biddlebourne, but *bad* Gudrun had been a schemer whose morals and manners could singe the wings off an angel.

Three cook-off entrants sat in folding chairs calming their nerves with Xanax or chamomile tea. Four others whispered among themselves near Oven No. 1.

But the eighth contestant, Eulalah Bee Pritchard, crowded near Edith Fay Smith and peppered her with questions. "What will happen to the other entries? Could the remaining contestants continue? Could Miss Wince's entry still be judged? Might someone take her place in the contest?"

Edith Fay, just off the phone with the sheriff, listened as long as she could to Eulalah Bee, then raised her voice, only a little.

"Ladies."

The contestants jumped to attention as if General Patton had come to lunch. The Glory Girls remained in a loose group near the east windows where they could see what went on in front of the church.

Edith Fay placed both hands on a shining countertop and peered at each woman in turn.

"Ladies, I deeply regret that today's cook-off is hereby postponed due to the untimely death of Ms. Gudrun Wince, principal of Biddlebourne High School, longtime community leader and recent candidate for membership in the Glory Girls. As I mentioned earlier, and as Sheriff Skiles agrees, this kitchen is to be regarded as a crime scene."

At that moment, though sunshine still beamed from the heavens and lilacs still perfumed the air like a hard-hearted hooker, the ground shifted under the cavernous, custom-designed kitchen of Glory Hallelujah Church in Biddlebourne, West Virginia.

In all the years since the Virginia General Assembly had established the town in 1813, Biddlebourne had recorded fewer than a dozen untoward deaths. Most of the fatalities stemmed from farming accidents involving either bad luck or poor equipment. One death had occurred when an illegal but popular whiskey still behind Johnny Ed Long's turnip farm blew up. The most recent fatality was that of twelve-year-old Audrey Jolene Hooper, who had crossed a pasture on her way to the skinny-dipping hole without first checking to see whether Leroy Joe Cline had let the bull out of the barn.

"Oooh," the assemblage breathed, acknowledging not only the horror of an unusual death in their town, but also the realization that Biddlebourne had become a place where mystery could attend death.

Edith Fay closed her eyes, folded her hands and said, "Ella Mae."

A buxom, white-haired woman in jeans and a soft denim shirt murmured, "Yes. Her family," and peeled away from the group.

Ella Mae's sneakers squinched as she walked to the main doors on the north side of the kitchen.

Every woman present—the Glory Girls and those who hoped to be—watched her go.

The smells of human effluvia floated into their nostrils, and the metallic air coalesced into millions of ragged motes. Several women swallowed nervously, and those closest to Gudrun's body stole glances at the not-so-lamented departed.

The room grayed as a massive nimbus obscured the sun over Glory Hallelujah Church.

All eyes focused on Edith Fay.

"Let's bow our heads," she said after a long pause. Even Buddy Lee dropped his chin. "Lord God of us all," Edith Fay said, "receive the spirit of our neighbor Gudrun Wince, we humbly pray, and help us who are still here to do right by her. May your truth be our guide in all things. Amen."

"Amen," said the women. Buddy Lee hiccupped.

Edith Fay cleared her throat and adjusted her eyeglasses. "I realize that this situation leads to many questions. All I can say with certainty now is that all of you contestants for the open position in the Glory Girls will be notified when the cook-off is rescheduled."

A hand waved nearby, and Eulalah Bee piped up. "Edith Fay, does that mean what we already cooked today won't be judged?"

"I'm afraid it does," Edith Fay said. "The cooking and the judging must be conducted under fair and stable conditions."

From the windows, Sheri Odell Ankrum, the Glory Girl in charge of the Clothing Subcommittee, got Edith Fay's attention and pointed outside.

"Can we take home what we cooked today?" someone else asked.

Edith Fay glanced toward Shari Odell and spoke carefully, "I would say that anything produced in the church kitchen today must remain here until inquiries are completed."

Several women quelled their disapproval of this decision. It would not do for a potential Glory Girl to disagree so soon—or perhaps ever—with Edith Fay Smith.

"Until the sheriff arrives with his staff, we have some things to tend to," Edith Fay said.

She looked around until she spotted a squarely built woman with her red hair arranged in a wiry pouf and her purple blouse rolled up to the elbows. "Bida June," she said, "will you please look this up in the book?"

Bida June Pyles removed her smock, revealing a lean and tanned figure, as she set out for the church library.

Edith Fay went on, "Ula Maude, take Buddy Lee to my office and give him a Coke. Then call Doc Weber and tell him what has happened, in case the sheriff forgets to do that."

Ula Maude Ferrebee adjusted her Bermuda shorts and walked over to take Buddy Lee by the hand.

Troops dispatched, Edith Fay cleared her throat and addressed the cook-off contenders. "As you see, we have taken the precaution of protecting the, um, scene so that the sheriff may conduct his investigation. I ask that no one go beyond the boundaries marked by Alwildia Louise and Fonda Renee."

"Are we free to go?" Eulalah Bee asked, earning more sideways glances.

A tiny huff escaped Edith Fay's lips, in many contestants' minds sealing the doom of Eulalah Bee Pritchard as a viable Glory Girl candidate, but Edith Fay replied evenly, "I was just coming to that. I think it best if everyone stays until the authorities have come and asked their questions. While we're waiting, I ask you to take your personal possessions and go to the Rhododendron Parlor, where I hope . . ."

A commotion outside the building stopped Edith Fay midsentence. Doors slammed, people shouted and a *thunk* indicated something heavy had landed on the concrete in front of the church.

At the windows, Shari Odell Ankrum and Lloyda Ruth Dent pressed their noses to the glass. "Oh, Lord Jesus, help us!" Shari Odell said. Her gold earrings glinted as she turned.

Edith Fay's heart jumped ahead a beat. "Ladies?"

Lloyda Ruth could only put her palms to her wavy white hair and shake her head repeatedly. But Shari Odell recognized their visitor.

"Now we got real trouble," she said.

He that is suffered to do more than is fitting, will do more than is
lawful. *Proverb*

CHAPTER THREE

"Gudrun was murdered. I'm sure of it."

Edith Fay took the phone from the pocket of her apron, pushed
two buttons and held up the screen for the pastor to see.

They stood in the pastor's office, the door closed against a
backgrund cacophony of booted footfalls, shouted orders and
backup beeps from emergency vehicles.

The pastor gasped as she stared at Edith Fay's cell phone and
took in the stark effects of Gudrun's slaying: the black blood on
the clothes, the right hand curled into a claw, food and gore
congealed in grim, syrupy splotches.

"Poor Gudrun," Annie said. "She seems so . . . so still. I do
hope she did not suffer long. This has never hap . . . But, wait, is
that broccoli there . . . on the floor?"

"Yes, quite surprisingly."

No dish of any merit in Biddlebourne contained broccoli, first
because broccoli was not amenable to human digestion and second
because broccoli was not locally produced. Hogs could tolerate
broccoli because they could tolerate anything, so if a Biddlebourne
cook somehow came to possess broccoli, it could at least be fed to
the pigs. But a pig trough was the only place people served
broccoli in Biddlebourne, and the nearest place they could
intentionally obtain it was fifteen miles away in Spartansville.

So, of course, broccoli on the floor was as puzzling to Edith
Fay and Annie Ido as blood on the floor, and perhaps more so,
since the human heart might contrive what the human stomach
simply could not digest.

The women quieted for a moment, their brows as furrowed as
the wrinkles on Boyce Ed Reinhardt's baby bulldog. They heard a
familiar voice shouting close by and turned toward the door at the
same time.

The door opened and a tall man of hollow cheeks, crooked
bowtie and grizzled pompadour rushed in. He halted just inside the

room and looked the women up and down as if they were livestock at the Skyler County Fair.

With no introduction or apology, he said, "I'm here to investigate a complaint about your kitchen." Behind him, the church administrator, Belle Watkins, stopped yelling and gestured to show that the hollow man had managed to reach the pastor's office without registering at Belle's desk, a requirement plainly stated in the vestibule.

"Thanks, Belle," the pastor said with a smile. Belle mouthed *sorry* and pivoted away.

"Now then, sir, I believe we have not met," Pastor Annie said.

He held up a yellowed card covered with minuscule script. The women squinted at it. "Emerson Duty, Skyler County Department of Public Health," he said, pocketing the card.

Edith Fay said, "Mr. Duty, this is the Reverend Annie Ido Scovill, our pastor, and I am Edith Fay Smith. I . . . help out in the kitchen here."

"Ah, yes," he said. "As I was saying, there has been a complaint."

"What kind of complaint, Mr. Duty?" the pastor asked.

"That your organization has not adhered to regulations regarding public health."

"To which regulations do you refer?" the pastor asked.

"I cannot comment at this moment. I am here to conduct an inspection. Please accompany me to the kitchen."

The announcement that the vaunted kitchen of Glory Hallelujah Church might have violated any standard of public sanitation so staggered the women that both momentarily stood mute in disbelief.

"But, Mr. Duty," Edith Fay managed to say, folding her hands over her apron. "We maintain the strictest standards of cleanliness in our kitchen. We have an entire team whose sole ministry is the sterilization of surfaces and equipment. We have never received a complaint."

The pastor added, "Nor have we been notified in writing of any such complaint, as I believe is the correct procedure."

Mr. Duty's response was to pull a clipboard from his brown box of a briefcase and a ballpoint from his shirt pocket. He clicked the pen repeatedly and perused the pad. When the women stayed put, he said, "I see by the sign in the lobby that the kitchen is in the south wing."

"There are . . . extenuating circumstances in the kitchen at this time, Mr. Duty. The area has been cordoned off because of an occurrence earlier today. I fear that an inspection at this time could seriously jeopardize another, more serious investigation that is under way." The pastor took a long breath after her appeal.

But Emerson Duty shook his head and pursed his lips. "Ms. Scovill, there are always extenuating circumstances. My orders are to conduct an inspection today—an inspection on all points—of the kitchen at Glory Hallelujah Church," he said, pronouncing the *J* in *Hallelujah*, "and I have driven here today from Spartansville for that purpose. I suggest that we proceed so that I may file my report in a timely manner."

Pastor Annie took a phone from her skirt pocket and said quietly, "Edith Fay, perhaps you will escort Mr. Duty while I make some calls."

Edith Fay nodded slightly, strode to the door and said, "This way, Mr. Duty."

At 309 Muzzy Road, in the Biddlebourne Heights subdivision, where the husbands hired teenagers to mow their lawns and the wives made their biscuits by opening cans, Laverna Inys Wharton lay on her bed sneezing and shaking.

Crazy thoughts careened through her head like blind chickens vying for the last kernel of corn in the coop. Sweat soaked the armpits and neckline of her silk chartreuse dress and stuck her straw wedgies to her feet. Her heart pounded and burned.

"Laverna, I'm home!"

William! Early! Laverna forced herself to rise. Giving quick silent thanks for her long, dark curly hair and big brown eyes, she went to her dressing table and applied a thin coat of glow-lotion to her face, neck and arms. She tossed off her sweaty garments as she ran to the closet, then put on a pink tank top and red shorts that fit her perfectly.

Over a late lunch of boiled hot dogs and leftover rice, Laverna learned that William had left work early to watch a Pirates baseball game on television. She listened politely and held her breath to avoid yawning while William spoke of his morning at the office.

After a while, William stretched and said, "I think I'll watch the game in the den."

"All right. I have a few things to do."

Laverna made sure William had enough snacks for the game and any extra innings, the *Skyler County Sentinel* and *Newsweek* for the commercials, and his Pirates coverlet in case the air conditioner ran amok again.

In the kitchen, she rattled the cookie sheets in the cabinet, ran the blender with water in it, and noisily worked up a batch of instant pudding with her stainless-steel whip in her stainless-steel bowl.

The time came at last. Laverna went to the door of the den and looked in. William was ensconced in his recliner and fixated on the TV screen. "I'm going out for a dip," she said. William waved a hand but did not look away from the game.

She went to the bedroom she shared with William, threw her clothes on the floor and put on the black one-piece swimsuit she had bought when she was a junior in college. She didn't swim enough to wear out a bathing suit but found that the wearing of a swimsuit often advanced her goals.

Laverna grabbed the biggest beach towel from the linen closet in the hall, walked to the double sliding glass doors and stepped onto the poolside patio behind the Wharton home. She turned on the CD player that sat on an umbrella table and threw her towel onto the bulky bin that held pool equipment.

After doing ten splashy laps to the beat of the Rolling Stones, Laverna slipped out of the water and walked past the blaring music player to the deck box. There she lingered only long enough to remove one item and wrap it in her towel before tiptoeing back inside.

Without showering or changing, Laverna went into the huge closet, the one with the built-in shelves and adjustable racks and dozens of cubbyholes for her shoes and purses. She locked the closet door, something she often did because she also kept her good jewelry in the closet.

Laverna steadied herself on an underwear shelf and soothed her mind with thoughts of her goal.

Yes, now that she had turned forty she would become one of them. She would go about doing good.

She would prove that she was a woman of worth, that she deserved a position of leadership.

Confidence shored, she knelt in front of the rack that held her slacks and skirts, reached past the clothes and touched a latch. It flipped up easily, and she crab-walked into the space it concealed.

Laverna pulled the treasure in behind her, tossed the beach towel aside and gazed at the object that would change her life, and the lives of her children—if she ever had any—and the lives of their children.

Mayor Jass Pinbiddie, unable to reach Cassie by phone and facing an hour and nine minutes to kill before meeting her, shouted for Marthleen Lewis and picked up his deep-black Mont Blanc Meisterstuck to sign the latest batch of proclamations.

Almost every group, club, cause, interest and political view in Biddlebourne had been the subject of a mayoral proclamation. There had been, in addition to other auspicious occasions, Bread and Butter Pickle Appreciation Days for the farmers who produced boxcars of cucumbers, Hip Replacement Week for the county's numerous nursing homes that picked up nice insurance fees for postoperative rehab, and Treat the Teacher Month so Biddlebourne's restaurants could ease the post-Christmas lull by selling gift cards to parents who had forgotten to provide such for their young-uns' longsuffering educators.

Mayor Pinbiddie could not stop the community's various coalitions and trade machines from expressing gratitude for his help. He considered the cash, liquor and investment opportunities they gave him the same as gratuities given to waiters, caddies and others who helped. Helping was the key, and Jass Pinbiddie was a powerful helper.

"What do you need, Jass?" Marthleen stood at the door, pigtailed, petite and juggling her purse as she pulled the strings tight on her lunch bag. "I'm on my way out."

"Where you goin'?" Mayor Pinbiddie was the only town official who had a personal secretary, and he took *personal* to mean that Marthleen would take his Chevy Blazer in for maintenance, pick up his Viagra at Elderdon's Pharmacy and keep him informed at all times of her whereabouts so that he might send her on personal errands.

Marthleen disagreed with the mayor's interpretation of almost everything, especially the meaning of *personal secretary*, but needed the job and liked the spotlight that shone on the mayor's office. She humored Mayor Pinbiddie—to an extent.

"To Glory Hallelujah," she said. "What can I get you before I go?"

"Aren't you a Lutheran? Why are you going to Glory Hallelujah Church?" A strange feeling fluttered through his chest.

"I just heard that Gudrun Wince got hurt bad there—at that big cooking contest. Thelma Blivins emailed me about it, but I said, 'That's baloney. Nobody gets hurt at a church.' But she said, 'Yeah, for sure it happened,' and then I heard the ambulance go through, and now I'm going over to the church. What do you need?"

Jass Pinbiddie grabbed his chest because, suddenly, he could not breathe. He felt and heard blood pushing, pounding, rampaging through his veins but lacked the power to make his lungs work.

He gagged, paled and crumpled like an empty paper sack onto the handsome, hand-rubbed executive desk presented him by the grateful members of the Biddlebourne Chamber of Commerce.

One chicken. One *Gallus domesticus* done to such tender and tasty delectation that the humiliation would end. That was all Laverna Inys Wharton wanted.

She fingered the magical artifact that would, finally and forever, bring her to the position of prominence she deserved in Biddlebourne. She let its heft tease her hopes, its glowing rosewood titillate her fantasies, its infused aromas fill her nostrils. The beauty of Gudrun Wince's heirloom recipe box was marred only by the bits of rust on the tiny hinges of its lid.

No matter. Laverna gripped the box. This was the pivotal prize of her life, the prize she had labored years to conjure, lied to obtain and now risked her soul to employ.

Gulping air to keep from passing out, she gently tipped the lid back and gazed in wonder upon the collected culinary knowledge of six generations of Biddlebournians.

Wearing thin plastic gloves to protect the box's contents—and herself—Laverna counted out 103 recipes scribbled on scraps of paper ranging from notebook sheets to brittle butcher paper, 156 torn out of various magazines and newspapers, 17 apparently clipped from cookbooks, 33 written longhand on lined tablet paper, 19 typed on onion-skin paper, and 95 printed in blue ink on unlined pink note cards.

"Hmm," Laverna muttered, surprised by the condition of the pages. Many bore food stains, tears or smudges. The onion-skin paper was badly faded. Paper fragments choked the bottom of the box.

Never mind. She would copy the recipes into a notebook, carefully preserving the valuable ingredient lists and instructions in her own hand, and, yes, in time adding notes and codes of her own as she recreated these 423 delicious dishes.

But when she began sorting the recipes for indexing, Laverna grew more concerned and began to sneeze and sweat. Except for those removed from cookbooks, newspapers or magazines, the recipes did not look right.

The most valuable recipes, those handed down by great-grandmothers and great-aunts, seemed truncated. For instance, ingredients for Country Spaghetti Sauce read as 2slbacsli, 1#gb, 1onch, 1smgpch, 1smtomp, 1ctomj, 1ctoms, 1Tws, 1clgar, 1Tsug, 1pkgspg. The directions were just as arcane: Fryba, addgb, on, gp. In seppan put tp, tj, ts, ws, gar and sug in pan. Add 1stmix. Slow3hrs. Spoverspg.

She put down the Country Spaghetti Sauce and picked up Mrs. Simpson's Creamed Turkey, and Grandma Jones' Cornbread, and Aunt Louella's Baked Cabbage.

"Nooooo!" she screamed.

Glory Girls Rule No. 3—All members of the Glory Girls service organization of Glory Hallelujah Church, Biddlebourne, West Virginia, shall be nominated and chosen from the membership of the Ladies Aid Society of Glory Hallelujah Church. All members in good standing of the Ladies Aid Society are entitled to nominate and to vote upon Glory Girls selections. *Glory Girls Book of Bylaws,* adopted May 1958.

CHAPTER FOUR

When Jass Pinbiddie woke up, he was glad, but not glad enough to forget why he had fainted, and certainly not glad enough to stay where he'd been put. Grunting, he heaved himself from the floor and onto the chair recently vacated by that pain-in-the-butt preacher woman. His shoes had been removed for some dim reason, so he reached for the lopsided loafers.

"Jass, ya gotta take it easy. Doc'll be here soon as he's done with Miss Cassie over at the church," said Boyd Eddy, 87, the backup to the backup for Biddlebourne's main emergency medical technician.

"Oh, my God," Jasper moaned. Cassie needed him. His little Cassie needed the help of the most powerful man in Biddlebourne, in all of Skyler County.

"Where ya goin,' Jass?" asked Marthleen, who had laid her purse and lunch bag on his desk and now tried to keep him seated. But the mayor shoved her away and lurched out of the room.

Jasper Pinbiddie was denied entrance to Glory Hallelujah Church by a deputy sheriff whose mother he had once dated and whom Jass had quite possibly fathered. The mayor turned to Marthleen, who had accompanied him out of fear of losing her job and simultaneously missing out on the juiciest piece of gossip to hit Biddlebourne since the Moose Club hired a stripper for the Labor Day wienie roast.

Jass made his right hand into a fist and slammed it repeatedly into the palm of his left hand. He marched back and forth in front of the main doors of the church. He held his head, swiped at mosquitoes and jabbed a finger in the air at the deputy, who only continued eyeing the mayor.

"For God's sake, find out what's happening!" Jass yelled at Marthleen.

"Well, Jass, I think we know what's happening."

"And what is that? How do you know?"

Few people liked working with Mayor Jasper Pinbiddie, a fact of which—and the reasons for which—Marthleen was aware. Jass told himself that being mayor of a West Virginia town with 9,743 inhabitants entitled him to the rights and privileges parallel to those of the president of the United States.

Jass believed, sincerely and fervently, that he held titular command of the constabulary of Biddlebourne, much as the country's president commanded its military. He believed he held rightful privy to, and direction of, the plans and actions of all municipal departments, agencies, personnel and materiel. He believed his was the final, indisputable word on all matters public—and many matters private—in Biddlebourne. His interference in and occasional ruination of public services in the town were ongoing and infamous.

Yet, election after election, voters returned Jass Pinbiddie to office by margins ranging from substantial to overwhelming. Marthleen maintained the private opinion that Biddlebourne voters simply preferred the known politician—no matter how greedy his motives or low his behavior—to the unknown one.

Marthleen did admit, though, that Jass had collected a sizable portion of his political clout by his own sweat as owner and operator of Biddlebourne Feed & Grain. Few Biddlebournians could avoid trafficking with Jass at the Feed & Grain. Farmers, ranchers and gardeners needed the animal feed, tilling equipment and herbicides that he sold. Pet lovers and 4-H families needed tack, leashes and kibbles. Proud homeowners needed lawn mowers, water hoses and deck paint.

The only store in town that even marginally competed with Biddlebourne Feed & Grain was Vinny Clark's All-American Hardware, which had lately fallen into the hands of lackadaisical caretakers after Vinny's incarceration on an arson charge.

Thus, there being no other store dedicated so specifically to the needs of Biddlebournians within twenty miles in any direction, customers trooped by the dozens daily into Jass Pinbiddie's emporium and presence.

Therefore, when Jass was not sitting in his mayor's chair at the Biddlebourne City Building, he was sitting in his owner's chair at

Biddlebourne Feed & Grain. Of course, he persistently used both locations to his political and financial advantage.

What Jass may have lacked in social finesse, he made up in business savvy. He granted discounts to repeat customers. He held regular sales on needful merchandise, all advertised in hand-lettered signs posted both at the store and the Biddlebourne City Building.

His Honor Jasper E. Pinbiddie made contributions to the school athletic teams, the marching band, the 4-H clubs, the church youth groups, the Little League teams, the Girl Scouts and Boy Scouts, the basketball league, the garden society, the Moms & Tots program, the Friends of the Library and the classic car association.

The Lions, Kiwanis, Rotary, Masons, Eagles, Elks, Moose and Odd Fellows all claimed Jass as an honorary member, as did the American Legion, Veterans of Foreign Wars and, for reasons known only by a few, the Gold Star Mothers Club.

The full facts were that if a donation bought Jass Pinbiddie his name or picture on a program, poster or T-shirt—or to the mind of a potential voter—he was there with his checkbook and his $800 fountain pen.

This symbiotic relationship produced a profound, if unspoken, understanding between Biddlebournians and their mayor.

Awareness of that relationship flashed through Marthleen's brain in an instant, causing her to act on a rare piece of bad judgment. "All right, Jass, all right," she said. With determined steps, she walked toward the deputy, adjusting her blouse buttons and her smile as she went.

"Just over eight thousand square feet," Edith Fay replied as she keyed in the combination for the ten-foot-high doors of Hearth House, the picnic pavilion occupying the west side of the Glory Hallelujah Church complex. *If she distracted Mr. Duty long enough*, she thought, *Gudrun's body would be gone from the church kitchen before the inspector reached it.*

"I would say your math is off—quite a bit, Mrs. Smith," Mr. Emerson Duty responded. "This shelter can be no more than twenty-five feet wide and sixty feet long. That would make it, ah, fifteen hundred square feet." He wrote numbers on his clipboard.

Choosing not to correct the inspector, Edith Fay smiled in a way that did not reveal her clenched teeth. Dry heat rolled out of the building as fourteen doors—seven on each length of Hearth House—thrummed into overhead slots.

She inhaled the hickory-tinged air and felt better. "Please call me Edith Fay, Mr. Duty."

When Mr. Duty said nothing, Edith Fay went to the electrical box and flipped switches. Five huge ceiling fans whirred into action, and a pair of stainless-steel panels opened at one end of Hearth House. Behind the panels, a bank of recessed compact fluorescent lights slowly illuminated a wood-fired grill with sixteen cook plates. Multiple cooking tools hung from a long iron rod suspended over the grill. Each tool was encased in a clear plastic bag secured with a twist tie.

"How many served here?" Mr. Duty asked.

"There are, as you see, twenty-six tables, each seating ten. Thus, we serve two hundred sixty in one seating, either buffet style—she pointed to the buffet tables—or sit-down if it's a wedding or funeral event.

"Here in Hearth House we use only high-quality disposable plates, utensils and cups, all of which are stored in original packaging until time of service. Cookware and serving bowls, platters and pitchers are washed in our commercial-grade dishwasher before and after each use.

"The grill is scrubbed after each use and sealed behind these locked doors when not in use. A licensed pest-control company maintains a monthly service schedule in all our food-preparation and service areas.

"In addition, our code committee thoroughly checks the main kitchen and Hearth House facilities every Saturday. All prep surfaces are sprayed with disinfectant before the refrigerators may be opened for meal preparation or service.

"Any meat cooked in Hearth House is chilled until it goes on the grill and is served within fifteen minutes of being cooked. We use thermometers to constantly monitor the temperatures of meat on the grill. Leftover meat is disposed of immediately—on the rare occasions when there is any.

"Cold foods come chilled from the main kitchen to Hearth House," she continued. "They are placed immediately in the buffet chiller and held there no longer than two hours."

She pressed a set of invisible buttons, and one buffet table opened to display thirty-six stainless-steel trays, each covered with clear, hard plastic. Refrigerator motors activated beneath the trays.

"Hmph," Mr. Duty said. He walked around the huge grill several times, opening the doors and drawers underneath. Then, slowly, he picked up the grill plates and made a stack of them, and removed the tools from the rod above.

With no comment to Edith Fay or glance in her direction, he rubbed his thumb along the grill plates, smelled the grill plates, held them up to the light at different angles, and left them in a heap on the concrete floor. "You will need to wash these again after my visit," he said as he moved to the tools.

Mr. Duty pulled each implement from its bag and made a line of tongs, spoons, knives and long-handled forks on the stove. He withdrew a fluorescent light from his case and shined it on each item.

The procedure took more than ten minutes, during which, Edith Fay texted each and every Glory Girl to set a luncheon meeting for 12 noon Friday at her home. Given the location, the Glory Girls knew not to mention the meeting to anyone else.

Another *hmph* came from Emerson Duty. He continued writing on his notepad. Edith Fay could not see what he wrote, but she didn't have to see it to know that the grill stove of Hearth House, like all the cooking equipment operated by the Glory Girls of Glory Hallelujah Church, was spotless.

This was because, even though Edith Fay was the elected president of the Glory Girls, she had a service specialty just like all the Girls. Her specialty was food and the selection, purchase, storage, preparation and serving thereof. A horde of helpers carried out her instructions, but she held herself responsible for the cleanliness and functionality of the cooking appliances, equipment, tools and serving ware entrusted to her care.

Edith Fay had long ago worked at the Skyler County General Hospital in Spartansville preparing surgical packs for the operating room. Every scalpel, every forceps, every dressing and every other supply that left her unit was free of contamination. This was essential to the surgeon's work, to the patient's care and to Edith Fay's sense of rightness. These skills and sensibilities came with her to Glory Hallelujah Church.

This was why Edith Fay could relax and enjoy the June breeze in Hearth House while Emerson Duty toiled over his notes and repeatedly jerked his head up in the apparent but futile hope of finding Edith Fay Smith wringing her hands with anxiety.

At 1:50 p.m., Emerson Duty stabbed the pen back into his pocket. "Take me to the main kitchen."

'Tis action makes the hero. *Proverb*

CHAPTER FIVE

"Good Lord, I don't believe this."

Sheriff Dooley Skiles rubbed his head and paced while Cecil Weber, M.D., worked with the body of Gudrun Wince. The sheriff's expression, equal parts consternation and bewilderment, tugged his mustache into a flat steel slash over his lip.

"What don't you believe? That she's dead or that she's dead here?" asked Doc Weber. His full white hair pooched out as he leaned over to pluck a form from his bag on which to note that at least he believed Gudrun Wince to be dead, and dead right here in Glory Hallelujah Church.

"Both," said the sheriff, scanning the room to make sure all the exits were covered by his people.

"For what it's worth, it looks like she was stabbed. We'll get an official take on cause of death, of course, but there's at least one stab wound. Looks pretty deep," Doc Weber said. He rolled the body on its side to check the back.

"No wounds in the back," the doctor said. "She was dead when I got here. I wrote 12:40 p.m. for time of death. The ladies said nobody touched the body or any of the stuff around it."

"Is it an obvious homicide, Doc?" Sheriff Skiles asked.

"Sure looks like it."

Dooley shook his head and automatically pulled a notebook from a hip pocket, feeling the gaze of everybody in the room on him. At forty-seven, he was 210 pounds and six feet two inches of broad-shouldered energy. More than one woman had stumbled over his blue eyes, muscle-hugging black uniform and trim buzz cut.

If Sheriff Dooley Skiles seemed baffled, it was because he was. But if he looked inept, it was a façade.

Dooley had deep roots and a long reach in Skyler County. His great-great-grandmother Bridgett Edgett Kearns had disembarked at New York Harbor in 1889 after crossing the Atlantic aboard the Majestic from Dublin via Liverpool. She slept that night in a tent she pitched in the shadow of the Statue of Liberty, alone because her husband Bartholomew had died in the crossing and had been unceremoniously buried at sea.

It took Bridgett Edgett Kearns six days to beg rides to Skyler County where her brother Paulie Edgett lived, nine weeks to meet and marry Golden Skiles, and seventeen years to become the mother of six sons and five daughters, all of whom married in-county and followed the fine family tradition of begetting multiple offspring.

So numerous were the descendants of Golden and Bridgett Skiles, and so varied their achievements, it could reasonably be said that everyone in the county was either a Skiles, related by blood or marriage to a Skiles, had attended school with a Skiles, had played football or volleyball or softball with a Skiles, or was employed by or with a Skiles.

Therefore, in the early '90s when Dooley Skiles at age twenty-eight placed his name on the ballot for sheriff and that fact was reported on page one of the *Skyler County Sentinel*, heads nodded throughout the surrounding valleys, hollows, bottoms and glens. The incumbent, Obey Wade, wisely declined to run again, and Jacob Lemasters just as prudently quit painting "Jake for Sheriff" signs in his shed.

While Dooley Skiles initially lacked experience, he made up for it with hard work, careful thought, a propensity to listen before taking action, and—in the spirit of his great-great-grandmother Bridgett Skiles—an unbendable determination to do his job well.

However, in more than twenty years as top county lawman, Dooley Skiles had handled only two outright killings and had "solved" each within twenty-four hours, in the first instance because Franklin Jones turned himself in after fatally punching out Joey Morris for impregnating his sister, and in the second instance when a carload of inebriated teenagers struck and killed "Old Henry" Bascomb and were too drunk to run away before the sheriff arrived on the scene.

Thus, the death of Gudrun Wince presented Dooley's first true murder investigation. He scratched his chin and made a quick mental list of all the possible murder suspects, including Buddy Lee Delbert, the church staff, delivery people, photographers and reporters, the other cooking contestants and—heaven help him— all the Glory Girls of Glory Hallelujah Church.

Nearly three dozen people, he realized, had to be interviewed and their stories checked and cross-checked. It would be a huge undertaking for any sheriff's department in West Virginia, but especially so for his understaffed unit.

The investigation would entail lots of work. But lots of work was where Dooley Skiles excelled.

He glanced toward a chair next to the pizza oven where Buddy Lee Delbert sat gobbling lemon cookies, but he walked toward Ella Mae Pugh, who'd been identified as his liaison for the Glory Girls. *Liaison, for crap's sake! How did the Glory Girls come up with this stuff?*

Ella Mae, the Girls' second-in-command, also took her work seriously. She stepped toward the sheriff and offered her hand in greeting. "Sheriff, thank you for getting here so promptly. We'll cooperate in every way we can with your investigation."

"Thanks, Ella Mae. I already talked to Buddy Lee a little, but he's too rattled to tell me much now," the sheriff said. "He'll have to come over to the station later."

"Yes, I understand," Ella Mae said. "I'll bring him over in my car. I understand he is between vehicles at the moment."

"Why was he even in here while you folks were having a cook-off?" Dooley asked.

Ella Mae held a hand to her forehead and swallowed. The discussion, or debate, about Buddy Lee's participation in the contest had occupied the better part of the Girls' April meeting. Memories of it were still vivid in Ella Mae's mind.

The request for help with Buddy Lee Delbert had come to the Glory Girls through an approved channel—as a note presented by a church member to the Ladies Aid Society, a committee of which gauged the merits of the request and forwarded it to the Glory Girls. Ula Maude Ferrebee, the Glory Girl in charge of the Community Health and Recreation Subcommittee, had read the note:

Dear Ladies,

I'm writing on account of my nephew Buddy Lee Delbert. He's 27, as I reckon you know because he was born the same year as Ula Maude's boy Clemson Lee and everybody said they stuck together like two Lees in a pod. Anyway, Buddy Lee has had a lot of misfortune in his life. His mama died young, and his dad couldn't hardly take care of him and his three sisters. I'm about all he's got now that his daddy's gone off with Sue Lynn McAbee to make a new start in Kentucky. All in all, Buddy Lee was lucky to graduate high school, but then he flunked out of the Army and the junior college. He tried a lot of jobs, but none of them suited him just right. He's a good boy. Claude and me think he could do real good if he could just get himself a job that he likes. Then he could get himself a nice girlfriend and settle down nice like the other boys his age. I'm asking you Glory Girls for help because Buddy Lee don't like anything better than eating, and we figure he could get a job in the food-making business some day. Nobody knows eating like you Girls. His sisters is all married now. Buddy Lee will be the last of the Delberts around here if he can't get a job so he can get a wife. Anything you can do will be appreciated.

Sincerely yours, Audra Pitts

Several Glory Girls wanted to honor this founding family's request to provide kitchen experience to a disadvantaged young man, but others worried that Buddy Lee would gum up church dinners the way he had gummed up almost everything else he had attempted.

Their discussion had touched on the possibilities of spiffing up Buddy Lee's appearance, finding him a suitable girlfriend, polishing his work resume, paying his tuition to a trade school, teaching him better manners, improving his reading skills, separating him from his video games and cleaning his fingernails.

At one point, all the Glory Girls had slapped their address books onto the table and called out the names of granddaughters, nieces, neighbors, waitresses, Sunday school teachers, child care workers and other young women who might be encouraged to see past Buddy Lee's abashed public self to his reportedly winsome inner self.

"Gwennie Morley?" asked Fonda Renee Postlethwaite. "She loves kids and is very patient."

"Way too tall," replied Floyda Ruth Dent.

"What about Ann Elaine Zerbinger?" said Fonda Renee. A stunned silence greeted the suggestion. After a while, Mary Ellen Brinkman said simply, "Too smart."

"Linda Louise Orbell?"

"Can't cook," proclaimed Alwildia Louise Doak. Nods came from the Girls.

"Ella Mae," the sheriff said, "you with me?"

"Oh, Dooley, excuse me," she said. "I was just remembering that the Girls decided a couple of months ago to give Buddy Lee some kitchen experience to aid in his job search."

"Oh?" the sheriff said doubtfully. "What was he supposed to be doing at the cook-off?"

"He was here to help the contestants with the heavier and more tedious chores."

"I don't get it. What chores couldn't they do on their own?" The sheriff had yet to meet a woman who couldn't lift a hind quarter of beef off the bed of a pickup truck and carry it to her basement.

"Some of our heavier pots are stored on back shelves, and at least one competitor has bad arthritis. Buddy also ran errands for the cooks. . . ."

Sheriff Skiles frowned. "Errands? Where to?"

"He removed garbage and packaging from the cook stations, for one thing, and took those items to the compost bins, trash cans or incinerator. He fetched ingredients from the cupboards and refrigerators. I overheard that he went to Value Mart to buy unsalted butter for somebody."

"I don't know. . . ." Dooley squinted at Buddy Lee, trying to picture the young bumbler pulling off a slaying in the presence of more than a dozen people.

"What does Doc Weber say?" Ella Mae asked.

The sheriff opened his mouth to answer, but everyone's attention suddenly turned to a sound like that of a bawling calf.

"Cassie, my little Cassie, oh Cassie! God, tell me it's not true!"

Jass Pinbiddie exploded into the kitchen, shouting, groaning, flinging his arms and trying to shake Marthleen Lewis off his sleeve.

"Now! I will see it now!" The veins of Emerson Duty's neck pulsed against his bowtie as he spat the words at Edith Fay Smith.

"The main kitchen? Of course, Mr. Duty. As soon as I've provided the details of the layout to you."

They stood in Edith Fay's tiny office leaning over a hand-drawn diagram of the south wing of Glory Hallelujah Church.

Edith Fay's demeanor betrayed not a whit of the turmoil inside her. She believed that every family in Biddlebourne depended on her—families who needed help with food, with shelter, with jobs, with safe places for their children to learn and play, with managing their budgets, with living alone in their senior years, with a thousand needs that the Glory Girls of Glory Hallelujah Church understood to be their ministry in this little corner of Appalachia.

But by far the largest ministry of the Glory Girls—and the most essential to the community—was Family Ministry Day, an outgrowth of the congregation's Seven Paths of Discipleship program.

Family Ministry Day occurred at Glory Hallelujah Church every Tuesday, when the Girls, along with Pastor Annie, taught classes, distributed food and clothing and used furniture, facilitated visits by specialists in every kind of family crisis and need, provided child care for parents and elder care for adult children, arranged job counseling and carried out dozens of projects, large and small, to better Biddlebourne.

Family Ministry Day began officially at 9 a.m.—after the Girls had been in prayer and other preparation from 7 a.m.—and lasted until the last child was picked up by the last parent well after sunset.

Family Ministry Day occurred every Tuesday of the year, including Tuesdays on which Christmas Eve, Christmas Day, New Year's Eve, New Year's Day and the Fourth of July fell.

No Family Ministry Day was identical to another except that child care and lunch were always free. The twelve subcommittees of the Glory Girls rotated so that on any given Tuesday only three subcommittees led a program, workshop, class, project, or giveaway of food, clothing or furniture.

The work was so consuming that membership in the Glory Girls was open only to women who had no children at home. As recompense for their deep personal sacrifices and unstinting toil, the Girls reaped the glorious reward of never having to turn away any honest applicant for help.

If an applicant's truthfulness was in question, the Girls asked around until it was no longer in question.

If a truthful need was presented that the Girls could not meet immediately, the Executive Board confabbed until a solution was found.

If a program fell through or got otherwise botched, the Girls followed up until it was done right.

If the Junior Chamber of Commerce wanted to partner with the Girls on a community event, the Girls agreed to participate.

If the owner of the yarn emporium needed advertising and wanted to hold a knitting seminar, the Girls agreed to do it.

If the Biddlebourne High School Band Boosters wanted to hold a fundraiser to buy new uniforms, the Glory Girls pitched in.

In short, much of what was needful and helpful in Biddlebourne happened because of the Glory Girls.

Edith Fay Smith had no intention of letting one smug county health inspector spoil any of the Girls' work. No, indeed. Edith Fay Smith had resources, and at that moment she decided to bring some of them to bear on the current situation.

Mr. Duty tapped his pen on the paper and opened his mouth, but Edith Fay was quicker.

"I'll just give you the basic statistics first—so you'll have an idea of the scope of our food operation. The main kitchen has 2,592 square feet of food preparation space. The indoor dining room occupies another 2,592 square feet, and the open-deck dining area is 864 square feet. And, as you know, Hearth House covers 2,016 square feet."

"Ah, totaling 8,064 square feet," said Emerson Duty, reluctantly impressed.

"Exactly, Mr. Duty," Edith Fay responded enthusiastically. "See." She pointed to the diagram.

"The main kitchen is seventy-two feet long and thirty-six feet wide—the same dimensions as the indoor dining room, which is next to the kitchen. We put the delivery bay on this side next to the driveway. There are four upright freezers and four refrigerators right next to the bay to save time unloading groceries."

"That's all good and well," Mr. Duty noted grimly. "However, I am not here to inspect the size of the operation, but rather its sanitation. We must proceed."

"We have five primary food-preparation stations, each sixteen feet long by four feet wide. There are two food-holding stations of the same size equipped with warmers and chillers. We have a bank of restaurant-size ovens. . . ."

"Ms. Smith, to repeat, I am not here to count. I demand that you show me at once to the main kitchen." Mr. Duty's face darkened.

"The blueprints are in the control room, but this shows the general outline. The south wing holds the main kitchen, indoor dining room and open-air deck dining."

Back straight and steps brisk, Mr. Duty made for the door. Edith Fay stepped in front of him and smiled. "I must add that the service wing also contains the youth assembly room, the dance and drama studio, the choir's practice auditorium and the fifty-plus gym."

Mr. Duty hugged his official box and looked past Edith Fay.

"And on one side of the main kitchen is the serving counter that we use for most of our own events, and occasionally for events that we cater. We can accommodate 320 diners at a time indoors, plus

132 on the deck in clement weather. Exits on both sides of the kitchen and the dining room more than meet requirements of the state fire code."

Mr. Duty cleared his throat. In flat syllables, he said, "You will allow me to pass, Madame, or I will call the sheriff for a security escort."

He sidestepped Edith Fay and stalked to the door.

"And in the main kitchen, our commercial-grade dishwasher can sterilize glasses at the rate of . . ."

"I'm coming, Cassie, I'm coming!"

Mayor Jass Pinbiddie wanted only to hold his sweet little Cassie one last time and to tell her she was the only real woman he'd ever known. Clamping his right fist over his left shirt pocket, he barged out of his secretary's grasp toward the spot where his lady love lay cold under the official cloak of death.

But Marthleen Lewis, who saw her job evaporating if she didn't stop this spectacle, hooked both hands onto the waistband of the mayor's trousers from behind, planted her Skechers on the tile and pulled.

Despite his two-hundred-pound weight advantage, the mayor sank to his knees with a thick thud of fabric and fat. Marthleen gasped. The sheriff came running.

But the mayor leapt to his feet, dodged Dooley Skiles, scuttled to Gudrun's side and flung himself onto her body. Moaning and trembling, he wailed, "She's gone. Oh, help me. She's gone!"

Of course, it took only seconds for the nearby Girls to grasp that the mayor had more than official interest in Gudrun.

However, it took longer for Sheriff Skiles to figure out why he had to pull Jass away from the body and chase him across the kitchen before Doc Weber could stick him with a syringe of tranquilizer and the two of them could put Jass on a folding chair.

"Phew, what in the . . . was that all about?" the sheriff asked Mary Ellen Brinkman, who had helped him corner Jass beside the salad-prep counter.

Mary Ellen stared at Dooley, wondering whether he had just arrived from Jupiter. She liked the sheriff, and he had been fair in 2002 when the Glory Girls had lost track of $4,386 in dinner proceeds and a Glory Girl's granddaughter turned out to be the culprit.

"Shoot, Dooley, looks like old Jass had himself a girlfriend," she said, trying not to smile because she had an overbite and also because the situation was, after all, tragic.

Watching Doc Weber tend to Mayor Pinbiddie, Dooley scratched his chin and considered the lightning-bolt revelation that Jass had very likely been the lover—no, make that *one* lover—of the deceased and therefore was a suspect in her slaying.

The mayor's relationship with Gudrun—and Dooley didn't necessarily accept Mary Ellen Brinkman's assessment of it—added a dimension of political intrigue to the investigation. By all reports so far, Jass Pinbiddie had not been at the cook-off and could not have personally done in Gudrun. But, Dooley knew, Mayor Pinbiddie had enough friends and influence to cause almost anything to happen in Biddlebourne.

Though Sheriff Skiles was more lawman than politician and preferred straightforward methods, he had enough canny Irish blood in him to realize that, at this very moment, his job was on the line.

He knew that if he lost his job, Jass Pinbiddie could block his every effort to secure any other job in or around Skyler County. And that if he kept his job, Jass Pinbiddie could throw enough monkey wrenches into the works to make the sheriff appear incompetent and even cowardly.

This was one heck of a situation.

Jass had his feet propped on an overturned crate while the doctor checked his vital signs and Marthleen Lewis fanned him with a handful of paper plates.

Nobody in the room was saying much, fearful as they were of inciting Jass to more mayhem, so everyone heard what Marthleen said next to Jass. "So, Boss, how long you and Gudrun been . . . uh, special friends?"

Sheriff Skiles took a step forward and put his right hand on his sidearm as Jass stiffened and gave Marthleen a long, hard look. Jass tore the blood-pressure cuff from his arm, plucked a wadded handkerchief from his pants pocket, blew his nose, narrowed his eyes in Marthleen's direction, and straightened himself on the chair.

"She was a friend to us all," he said. Then he clamped his mouth shut and stared past the doctor, the Glory Girls and Marthleen in the direction of Sheriff Dooley Skiles.

Dooley met his gaze and nodded ever so slightly, signaling he knew that Jass knew he'd be asking him a lot of questions about the death of Gudrun Wince—and that the mayor might be indisposed at the moment but still wielded enough power to influence the outcome of a murder investigation.

In a corner of the kitchen, Ella Mae Pugh answered her phone and listened while Edith Fay Smith told her that, despite Edith Fay's employment of her best stalling tactics, Mr. Emerson Duty of the Skyler County Health Department was at that moment speed-walking to the kitchen for the purpose of closing it down.

Glory Girls Rule No. 4—Any nominee for membership in the Glory Girls service organization of Glory Hallelujah Church, Biddlebourne, West Virginia, shall have served at least one full year (12 months) as a general officer (president, vice president, secretary, treasurer or chaplain) of the Ladies Aid Society, and shall have been absent from no more than one general monthly meeting in each of the five preceding calendar years. [Exceptions may be granted by the Ladies Aid Society Executive Board and are limited to absences related to illness and/or natural disaster.] *Glory Girls Book of Bylaws,* adopted May 1958

CHAPTER SIX

The back room of the American Legion hall smelled foul and looked worse.

Upon hearing news of Gudrun Wince's death, the men who as boys had endured her pitiless discipline rose as one and dashed their beer bottles on the walls. They cheered, upended a crate of cabbage that would never become cole slaw, smashed a case of olives, kicked open several bags of garbage waiting to be picked up, and broke a jug of cleaning ammonia. In the melee they also accidentally broke most of a case of Leinenkugel's Canoe Paddler. That unfortunate event immediately stopped the merrymaking.

Foamy puddles, glass shards, wood splinters and vegetables used and unused covered the floor.

The combined stink of ammonia, offal and hops drove Bucky Feinmeister to open the door of the windowless room and Arnie Coker to yell through the doorway, "It's okay, folks. Just a little accident. Everything's under control."

No one in the outer room so much as looked in Arnie's direction, first because an officer of the law was not to be openly contradicted, second because they were engaged in several modes of gambling that required the acquiescence of the esteemed deputy sheriff.

"Wow, I didn't see this coming," Arnie said as he stepped over the mess to leave. "Wince the Witch is dead. I wonder if anybody'll care."

"Doubt it," said Harley Baker, bending to scoop trampled olives into a dustpan. "Where'd you say it happened?"

"Glory Hallelujah Church."

"Jeezoweez!" said Harley. "How?"

"Not sure," the deputy replied. "Thing I do know is that Jass Pinbiddie musta had a thing going on with old Gudrun. He's bawlin' and carryin' on over her at the church. Beats me what he saw in her, but it looks like they were hot 'n' heavy."

The other men, all previously unaware of Jass and Gudrun's affair, nodded, wide-eyed that such hanky-panky could happen secretly in tiny Biddlebourne and in profound admiration of Jass for keeping it so.

"Well, I gotta go, boys," Arnie said. "The sheriff needs me. Take care of things. Hear me now. I mean take care of everything."

The boys finished cleaning the storeroom with a fervor and speed they exercised nowhere else and regrouped to the chairs, cell phones in hand instead of beers.

"Whatta we gotta do?" asked Bucky, who kept things moving when Arnie Coker wasn't around.

Harley Baker pulled at his black-and-white suspenders, deep in thought. He was the analyst of the group by virtue of having operated a gas station for more than four decades. The merchandising and marketing of petroleum products, tires and wiper blades were no mean accomplishment, they all agreed.

"Well, gentlemen," he drawled, straightening in his chair and letting his feet fall from a keg. "We need to do two things, I reckon."

Someone in the main room next door yelled, "Woohoo, jackpot!" But the men in the back room were too intent on Harley's coming announcement to open the door and find out who had won the big prize. They unconsciously shifted in their chairs and waited.

"Numero uno, let's circle the wagons for our friend Jass."

"How we gonna do that?" asked Rymer Neff, who though skilled at arm wrestling and horseshoe pitching, rarely had an original idea and leaned heavily on his brethren for theirs.

"We go to the feed store and tell anyone who asks that His Honor has merely been to the church to express his outrage that a citizen of our town has been killed. Oh, and to pledge his assistance in capturing her killer."

"You mean we should sit in his chair and tell that to the customers?" Rymer asked.

Even Harley, who'd been best friends with Rymer since first grade, was astounded by Rymer's lack of subtlety.

"Nah, we go on over kinda casual and sit around the table where we can overhear what the customers are saying when they check out. And if somebody starts to say somethin' we don't like about Jass, we stick up for 'im."

"Oh, okay," said Rymer, slumping back in his chair with a thoughtful expression.

"What else we gotta do?" pressed Bucky.

"After we shake off any problems over to the feed store, we make sure Jass don't get nailed for the murder," Harley said.

The men nodded, each bringing to mind all the ways in which the mayor had aided, abetted or even concealed their own offenses large and small.

Even if Jasper Eugene Pinbiddie had killed Gudrun Cassandra Wince—an act of which each of these men knew Jass was capable—he would never be convicted of the charge if the backroom boys had anything to say about it.

No food establishment named in the annals of the Skyler County Department of Public Health had ever before failed an inspection as fully and abysmally as did the kitchen of Glory Hallelujah Church the day Gudrun Wince died.

Mr. Emerson Duty's pen ran out of ink and had to be replaced, so numerous were the violations of public health law committed by the food service operation of Glory Hallelujah Church, most notably the presence near a cooking surface of a dead human body but also including the presence of human blood on and around cooking surfaces, cooking vessels on the floor, cooking utensils on the floor and food on the floor.

The effects of those infractions were exacerbated by the facts that yellow caution tape barred Emerson Duty from the immediate vicinity of Gudrun Wince's body, that nevertheless he saw for certain there was no hairnet on the head of the late Ms. Wince, that paramedics had wheeled an obviously unsanitary conveyance into the room for the purpose of removing her body, that the room stank of human secretions and that a panful of garlic had over-roasted in the hubbub created by Gudrun's passing.

Edith Fay Smith, whose visionary leadership had made the Glory Hallelujah Church food ministry a model of community service, had never been so mortified. Not when twenty-five out of two hundred educators had been denied homemade cherry pie at the annual retirees' banquet because of a miscount by the Glory Girls. Not when three raw turkeys had been left to decompose inside a banana box because a new Glory Girl presumed that only bananas arrived in banana boxes. Not even when Laverna Inys Wharton had brought an abominable Spam casserole to a church picnic and printed *EDITH FAY SMITH* in big, ugly letters on the dish.

Edith Fay stood stoically as Mr. Duty filled page after page with words and numbers that threatened the reputation of the Glory Girls, the future of the Glory Hallelujah Church meal ministry and the underpinnings of the church budget.

"Our office will communicate with your office," Mr. Duty said, smartly sliding his replacement pen into his pocket. "Meanwhile, I am shutting down this kitchen."

"Mr. Duty, I assure you that this . . . uh, situation will be cleaned up and the kitchen sterilized within twenty-four hours."

Mr. Duty looked at Edith Fay over the top of his glasses and smiled for the first time since entering the church. "Ah, yes, I'm sure. But rules are rules. Food may not be served again from this kitchen until I or one of my colleagues has inspected it and found it within guidelines."

"How long will it take to schedule another inspection?"

"Call my office when you're ready," he said, handing Edith Fay a wrinkled business card. "Good day."

As Mr. Duty walked away, Edith Fay fought back tears. She would not, could not, cry over blinked milk—or spilled broccoli, as it were. She must remain objective. She must exercise leadership. She must set an example of calm and reason for the other Glory Girls.

She must also muster the courage to inform Pastor Annie Ido Scovill and the church council of the closure—and to bear the unspoken censure sure to follow, not from church leaders but from other citizens in want of their freshly cooked, politely served, filling, nutritious—and cheap—dinners.

The eleven Glory Girls had to squeeze together to fit into Edith Fay's office, to which they had been dispatched by Sheriff Dooley Skiles while state forensic techs worked in the kitchen.

Dooley had also posted Deputies Bobby Gibboney and Arnie Coker to watch the crime scene and Chief Deputy Stan Neiswonder to watch them, ordered Deputy Lou Shilky to string police tape all around the church, and had Doc Weber take Mayor

Pinbiddie to the choir room and occupy him until the sheriff could get there.

In addition, Dooley escorted the church custodian out of the building, then shook a forefinger at the people lounging under the side portico in hopes of seeing something good.

When Pastor Annie Scovill joined the Girls, they had to scooch together to give her a seat on a crate of cucumbers from which pickles were to be made.

Edith Fay spoke without preamble. "As you may already have heard, the church kitchen has been closed by the county health department because of so-called infractions noted today by an inspector."

Of course, the other Girls had already heard this awful news—from Mary Ellen Brinkman, who now raised her hand.

Receiving Edith Fay's nod, Mary Ellen said, "When we get the okay, the sanitizing team will work night and day to get the kitchen sterilized. We've already discussed it. We'll cover everything, have the exterminators over for good measure, and then we'll do the checklist again."

"Thank you. We all thank you," Edith Fay said. The others offered sedate applause.

Edith Fay continued, "Ella Mae, has Gudrun's family been told yet?"

Ella Mae Pugh, who sat on a case of canned wax beans destined for the food pantry, patted her frayed hairdo.

"I called her secretary at the high school—you know her, Jeannie Milton's niece, Patty Leta Keys—and she said Gudrun never mentioned any family at all. Patty Leta thought Gudrun might have come from Arkansas."

A mumble of surprise swept the room. "I thought Gudrun's people were from Marys Mills and that she had a brother living in California," said Jo Claire Carsey.

"No, I'm sure her father came from over at Jerry Run and then moved to Spartansville," rejoined Lloyda Ruth Dent. "She told me so herself."

"Well, she told me that her mother's parents immigrated from Belgium and her father's parents moved here from New York, but that her parents and grandparents all died before she was thirty," Ula Maude Ferrebee added.

Several people spoke at once to offer other views on the past and parentage of Gudrun Wince.

"Ladies, ladies," Edith Fay said finally, turning to the pastor.

The room stilled. Pastor Annie Scovill reached into her briefcase and brought out her copy of the church membership roster, in which she kept tidbits of demographic data for each church member.

Dog-eared and coffee-stained, the roster never left the pastor's side. And was never opened to the eyes of others.

She carefully opened the roster to the *W*'s. Under Gudrun's name were various notations that had nothing to do with the question at hand, followed by only one comment that might: *Ran away from home at 15.*

Pastor Annie paused to consider that notation.

The Girls' silence communicated their curiosity. Where was Gudrun Wince's family? Given Gudrun's age, thought variously to be between forty-five and sixty, could her parents still be alive? Were there brothers and sisters to swoop in and demand answers? Had she ever been married? Had Gudrun ever brought a family member to a Christmas service, homecoming or wedding? Why hadn't any of the very knowledgeable, very connected members of the Glory Girls service organization of Glory Hallelujah Church ever noticed how alone Gudrun Wince had actually been?

The pastor closed the roster, put it back in the briefcase and shut the case. She folded her hands on her lap and wet her lips. "I'm sorry, ladies, but I have nothing that tells us who or where Gudrun's family are."

When no one spoke, the pastor continued. "However, I'm sure the sheriff will want to speak with the family. I'll coordinate with him to find them and learn their wishes with regard to the funeral and other matters."

Edith Fay drew in a deep breath and said, "Very well. Thank you, Pastor. Now, Bida June, what did you find out in the book?"

Bida June Pyles had a copy of the Glory Girls Book of Bylaws in her lap and stood to read from it. "Here on page eighty-six . . ."

She was interrupted by Belle Watkins, who knocked thrice loudly on the door and burst into the room. Her cheeks were pink because she had been running.

"Edith Fay," she said, gulping air, "you have a call on line three. The intercom system is out again."

"Thank you, Belle, but would you take a message?"

"No! I'm sorry. I mean, probably no. I think you'll want to take the call."

"All right." She picked up the phone on the desk that once housed a sewing machine.

"This is Edith Fay Smith."

Quiet for the sake of Edith Fay's conversation, the others could hear, and see, her half of it.

"Yes, we do."

"About fifty dinners a year."

"Twelve of us."

A laugh. A pen picked up. "I'll talk it over with the others. May I get back to you? Yes, ready. Was that area code 404? Okay, got it. Yes, by Saturday. We'll be in touch."

Edith Fay ended the call and, not being one to pussyfoot, said, "Ladies, *Home Cookin'* wants us!"

Squeals of delight broke out. Zula Ruby Hissom made her black pageboy fly as she happy-danced, and Bida June Pyles whooped the war cry of the Biddlebourne Bulldogs, the town's famously competitive coed softball team. Even the staid Mary Ellen Brinkman grinned and clapped softly.

Home Cookin' was to the women of Glory Hallelujah Church what *Sports Illustrated* was to a high school football coach or *The New Yorker* was to a college sophomore studying journalism. It was the holy grail of amateur cooks, the Olympics of casserole and cookie making, the Pulitzer Prize of home recipe innovators.

Edith Fay held up a hand. The women hushed as one. "They want us for the cover feature in next year's Bridal Edition."

All present now realized something more. Not only had the Glory Girls of Glory Hallelujah Church been invited to appear in one of the country's top cooking publications, but they also had been chosen as the face of *Home Cookin's* most popular issue, the one published in February for brides of June and beyond.

"That means," Edith Fay continued, "that photos must be taken, recipes collected and interviews conducted no later than August thirty-first—this year."

The Glory Girls had been photographed and interviewed often enough by newspapers and magazines to know that editors took months to complete pre-publication tasks. *The West Virginia Culinary Archive Journal*, for instance, had spent fourteen long, pre-Thanksgiving days with the Glory Girls in November 2007 for an article that appeared exactly one year later.

"We have to let them know within forty-eight hours if we can do it," Edith Fay added. "They need to be here seven full days—to see what we do every day of the week."

"August 31st is only 67 days away," the pastor said, church calendar in hand.

The Glory Girls got out their own calendars.

"We don't know when we'll be able to use the kitchen again," Mary Ellen noted.

"We have the Biddlebourne High homecoming dinner on September eighth," said Lloyda Ruth.

"And the July Fourth cookout in Hearth House." Mary Ellen again.

"The Asher wedding reception June 28th."

"Refreshments every night for vacation Bible school, July 9th through the 13th."

"Seventy-five pies for the VFW picnic on August 11th."

"Plus the rescheduled cooking auditions," Edith Fay noted.

"And quite possibly a funeral dinner after Gudrun's service," the pastor added slowly.

Edith Fay flipped pages back and forth in her calendar, first studying July, then August, September, October, November and December.

After a full minute of page flapping, she said, "All in favor of scheduling the *Home Cookin'* visit August 12th through the 18th, raise a hand."

Ten hands went up. None stayed down except the pastor's, it being understood that ministers of the Gospel had their decisions and ministers of food had theirs.

The Glory Girls forgot all about Bida June's report.

Meanwhile in the choir room, Mayor Jass Pinbiddie faked another fit to further delay talking to Sheriff Dooley Skiles. In the Rhododendron Parlor, eight frustrated cook-off contestants fumed and used their time and cell phones to tell kith and kin what hadn't already been broadcast by busybodies and law enforcers.

Glory Girls Rule No. 5—The ministries of the Glory Girls service organization of Glory Hallelujah Church, Biddlebourne, West Virginia, shall occur equitably in twelve (12) subcommittees of community purpose and need. *Glory Girls Book of Bylaws,* adopted May 1958

CHAPTER SEVEN

At 200 Bailey Street, the mayor yanked off his shirt, shoved Doc Weber to the door and said, "I'm feelin' fine. You can go now."

Cecil Weber, M.D., named after former Governor Cecil Underwood, a close family friend, had been the fourth generation of Weber medical students to graduate with honors from West Virginia University. But he counted as his most valuable education that which he had received directly from his father, grandmother and great-grandfather.

Those forebears had imparted to Cecil Weber an oral history of county and town ranging from reports of which families had to be watched for heart disease to stories of which ones couldn't endure a hangnail without wailing for painkillers.

But the Weber family medical legacy also named those who'd had secret surgeries, the ones who'd been shot and the reasons why, the victims and sometimes the perpetrators of incest and other forms of molestation, the alcohol and drug addicts, spreaders of venereal disease, and people who didn't pay their doctor bills.

"Jass, you kickin' me out?" Doc Weber said good-naturedly.

"Git! I got things to do!"

Doc Weber was used to the sultry comments of women who wanted more than a physical examination, the kicks of children after immunizations and the shouts of octogenarians who could not hear and refused hearing aids.

However, Doc Weber expected civil behavior from the professionals around him, and he grudgingly considered Mayor Pinbiddie a professional.

But Cecil Weber, M.D., merely tucked this latest rudeness of Mayor Pinbiddie into his memory and said, "Well, sir, we all have things to do. Besides, here comes the sheriff, and it looks like he means business."

The doctor walked out the front door and nodded at Dooley Skiles as he walked in.

"Jass," Dooley said, "I just got a few questions. . . ."

Demonstrating a remarkable recovery from his recent indisposition, Jass lumbered up the stairs two at a time. Standing shirtless in the landing, he said, "I ain't got nothin' to hide. I'm gonna take me a shower. Wait in the parlor. I'll be down in ten minutes."

Before the sheriff could agree or disagree, the mayor ducked behind a door and turned a spigot on full blast.

Sheriff Skiles figured if he left now, he'd just have to corner Jass later. If he stayed, with any luck he might be able to eliminate Jass as a suspect in Gudrun's death or put the crime squarely at his feet.

He decided to wait for Jass to shower.

Dooley had never before been in Jass Pinbiddie's house while Jass lived in it. It had been built in the late 1800s from locally quarried stone with the turrets and gargoyles of the Victorian age. The original owners had proudly maintained the house, and so had the families that later occupied it.

But Jass Pinbiddie had bought the three-story property at auction in the housing bust of '09. Since then, Jass had neglected the upkeep of the grand dame's grounds, from which weeds, wrecks and weather's residues reigned all through the year.

Now from the central vantage of the parlor, Dooley got a close look at what Jass had done with the interior of the house: apparently nothing. The place was filthy, with torn and smudged wallpaper, footprints and food stains on antique oriental rugs and sticky grime on elegant chandeliers.

Every table, counter and cabinet bore debris formed of old newspapers, adult magazines, tools, ledgers, takeout cartons, Pabst Blue Ribbon bottles and Mountain Dew cans, and dirty clothes.

In the hall, atop a mahogany armoire with stained-glass insets, lay two shotguns under a heap of greasy cleaning rags and a bottle of Hoppe's Elite Gun Oil.

Glancing at his watch, Sheriff Skiles walked to the opposite side of the parlor. On display side by side were two nicely framed eight-by-ten color photos. One pictured Gudrun Wince in a red sequined dress, signed "You do it for me, Love, G."

The other photo was a straightforward likeness of Pearl Gay Osbourn, owner of the Biddlebourne Hoot 'n' Scoot, in a tight yellow sweater and blue jeans, signed "Sweet Cakes, you're the best, All my love forever, Pearl Gay."

Sheriff Skiles did two things. He decided Mary Ellen Brinkman had likely been right about Jass and Gudrun, and he opened his notebook to add Pearl Gay Osbourn to his list of suspects.

Because Jass' ten minutes had come and gone, Dooley returned to the foyer and hollered up the stairs.

"Jass, you ready yet?"

No answer.

"Mayor, let's get this over with," Dooley yelled as he began to climb.

There was still no response, so Dooley hurried to the door behind which Jass had disappeared.

He knocked, the door fell open, and he saw not only that the bathroom was empty but also that it lacked any sign of recent use except for water running steadily from the showerhead. There were no towels wet or otherwise, no shaving implements, no toiletries and—most tellingly—no dirty clothes or spilled mouthwash. Except for a sheen of water where the shower had sprayed beyond the open stall, the bathroom fixtures stood in grubby, dry testimony to Jass Pinbiddie's deceit.

"That son of a gun," Dooley Skiles said quietly.

Dooley turned and climbed the stairs to the attic. Working his way down, he inspected every room, closet and cubbyhole on five levels including basement and attic. Then he left the house and did the same in the backyard shed and three-car garage.

There was no sign of Mayor Jasper Eugene Pinbiddie.

"Look at this," Edith Fay said, again holding up her cell phone.

The other Glory Girls had left to select their best recipes for the *Home Cookin'* shoot. Edith Fay and the pastor had just spot-checked the building for stowaway gawkers.

Pastor Annie leaned in and adjusted her trifocals. "Poor Gudrun. Yes, I see the stab wound."

"It's what's not there, not what is," Edith Fay hinted.

"Well, I don't see her purse, but I suppose she put it in the cupboard."

"No, she did not. It wasn't anywhere around her. And neither was her recipe box."

"What? Her recipe box is missing? Oh, my. Did Sheriff Skiles take it?" Annie leaned back and put a hand to her forehead.

"Huh-uh. I just got a call from Dooley, and he said he didn't take anything from the scene yet."

"Oh." Both women silently considered the ramifications of a missing recipe box.

At Glory Hallelujah Church, a recipe collection was nearly as sacrosanct to a serious cook as the Holy Bible. Each compilation represented years of searching, experimenting and winnowing. Recipes were rarely used as found but were improved upon, halved or doubled according to family size, tweaked to prevailing tastes and budgets, adjusted for a hundred variants important only to a particular cook.

Many a Biddlebourne girl began collecting recipes around puberty, tested those recipes on sundry boyfriends and later married the man who responded best to her cooking. A recipe box took the place of a hope chest for many young women, and more than one suitor in the county had presented a handsomely engraved recipe box to a girlfriend as token of affection and signal of intention.

"That's not all," Edith Fay said. "Look at this." She pushed buttons on her phone and displayed an image of the broken casserole dish and its splattered contents that rested next to Gudrun's body.

"That looks like . . . what?" the pastor said, rubbing her chin.

"I don't know either," said Edith Fay. "For all of Gudrun's bragging, I thought her entry might be the best dish we'd ever seen in the cook-off. She called it Mammy's Marvelous Biscuit Casserole, but I don't see biscuits there."

"And I don't see marvelous," Annie opined.

The church bell chimed six times, startling both women. "I have a meeting at seven, and I need to stop at home first," the pastor said.

"Then I'll bring you up to date as quickly as I can," Edith Fay said. "Dooley interviewed the cook-off contestants and let them go home. I asked him if they offered anything useful, but he wouldn't say either way.

"He did ask me, though, if I'd seen Jass Pinbiddie. I thought that was odd, seeing as how Doc Weber took Jass home 'cause he was feeling so poorly. I told Dooley that, but he was way ahead of me. Said Jass had to leave the house . . . suddenly."

"Hmm," said the pastor.

"On other fronts, we've already had a dinner cancellation. The Boormans. Afraid the kitchen won't be open by next Friday. They moved the rehearsal dinner to the Daniel Boone room at the Gentry Inn."

"You don't think any of the big fundraisers will be canceled, do you?" Annie asked uneasily.

"I doubt it. Our next big one is the homecoming banquet. There's no other place in Biddlebourne that can hold that many diners. Besides, three of the Glory Girls are on the homecoming committee."

"That's good news," the pastor said. "The church budget needs the six thousand dollars that homecoming brings in. The way things are going, it may be our last big dinner that's tax-free."

Both women painfully realized that an indefinite closing of the Glory Hallelujah Church kitchen could undermine the many community services and projects carried out by the congregation. Church members pledged their tithes, and offering plates brimmed, but it was the delectable meals organized by the Glory Girls that reliably brought in the most money. Even a temporary interruption in food service would hurt.

The pastor spoke again as she rose to leave. "Of course, the prayer team knows about Gudrun and the kitchen closing. And I've put in a few discreet inquiries about our surprise inspection. We need to know who's behind it. I may have some answers soon."

Joining the pastor at the door, Edith Fay nodded. "Call me if you need me. I have to go too. Dooley's coming to the house this evening."

Edith Fay didn't mention what she would be doing before the sheriff came to call.

She got in her car, turned on the air conditioning and tapped the speed dial on her phone.

"Ella Mae," she said when her call was answered on the third ring, "I'm sorry to have you ask you this, but I must."

"What is it, Edith Fay? I'll do whatever I can. You know that."

The top Glory Girl dug in her satchel for notebook and pen. "Here's what I want to know," she said. "This will take a while, so I hope you don't have dinner on the stove."

"I'll take it off," Ella Mae said.

"What's that smell?" William Wharton demanded.

Laverna turned from the oven and smiled. "Do you like it?"

William, who at the bottom of the ninth inning in a tight game between Pittsburgh and Cincinnati had felt compelled to roust from his recliner and trot to the kitchen, held one hand over his nose and used the other to turn on the vent fan.

"Holy cow, it smells like, like those tires that burned for three days over behind the race track. What are you baking in there? Tennis shoes?"

Without a word, Laverna switched off the oven and bent to retrieve a pan that held the remains of a whole Alaskan salmon for which she had paid $19.99 a pound at the Sparkelette.

The unfortunate fish had been snagged by an Inuit fisherman, sold to a dockside wholesaler, quick-shipped to Richmond, Virginia, and trucked the next day to Biddlebourne only to be immolated by Laverna Inys Wharton in her first go at the misbegotten recipes of the late Gudrun Cassandra Wince.

The salmon lay shrunken, shriven of its nutritious fatty oils and surrounded by charred tomato and eggplant slices. Sickly smoke wafted from it in the direction of the vent fan, which William had set on high.

"You know I like my steak medium rare," William commented.

"It's salmon!" Laverna sneezed five times and sank into a chair at the dinette. "I was smoking it for dinner."

Glancing toward the den and the televised sound of hysterical cheers, William looked over his shoulder as he left the kitchen. "Don't worry," he said. "We can have pizza."

Alone while William hurried back to his game, Laverna swallowed hard and picked up the yellowed card on which an illustrious Biddlebourne cook had long ago penned the heading *Bkd slm*.

She took a clean recipe card and again tried to unriddle the ingredient list: 1 lg slm, 1t st, 4T sp, 4T ss, 3clgl . . .

All truths are not to be told. *Proverb*

CHAPTER EIGHT

"You lousy two-timer. You gotta lotta nerve coming here!"

Pearl Gay Osbourn brandished a garden spade, its pointed blade mere inches from Jass Pinbiddie's crotch. The mayor, who'd canceled the evening's town council session, used his hands to protect his genitals and his feet to back away from the enraged woman.

"Baby, I can explain," he shouted as Pearl Gay pinned him to the Coca-Cola vending machine at the Hoot 'n' Scoot. Fortunately, the store and its drive-through window were free of customers at the moment, though that could change quickly if anyone decided to come by and toot for a six-pack of Budweiser or a carton of Marlboros.

"Like hell! I got all the explanation I need from my customers. How long you been playin' around with that hag Gudrun Wince? Huh? How long?"

"It was just business, Honey. I swear! Geezooey, Pearl Gay, get that thing away from me, would ya?"

Jass' efforts to placate his second-best mistress gained him nowt. Pearl Gay dropped the shovel and picked up a metal chair. Straining the tensile strength of her bright orange tank top and canary yellow leggings, she corralled him against a wall and clobbered him with the chair until he slid to the floor with arms and legs curled into a shield.

A horn sounded at the service window on the other side of the store. Pearl Gay said, "You get up from there and I swear I'll finish the job." Jass stayed put because he could neither outrun nor outfight Pearl Gay, who spent much of her time stacking beer cases.

"Thanks, Carl. Appreciate the business," Pearl Gay said sweetly as Carl Jenkins drove away. Pearl Gay went to the front of the store, put up a ragged *CLOSED* sign and turned out the exterior lights. Turning toward Jass, she screeched, "Okay, just for the fun of it, tell me what kinda business you coulda had with *her*."

"Can I have a Mountain Dew?" he asked.

"No, you . . . you jackass! Talk! Now!"

Stretching out his legs so he could hitch himself up on the wall, Jass smiled feebly and licked his lips. "Me and Gudrun had a little arrangement, that's all," he ventured.

"What kinda arrangement?" Pearl Gay sat at her smoking table but kept both hands on the chair-turned-weapon.

Jass Pinbiddie didn't want to tell Pearl Gay about all his arrangements with Gudrun Wince, such as their profit-skimming from high school sports concessions, their bid-rigging with vendors and contractors and their bribe-taking from job candidates.

"Aw, Honey, you probably already know about it," he said placatingly. "Me and Gudrun just wanted to do right by all the other businesses in town and put a tax on the food they serve over at that Glory Gladtomeetcha Church."

Pearl Gay was not amused. "What the heck are you talkin' about?"

Thinking fast, Jass said, "Well, as you know, there is a business tax paid by all store and restaurant owners in Biddlebourne."

Pearl Gay nodded and Jass continued. "I got to thinkin'. Who gets away scot-free on taxes? Who serves hundreds, no, thousands of meals every year and never pays a dime to the city treasury?"

"Okay. I get it. You sayin' that church ain't payin' its fair share?"

"Yes, exactly," Jass said as he struggled upward and dropped onto a chair next to Pearl Gay. "See, I figured that all the store owners like yourself could pay less if the church just paid their fair share.

"But when I proposed my little idea, that pastor woman went off like a firecracker and put up all kinds of ridiculous objections, even got some of the council on her side, though they're tryin' not to let on.

"So that's when I thought of Gudrun. I swear it was all business, Honey. I went to her for help in getting inside that Glory Girls gang. She decided to run for a spot they got on their high and mighty board, or whatever they call it, so she could be on the inside and give me information that could be . . . ah, helpful . . . about taxes, that is."

"Would my taxes go down if the church paid taxes?" Pearl Gay was a wounded lover, but she was also a businesswoman, though she had ignored at least two honking horns while she and Jass talked.

"Why, Honey, they sure would," he improvised. "I figure you'd go from, what, about three thousand dollars a year to, oh, maybe two thousand. Maybe less."

Pearl Gay looked straight at Jass as if to gauge his truthfulness by the set of his jaw and the shift of his eyes. She tapped the heel of one foot on the thin linoleum she'd laid herself when she built the store twenty-seven years earlier.

"Did you kill her?"

"What did you hear?" His voice was tentative.

"I asked you a simple question," she said. "Did you kill that battle ax Gudrun Wince?"

"How could I? I was in my office all afternoon."

"And you swear on your life that's all you had to do with Gudrun and you and her wasn't . . . playin' pink submarine when you got together about business?"

"I swear it," Jass said with his right hand over the general area of his esophagus. "But because of the . . . delicacy of my situation, I do need to lay low for a while. I was hoping you'd let me stay downstairs until I . . . sort things out in my head."

The Hoot 'n' Scoot basement was special to Pearl Gay and Jass, being where they had trysted every Thursday afternoon for eleven years when Jass' staff thought he was on buying trips and Pearl Gay's customers thought she was taking inventory.

Pearl Gay got up and fetched a Mountain Dew from a tall refrigerator. "I ain't sayin' I forgive you, but I'll let you stay," she said, handing him the Dew. "Just for a while, hear me? You drive your Blazer over here?"

"Of course not," he said with a grin. "I took the old hiking trail. Didn't meet a soul on the way."

"Well, at least you were smart about that," she said. "Now let's go and get you settled. Did I hurt you with that chair?"

Jass smiled and patted her rump as they walked toward the basement door. It wouldn't take long for him to get settled and start receiving "first aid" for his wounds. The bed and blankets were already there.

"I've been picking up some background on Gudrun, and I need . . . I need . . ."

"A reality check?" asked Pastor Annie as she closed the door of her office and headed for the coffee.

"Something like that," Sheriff Skiles said, walking to a window. "Thanks for coming back in to talk with me."

The late evening shade silhouetted the beech, sweet gum and poplar trees in the prayer garden.

"It's no problem," Annie said. "I have paperwork to do anyway."

Annie handed him a cup of the morning's coffee and carried her own to a padded armchair.

"Thing is," Dooley said with his back to her, "I'm finding out a lot of people had reason to dislike Gudrun Wince."

"I imagine you'd rather focus on the perpetrator than on the victim."

Dooley took the chair across from Annie. "That's right," he said. "The more I hear about her, the more suspects I find. I'd like to check some things with you to keep from going down any more rabbit holes than I have to."

"What we say doesn't leave the room. Okay?"

"Deal," Dooley said.

The sheriff gulped more coffee and said, "To start with, our deceased is . . . mysterious herself. She's been in town for decades, but nobody seems to know how old she is . . . was or how she earned her keep before she got here."

Annie drew in a breath. She had been concerned that Gudrun's background would have to come out, but there was no delaying it now. She consoled herself that in revealing information about Gudrun she would be helping to find her killer.

"She told me herself that she ran away from a foster home in Wetzel County when she was fifteen," Annie said. "She got a job in Youngstown."

Dooley nodded and wrote in a small spiral notebook. "That matches what I've heard. Do you know what year that was?"

"I checked my notes today. Gudrun came to Biddlebourne in 1973. She was born in 1951, so I guess that makes her . . ."

"Sixty-one," Dooley said. "Did she ever talk with you about her birth parents or foster parents?"

"No. She said only that she was unhappy with all her foster families."

"Do you know whether she changed her name?"

"We never talked about that."

Dooley scratched his head and drained his cup. "Word is she scraped up enough money to go to college. Any idea what kinda work she did?"

"She never said," Annie responded, "though she was clear she wanted to do something positive with her life. Gudrun yearned for a career that was respectable. I think that's why she chose teaching and worked so hard to move up the ladder at Biddlebourne High."

"She ever tell you when she came to Skyler County?"

"No, but she was here long before I arrived," Annie said. "I suppose those records are filed with the school board."

"Yeah. I haven't even started on records yet. I'm just talking to people for now. Speaking of which, I talked to several of the teachers at the high school. They didn't have much good to say about Gudrun. There've been reports that special cash accounts at the school—you know, things like the collection for flood relief—started going missing after she got there. But they were never able to get any direct evidence."

"I've heard the same rumors," Annie said. "A few of the women here at the church bear some animosity toward her too, I regret to say. They contend that Gudrun had the home economics teacher make dishes that she claimed as her own in order to gain approval in the Ladies Aid Society."

"Wow," said the sheriff. "Stealing credit for food that others made? That takes the cake—no pun intended."

"Like you, we have no proof," the pastor hastened to add. "But I'm curious about that. How did Gudrun become principal if she was surrounded by rumors of wrongdoing?"

Dooley rubbed his forehead. "I'm beginning to understand how that may have happened. This whole thing may be bigger than it looked at first."

The sheriff grew silent. Sensing he would say no more about Gudrun, Annie said, "Dooley, I need to know something else that may have nothing to do with Gudrun's death."

"What's that?"

"Do you know who made those bogus complaints about the church kitchen?"

"Lordie, I heard about that. You sayin' you don't know who did it?"

"I don't, and I'm sure the Glory Girls don't either."

"Well, all I can say is I'll keep my ears open. You gotta understand I have my hands full as it is."

"I understand, Sheriff," she said. "I hope the kitchen complaints aren't related to Gudrun. . . ."

"Amen to that."

"Well, I gotta get over to Edith Fay's," he said, rising.

"Sheriff, it's important for us to know whether Gudrun has any family living—because of the funeral. I'll make inquiries about that, if it's all right with you."

"I'd appreciate it," he said. "My team's stretched far enough as it is. Just let me know what you find out."

"I will," Annie said, dreading what might ensue.

Glory Girls Rule No. 16—Slots lettered A-1 through A-12 in the west parking lot of Glory Hallelujah Church, Biddlebourne, West Virginia, shall be reserved for Glory Girls at all times except for one hour preceding, during and one hour following all worship services on Christmas Eve, Christmas Day, Palm Sunday, Easter Sunday and Biddlebourne Homecoming Sunday. *Glory Girls Book of Bylaws,* adopted May 1995

CHAPTER NINE

Mr. Emerson Duty was on the hot seat.

Actually, it was a metal folding chair placed by his supervisor directly in front of her desk as if he were an errant child and she the omnipotent ruler of his universe.

Which she was.

Ms. Blaize Luzader, newly transferred against her will and preference to Spartansville from the Charleston office, riffled pages of notes she had taken about the closure of a church kitchen in Biddlebourne, some burg out in the county where Ms. Luzader had never been and hoped never to go in her rise to government greatness.

She wore her red power suit and black patent stilettos, the ones with the tiny bows on the side, and had her blond hair done up in a careful twist that showed off her long neck and modest but shiny earrings.

"I've had a number of calls today about you," she said.

"Oh?"

Ms. Luzader let her gaze fall from Emerson Duty's bowtie to his rumpled brown suit and then to one of the pages she held. "Your visit to this church here . . . uh, Glory Hallelujah Church in Biddlebourne . . . seems irregular."

"How so?" said Mr. Emerson Duty, a man of few words when those words were about his own competence.

"I believe you know how so, but I will tell you—for the record." She pulled a small tape recorder from a desk drawer and set it next to her left elbow. Clicking it on, she continued, "Let the record show that unit supervisor Blaize Luzader is speaking with inspector Emerson Duty at 6 p.m. on June 14, 2012, at the Skyler County Department of Public Health in Spartansville, West Virginia.

"Mr. Duty, will you please answer allegations that on Thursday, June 14, 2012, you unlawfully inspected and closed the kitchen of Glory Hallelujah Church in Biddlebourne, West Virginia?"

He swallowed so hard his bowtie danced over his Adam's apple. "My inspection of said premises was based on reports of irregularities filed with this office by responsible parties in Biddlebourne."

"And just who are those responsible parties, uh . . . Emerson?" she said, glancing at the fat personnel file upon which her subject's name was printed.

Emerson Duty was not one to shoulder blame belonging to others, but neither was he one to tattle, especially when his own culpability could thereby come to light. "I don't have their names with me. And, as the supervisor knows, all our active case records were compromised by today's shredding . . . mishap."

Ms. Blaize Luzader straightened her spine, causing her suit jacket to rise just perceptibly over her dainty bosom. *What's next in this hick town*, she thought, *the goat ate my records?* Again she rued the day she had been sent to this place, with its plodding staff and trivial cases.

However, she had to allow for the fact that the office clerk, one Miss Aveline Marsh, had on this, her third day of employment, mistakenly shredded a large batch of current case files instead of a larger batch of obsolete files that had been so designated and stacked behind the water cooler.

"That is no excuse," she said, although she thought it might be a legitimate excuse for Emerson Duty's failure to produce the names of his informants. "You know that all case files are to be reproduced in triplicate—one copy for the office, one copy for the case worker and one copy for the inspected party.

"Further," she said while paging through her notes, "I have been told that you failed to notify the inspected party in advance of the complaints filed against it, that you failed to give the inspected party the required seven days in which to answer any complaints, and that you closed the inspected party's operations on your own authority without seeking my consultation—and my required agreement."

"Who told you all those things?" he said before he could stop himself.

"That," she said icily, "is not for you to know. Suffice it to say that truly responsible parties have spoken with me of these matters."

Indeed, Ms. Luzader was certain that William Wharton was a bona fide attorney, that Shirl Burrows was the bona fide treasurer of Glory Hallelujah Church, and that Dr. Cecil Weber was a bona fide—and very longtime—benefactor of Glory Hallelujah Church and consultant to the Skyler County Department of Public Health.

The calls from these persons had been cordial but pointed. Each expressed a different aspect of the church's inconvenience and righteous indignation over Emerson Duty's spurious kitchen inspection. And each hinted, just as cordially, of questions that would be put to persons in higher places should Ms. Luzader fail to take their concerns seriously.

If there was one thing Ms. Luzader wanted to avoid, it was aspersions cast on her abilities toward the direction of higher up. Such reports, true or untrue, would stick to her own personnel record like old mascara, running rampant over the good parts and drawing attention to the bad.

"Emerson," she said, drawing out his name with a longsuffering breath, "do you deny that you committed the three offenses I have specified?"

Emerson Duty thought about it. He had been employed by the health department nearly forty years and would reap a generous pension in only twenty-four months. This was no time to speak or act rashly.

Though Emerson Duty was a cautious man, he knew he had done wrong. What he had done wrong was to presume that a new supervisor would take no notice of individual case files until she had decorated her office with diplomas, certificates, pictures and knickknacks and held expense account lunches with every staff member.

Still, Blaize Luzader apparently had little direct evidence of his misdoings—and might never have any, thanks to the ineptitude of the office clerk.

"I would like to speak with my attorney before I say anything else," he said. He crossed his arms over his wilted jacket and looked steadfastly at his supervisor.

Now Emerson Duty had really gone and done it. Picturing a hot conference room occupied by herself, Emerson Duty, attorneys, sundry support staff and her own superior, Ms. Luzader tried not to show her displeasure. She had intended to fire this duplicitous man on the spot, thereby clarifying who was in charge and who was a by-the-book administrator. But she did not want the regional director to associate Duty's shenanigans in any way with herself.

"Very well then," she said. "You are suspended with pay until further notice. Please remove yourself and your personal possessions from the building as soon as you leave this room. You will be notified when to return for the . . . next step in these proceedings."

Mr. Emerson Duty adjusted his bowtie, rose and walked out the door with his hands in his pockets, one on his cell phone and the other on the nice little packet of cash he'd received for his work in Biddlebourne.

Glory Hallelujah's people of prayer, numbering a full fifth of the congregation, were on it. In barns, fields, mines, offices, homes and a few taverns, they beseeched the Lord God Almighty to sort out the woes besetting the church in the form of assassination, inspection and taxation.

The most fervent petitions, however, flowed from the lips of Edith Fay Smith. Kneeling at an antique rocker in her sunroom, she wept and called out the name of each Glory Girl.

She sought strength for Pastor Annie and everyone else on the church staff, the town council, the church council and the high school faculty. She pounded the cushion of the rocking chair and told God about Gudrun Wince, Jass Pinbiddie and Emerson Duty.

And she shouted to God that her life's work was at stake, that the needs of the community should trump all the devil's devices, and that she dearly needed the Lord's help in her current circumstances.

After a while, when the bumps on the hand-braided rug made big enough dents in her knees, she arose and looked around her to regain a sense of balance.

Edith Fay Smith's home reflected her heritage. Built by her forebears in the irenic lull before World War I, it was designed in the Craftsman style with low-pitched roof, squared columns and deep eaves. But when Edith Fay became its owner at age twenty-seven after her mother died, she had used the energy of grief to add her own touches.

She placed flower boxes along the base and railing of the covered porch that ran along the front and sides of the house. In those boxes she planted, on the south and west sides, annuals including begonias, zinnias, marigolds, petunias and verbena, and on the shady side impatiens, browallia, oxalis, polka-dot plants and sweet potato vines.

The following May she sowed perennials in the ground around the entire house, focusing on seven varieties of hosta for the shady sides and dahlias, hyssop, crocus and fleabane for the sunny sides. In this flower border she left clearings six to eight feet wide in which she later transplanted juniper, boxwood and spruce plantings given to her by friends and neighbors.

Indoors, Edith Fay personally dismantled the small brick fireplace in the great room and, with her reciprocating saw, opened the resulting hole through to the kitchen. Then she hired Creed Fedderman to expertly line and trim the aperture with stones that she lugged up the hillside from the creek behind the house.

She used the old bricks to make a fire pit in the back yard.

When that project was done, she rested a week and went to work on the kitchen, installing new cabinets with the help of other women in the Ladies Aid Society and covering the floor with boards from what used to be a haymow in the ancient barn. She had the man at Biddlebourne Lumber split a red-oak beam from the barn and used the two halves to fashion mantels for both sides of her new fireplace.

Then she covered everything in the kitchen with heavy-duty tarps and had Bucky Feinmeister come out and rip three large holes in the ceiling. Into those openings, she installed solar collectors that stored energy from the sun and passed natural light directly into the kitchen 365 days a year.

The result was that Edith Fay Smith's home, hardly an eyesore before her ownership, became a showplace. It starred on every Skyler County home and garden tour whether the event was arranged by a local garden club or the state antiquities commission.

Edith Fay loved caring for her home, for she saw it as an extension of her parents, Julia Burdette Stealey Smith and Malcolm Gerard Smith. She had no siblings, living or otherwise, and had blossomed under Julia and Malcolm's affection and guidance from skinny, awkward child to gracious and accomplished woman.

No expense had been spared in her education. She worked four years in the Peace Corps after graduating from Wellesley College, then returned to Biddlebourne when her mother became ill and hung her diploma in her bedroom where visitors would not think her boastful for displaying it.

She had worked nearly two decades at Skyler County General Hospital, starting with the sterilization of surgical packs and moving up to the post of hospital administrator by the age of thirty-five.

However, an epiphany at age thirty-nine had given Edith Fay to understand that God was calling her to the leadership of the Glory Girls. She relayed this fact to the trustees of the hospital who, though astonished and chagrined, granted her request for early retirement. Her name and face were still fondly and sometimes fearfully remembered at that institution.

Now she lived on a modest hospital pension and an immodest income from oil and gas leases and a trust left to her by her industrious parents, who had raised beef and hogs, operated a lumber mill and cultivated apple and cherry orchards on the Smith farm.

The jangling telephone startled Edith Fay. It was late and she still expected the sheriff. She hoped he was calling to postpone their meeting.

"This is Edith Fay."

"Edie, I've been trying to catch you all day," yelled Thelma Blivins, who thought everybody on the planet was as deaf as she was.

Stifling a groan, Edith Fay said, "I haven't been home long. What's going on, Thelma?"

"I want to let you know I'll be glad to make the blueberry pies for the funeral dinner. What day is the funeral? Nobody seems to know."

Edith shook her head and frowned. Thelma was using the volunteer ploy to dig for details about the death at Glory Hallelujah Church so she could twist and expand those tidbits into a nonstop stream of gossip and rumormongering.

Neither the ploy nor the prattle amused Edith Fay.

"I haven't been informed of that," she said.

"Isn't that odd?" Thelma asked.

"What do you mean?"

"Well, it's been all day . . . she died ten hours ago . . . and I reckon someone might make the proper plans."

"We have been busy, very busy, today, as you might imagine. I'll ask Mary Ellen to give you a call when we know more." Mary Ellen Brinkman always communicated assignments to volunteers when there was a funeral meal at the church, a fact that Thelma Blivins surely knew.

Acting as if Edith Fay had not spoken, Thelma said, "I'll tell you one thing for sure. This will not be a well attended funeral, unless, that is, people come to make sure Gudrun Wince is dead."

"Thelma! That is quite an ungracious thing to say."

"It's true. Don't you agree?"

"No, I certainly do not. . . ." Before Thelma could say what else she thought, the doorbell rescued Edith Fay. "Someone's at the door. I have to go. I'll let Mary Ellen know about the pies. 'Bye."

With a relief she would not have predicted, Edith Fay opened the door to Sheriff Dooley Skiles.

The Faith Development Subcommittee of the Glory Girls service organization of Glory Hallelujah Church, Biddlebourne, West Virginia, shall organize and conduct three spiritual retreats annually: one for Biddlebourne women ages eighteen (18) years and better, one for Biddlebourne men ages eighteen (18) years and better, and one for Biddlebourne children ages thirteen (13) years through seventeen (17) years. *Glory Girls Book of Bylaws,* adopted May 1959

CHAPTER TEN

The polished star on Dooley's hat caught a twinkle from the antique chandelier, and the sheriff smelled the roses on the hall table as he stepped into the foyer and doffed his hat.

Closing the door, Edith Fay turned to him and said, "I figured we'd sit in the kitchen. I can give you a bite to eat. I s'pect you've not had your supper yet either."

The prospect of a late meal at Edith Fay's table made Dooley grin. As he followed her to the kitchen he couldn't help admiring her slender figure and bare feet.

Edith Fay had never married. Many a fine family in Biddlebourne had hinted to Julia Stealey Smith that a son would like to court her daughter. But the high school girl had been more interested in music and basketball, the college woman more attuned to world travel and service.

When Edith Fay came back to Biddlebourne to tend her mother, hearts fluttered in several young men who made their hopes known to Edith Fay. But she could not allow their attentions to distract her from Julia's care.

By the time Edith Fay established herself as a visionary leader at the hospital, most men were intimidated by her authority and more likely to give her a bar graph than a love note.

"How about roast beef and gravy piled up on buttermilk biscuits with homemade slaw on the side?" she said.

"That'd be real welcome, Edith Fay. Can I set the table?"

No man in Edith Fay's acquaintance had ever before volunteered to set her table. She smiled.

"That would be real nice, Dooley. The plates . . ."

"I think I know where everything is."

Dooley had sat dozens of times in Edith Fay's kitchen, ostensibly to plan departmental cooperation with the Glory Girls on crowd and traffic control at their numerous celebration and fundraising meals. But he'd paid attention to everything he saw and heard and had become a tacit fan of his hostess' home-cooked meals and home-grown philosophy.

Sheriff Skiles, considered a catch by many single women—and several married ones—in Skyler County, had a checkered romantic history. He'd been engaged at age twenty-three to his college sweetheart, Amanda "Sissy" Tennant. But Sissy broke up with Dooley when he left for the Navy, telling him she wasn't a waiting kind of girl.

After Dooley returned to Biddlebourne from SEAL service, he dated a string of young women who appreciated his Navy medals, muscled body and quick mind. But they did not appreciate his habit of working fourteen hours a day in his Uncle Harold's bail bond business.

"Dooley, didn't the Navy teach you what a man does at night?" one of his girlfriends had asked one day while they lunched at the Mug. Dooley had noticed the smiles of the other diners.

Three months later, Dooley ran for the sheriff's post.

After they stashed the dinner dishes in the dishwasher, Edith Fay and Dooley sat on opposite sides of the big farm table, Edith Fay doodling on her notebook and Dooley putting bookmarks in his.

He put his pen down. She put her pencil down. She asked if he wanted more coffee. He didn't.

She regarded him steadily, noting for the first time how square his chin was. "Go ahead and ask," she said.

"You know I have to investigate all possibilities . . . in a case like this," he began.

"Of course."

"I'm wanting to eliminate . . . um . . . certain individuals as suspects in Gudrun's murder."

Edith Fay nodded. "I understand that you cannot speak with me about all the details." She folded her hands over her notebook.

Dooley shifted in the oak chair, the rungs of which Edith Fay's cousin, Gail Smith, had turned on his own lathe over in Doddridge County.

Dooley turned a page in the notebook and stared at it. "Could a Glory Girl have done this to Gudrun?"

Edith Fay's expression remained neutral. She sat still and thought about Dooley's question. In all her years alongside the Glory Girls, she had witnessed nothing even remotely violent in them.

Chuckling, she said, "A couple of 'em have said *damn* in my hearing."

Dooley laughed politely. "Edith Fay, I really need to know. I'm up in the air on this investigation with nowhere to put my feet."

Chastened by his earnestness, she turned serious. "It would help me if you could share what the Girls have told your deputies. If there are any discrepancies or questions, perhaps I could help."

"I haven't picked up any discrepancies there," he said, which was the truth as far as it went.

"I don't mind your asking about the Girls," she said. "I realize all ten of them were in the kitchen when it happened."

"I need to know exactly where they were when the body was found. What were they doing? Monitoring the contestants?"

Edith Fay nearly panicked. She had put the same kind of queries to Ella Mae Pugh earlier and had carefully studied the responses of her top lieutenant. *Did Dooley know something she didn't?*

"It was the Girls' original plan to monitor contestants when they started the cook-offs way back when. But as it turned out, the contestants didn't like people looking over their shoulders. Said it confused them, kept them off balance. So now the Girls sort of patrol the kitchen in general during a cook-off and assist the cooks in small ways, such as locating special tools. They take turns sitting at the table where we file delivery invoices. They walk around the kitchen to keep an eye on the contestants. Sometimes they check in products at the delivery bays."

"How many deliveries did you get today?"

"We were due for paper goods, soda pop, coffee and tea, and maybe eggs if Johnny Ferrebee's chickens are laying. I'll check the invoices to see what arrived."

"And when it arrived," Dooley added. "I'd appreciate that. So the Glory Girls were in the kitchen but not observing each contestant one to one?"

"That's right."

"Anyone else around there today, I mean besides Buddy Lee and the delivery people?"

"Well, a photographer from the *Sentinel* came over around ten to take a shot of the contestants."

"Oh. You mean Winona Wilcox?"

"Yes," Edith Fay said, wondering why Dooley paused when he said the name.

"I'll get in touch with her. Were there any other cameras in use that you saw?"

"The contestants aren't allowed to have cameras in the kitchen during the cook-off. I didn't see any Glory Girls using a camera."

Edith Fay pushed imaginary crumbs off the table.

"All right," he said, checking his notes and dog-earing a page. "I looked all over the kitchen but didn't see anywhere someone could have hidden."

"Not unless he—or she—was small enough to hide in a cabinet . . . or a refrigerator," she added, "but I imagine your people looked everywhere."

"Hmm. What about knives? Were any knives missing at the end of the day?" he asked.

A crow chattered outside the window. They twisted to look, though they both recognized the bird's scratchy scraw, but saw only the lower boughs of a tall maple thrown into shadow by low-voltage lights.

"We didn't take an inventory of the knives, Dooley. I'm sorry. I should have thought of that. I hope it's not too late now."

"We haven't found the murder weapon yet. We aren't sure the killer used a knife, but we need a list of all the knives kept in the kitchen."

"I'll take care of the list first thing tomorrow," Edith Fay promised. "Um, may I ask what your deputies did with Gudrun's purse and recipe box?"

Dooley had personally collected all the evidence from the area nearest Gudrun's body. He had seen no purse or recipe box.

"Oh, all the evidence is tagged, counted and stored at the station," he said.

"I was wondering about her purse because it might help us locate her family," Edith Fay improvised.

"I'm sorry, but all the evidence has to stay at the station. I'm really not at liberty to discuss it," he said. "Your pastor promised to help track down her people. You might want to coordinate with her."

Dooley's cell phone dinged, and he read the text message. Edith Fay sat quietly and tried to decide where to look next for Gudrun's purse and recipe box.

"I need to get back to the office," Dooley said, "but before I go can you tell me if anything—anything at all—happened during the cook-off that was odd or different . . . or unplanned?"

"The only thing we did differently this time, as far as I can think of right now, was that we allowed Buddy Lee to come in and help. I doubt we'll do that again."

He drained his cup and said, "I hope you aren't blaming Buddy Lee for this. Innocent until guilty and all of that."

"Of course not," Edith Fay replied. "The main reason is that we require the contestants to bring all their ingredients. When Gudrun sent Buddy Lee to the store for butter, she broke a rule. And we opened the door to that by letting Buddy Lee help."

"All right. I understand. Just one more question. Did any of the contestants or the other Glory Girls do or say anything that seemed out of line to you?"

"The contestants were all nervous. I think you're aware that we hold the cook-off to make the final cut for membership in the Glory Girls. They wanted to do well and were on their best behavior—mostly."

"Uh-huh," he said. "I've heard the competition is like hand-to-hand combat." There was truth to his comparison. Women selected for the Glory Girls enjoyed a reputation far beyond the church and the community, and they competed fiercely for the privilege of membership.

"But among the Glory Girls," Edith Fay continued, "the only thing different this time was that Buddy Lee was there and the Girls had to oversee him as well as the cooks."

Dooley checked his watch. "I gotta go. Thanks for dinner. And please call me if you think of anything—anything at all—that might help us figure this out."

"Certainly, Sheriff."

Back in the foyer, Dooley swept his cap off the hall table and bowed like a modern-day Rhett Butler. Then he took Edith Fay's hand and gave it a playful kiss. "Ma'am, despite the circumstances it's been a pleasure," he said.

"For me too," Edith Fay said, suddenly feeling warmer than she should on a mild June evening.

One may see day at a little hole. *Proverb*

FRIDAY, JUNE 15

CHAPTER ELEVEN

The *big* question ambushed Dooley Skiles before he put bare feet to bare wood: Where was *His Honor* Jass Pinbiddie?

The house was still except for the breathing of Corndog the Coonhound, third in the succession of black and tans Dooley had owned since age seven.

At four-thirty the morning after Gudrun Wince's slaying, Dooley ruminated as he showered. If the mayor had gone on the lam, for sure he was tied to Gudrun's death, which actually would make Dooley's job a lot easier. However, if Jass had escaped only to cope with the loss of a girlfriend, his absence was purely personal but still sure to gum the investigation.

Then there was, as always, that confounded political angle. Mayor Pinbiddie could turn any situation political, as Dooley had painfully and repeatedly learned, most recently when he had presumed to provide a sheriff's escort for the visiting governor while the mayor had already arranged for state troopers—and himself—to ride at the front of the column.

Besides all that, slippery Jass Pinbiddie was known to leave town on business almost every Thursday and sometimes not reappear for three or four days. Dooley knew this because he'd spent countless hours trying to track down Jass and obtain his signature for various governmental goings-on that required his approval no more than the moon needed the mayor's permission to rise.

Was Gudrun's death on a Thursday somehow related to the mayor's regular Thursday travels?

Corndog, when asked that question, gave no answer but stood face down at his bowl waiting for breakfast. *Darn it all*, the sheriff concluded, *this case was less than twenty-four hours old but already had more roots than the king cedar that shaded Alf Smith Cemetery.*

Dooley poured a big helping of meaty kibbles for Corndog and wished he had a big mug of coffee and a plate of pancakes for himself.

Despite his frustrations, Dooley proceeded to the morning inspection of his home, necessitated by a patch of vandalism that had cost him $4,500 and thirty hours sawing and sinking posts to repair his back porch.

The run-through didn't take long, as the house was a double-wide mobile home outfitted more for function than fairness of appearance. The kitchen had a sink, one set of white fiberboard cabinets, an old refrigerator and an older electric stove. A brown velvet sofa, one metal folding chair, a television and a desktop computer sat along the walls of the living room.

The spare bedroom was Dooley's safe room where he kept his guns, bulletproof vests and other valuables. Of course, Corndog the Coonhound, as befitting a canine of considerable merit, slept in Dooley's bedroom.

Dooley ran a 20-minute route with Corndog, then explained at length to the dog that he would be home late because of the murder case. Corndog put on his sad face and went to the window to await Dooley's late return.

Dooley arrived at Value Mart by way of Larry's Drinkin' Depot, where the coffee was always fresh, hot and cheap and the doughnuts exactly the opposite. He caught Value Mart manager Bill Roy Muzzy as he opened the front doors at 5:30 a.m.

"How's it goin,' Cuz?" Bill Roy stretched out a huge hand and high-fived Dooley. They weren't really cousins but had played Little League ball together from the time their front teeth fell out to the time they discovered girls.

"Bill, I s'pose you heard what happened over at the church?"

"Yep. Whaddaya need?"

"Can you let me have your videotapes from yesterday, say 8 a.m. to 1 p.m.?"

Bill Roy clipped his keys to his belt and motioned Dooley into the store. "Let's go get 'em."

At the *Skyler County Sentinel*, Winona Wilcox was less eager to give up her camera footage. "The editor's been all over me, wants me to fill in the gaps on Gudrun just because I took a few pics for that contest," she complained.

Dooley had already fended off Wilford Nicklin, the *Sentinel* reporter assigned to Gudrun's case.

But the situation with Winona was different.

"I'm looking for the murder weapon," he told her in a low voice. "What if I let you take an exclusive photo of it—whenever we find it, that is?"

"Hmm," said Winona. "What I'd like is a picture of you standing in front of the church holding the murder weapon."

"Done."

"And a couple photos of the crime scene after it happened. It'll be like a swap—my *befores* for your *afters*."

"Sorry," Dooley said. "I can't do that. But I'll ask Edith Fay Smith to give you some stock photos of the kitchen."

"Aw, Dooley, that's boring. Let me take a picture of the counter where Gudrun was working. Just the counter. Just one shot," she wheedled.

Dooley considered the value of comparing Winona's pre-murder photos with the forensic shots the scene techs had taken.

"All right, one shot, but I'll set it up," he said. "Meet me over there about, say, three this afternoon."

Winona, who didn't have to ask Dooley's email address because they'd had a torrid fling several summers back, turned to her computer, pushed keys and said, "I sent you digitals of everything I took—about twenty shots. If you wanna take a quick look at 'em now, just click on this arrow right here."

He stepped to the computer and asked, "What time did you get to the church, Winona?"

"Ten-fifteen in the morning. I punched in here at ten and went straight to the church. I got there just before the actual cooking was supposed to start. Edith Fay said she didn't want me taking pictures while the contestants were trying to concentrate. They have a rule about cameras at the cook-off."

"So I hear. And you left when?"

"I don't remember exactly. It didn't take long to get the pics, but then they offered me coffee. So I had a cup with Ella Mae Pugh—she was my 4-H leader for years—and we talked a while. I guess around 10:45. Ella Mae might remember better."

"We'll see."

On his way out of the *Sentinel* building, Dooley flipped his phone open and punched numbers.

In Spartansville, Mr. Emerson Duty experienced a profound failure in his relaxation efforts.

When that harridan Blaize Luzader suspended him for his responsible and appropriate inspection of Glory Hallelujah Church, he had not planned to spend his time off consulting an attorney, as he had cleverly suggested to Ms. Luzader. He could handle his own legal affairs and keep the $1,000 he had earned in Biddlebourne.

No. His vacation would be spent on his long-neglected tennis game, his Civil War belt collection and his whacking of weeds that sprang in maddening profusion from every crease and corner of his small lot on Columbiana Street.

If he had time after those fun things, he might take Eleanor to visit her sister in Nashville, being careful to embark at an hour that would afford him the maximum number of meals in restaurants along the way.

Eleanor's cooking through the years had become—well, he hated to acknowledge it because it reflected poorly on his leadership in their marriage—boring and perfunctory. For example, Eleanor now considered it acceptable to serve him dry cereal for breakfast, a hasty sandwich at lunch and fried eggs for dinner. Perhaps Eleanor thought such matters were unworthy of her fullest attention. But Emerson fondly recalled that when they were newlyweds Eleanor routinely made such favorites as egg and sausage casserole for breakfast. Why, she'd even mixed the casserole the night before, properly refrigerated it overnight and baked it in the morning while he showered and dressed.

Lately, Emerson mused, Eleanor had formed the tacky habit of lolling late in bed every morning. Not only was she not making egg and sausage casseroles, she had taken to asking him to come back to bed, as if he also had nothing better to do and could while away his time sleeping.

At this very moment, he heard his name being called from the bedroom. He turned up the radio to drown out her pleading and picked up his morning newspaper.

But he could not concentrate on the news, even the obituaries, his favorite section. Blast that Eleanor. If she was not asking him to sleep when he was not sleepy, she wanted him to take her shopping, a task he detested because it began with his waiting interminably on hard chairs in various stores and ended with his carrying multiple bags and boxes to the car.

And that was not all. Her newest demand was that—of all the frivolous things on Earth—he take dancing lessons with her. So they could go out dancing when he retired, she said.

Thusly distracted from his own agenda, Emerson Duty sat miserable and dejected in his small kitchen, unable to enjoy a precious day off.

He mulled over his options, drinking Earl Grey and looking out the window, until Eleanor stopped calling his name and the sun slanted off the glass.

The more he thought, the more he realized his pain was not Eleanor's fault. She was not the person who had caused this turmoil, this restlessness, and had made Emerson feel as small as a gnat on a toad.

He rose from the table. It was time. Time for the devil to face the consequences of his actions.

The Persons Over Age 62 Subcommittee of the Glory Girls service organization of Glory Hallelujah Church, Biddlebourne, West Virginia, shall assist Biddlebourne residents ages sixty-two (62) years and better in mobility, nutrition, health, finances and social activity. *Glory Girls Book of Bylaws,* adopted May 1959

CHAPTER TWELVE

Edith Fay possessed as many church keys as the custodian, and she intended to use them Friday morning. She had forgone breakfast, yoga and devotions at home to get to Glory Hallelujah Church ahead of everyone else.

The deputies assigned to keep people out of the church were in their squad car with the strawberry scones and apple turnovers she had arisen at four to make from scratch.

She accounted for the knives easily by comparing the Glory Girls' tool inventory against implements in the kitchen.

Six electric knives, check. Twelve 12-inch butcher knives. Check. Twelve 10-inch butcher knives. Check. Twelve 8-inch chef's knives. Check. Twelve 6-inch hollow-edge chef's knives. Check. Six Santoku knives. Check. Twenty-four paring knives. Check. Four boning knives. Check. Eight bread knives. Check. Six carving knives. Check. Twelve pizza knives. Check. Sixteen miscellaneous utility knives. Check. Two hundred eighty-eight clam knives. Check. Two hundred eighty-eight steak knives. Check. Forty-eight butter knives. Check. Seven hundred forty-six *official* knives accounted for, none missing.

But Edith knew that lots of kitchen users brought in their own knives and forgot to take them home. A quick look in the various tool vessels of the kitchen turned up fifteen odd knives, and as Edith noted the number and locations of all 761 knives, she wondered whether Dooley would ever find the weapon that had been used to kill Gudrun.

Gudrun. Gudrun Cassandra Wince. The braggingest woman in Biddlebourne. The slipperiest member of the church when it came to spending time or money on a project. The gaddingest female in the county, if one could believe the gossip that swirled around her like September fog on a cattail swamp.

However, Gudrun Wince was the best principal ever to rule Biddlebourne High School, according to parents and faculty who appreciated her no-nonsense, take-no-prisoners methods.

Students, of course, disagreed. Over the years several groups of outraged teenagers had mounted vain campaigns to "Lampoon Gudrun" or "Mince Miss Wince." The school board, aware of improved statistics at the high school, dismissed all such pupil outbursts as the products of overactive hormones and imaginations, and kept giving Miss Wince stellar performance reviews and matching raises.

Edith Fay's problems with Gudrun were less publicized. For reasons Edith Fay was reluctant to consider, Gudrun had missed few opportunities to needle, provoke or otherwise aggrieve the Glory Girls leader.

When Edith Fay conducted a meeting of the Glory Girls, Gudrun, a longtime member of the Ladies Aid Society despite her aversion to actual church work, would "pop in" to ask ridiculous and sly questions that wasted time and energy.

When Edith Fay had a recipe published in the church newsletter or the Featured Cooks section of the *Sentinel*, Gudrun would write letters to the editor suggesting that the cooking time was off or an ingredient missing in "Smith's concoction."

When Edith Fay reported on the work of the Glory Girls as required at church council meetings, Gudrun, who had wrangled a seat on the council because she sharpened pencils used in the pews by visitors, disputed Edith's report whether it dealt with building expansion or juice cups for the toddler room.

With the knife inventory emailed to Dooley, Edith Fay sat at the Girls' kitchen desk and gathered Thursday's delivery notes, which she also sent to the sheriff.

Then, as daylight warmed the sills and kicked on the air conditioners, Edith Fay set about a private task. Starting in the west wing, she opened every portal to every office, Sunday school room, restroom, custodial closet, storage area, cloak room, conference room, chapel, closet and cubbyhole in Glory Hallelujah Church.

She crawled under tables, shone a flashlight into vents and grates, stuck her hand behind furniture and under rugs, poked the dirt in dozens of planters, unrolled the candles and hangings and tablecloths, sifted through crayons and scissors, took off toilet tank lids and seat covers, rifled the contents of boxes and jars, lifted cushions off chairs and settees, shook out choir robes and music folders, and unwrapped and looked into all the communion ware.

Edith Fay panted, sweated and grew grimy but found no sign, anywhere, of Gudrun Wince's purse or recipe box.

This was as much a problem to Edith Fay as Gudrun's slaying. The reasons were complex but began with Gudrun's unsupported claims to culinary accomplishment. The school principal had missed no opportunity—in person or in print—to tout her own cooking, which was a particularly egregious faux pas in Skyler County.

Gudrun had, for instance, while being photographed for a newspaper spread on the athletic teams at Biddlebourne High School, told the *Sentinel*'s Winona Wilcox that everyone came to her pre-game parties because of her fabulous dips and famous chili. Edith Fay had been to one of those parties, back when she had time to attend such events, and knew for a fact that Gudrun's chili came straight from a can and her dips from a carton. Edith Fay had found the containers in Gudrun's garbage bin when, in an effort to assist the hostess, she had taken out an overfilled trash bag.

Edith Fay had since concluded that Gudrun's self-congratulatory comments masked something dark. She also had feared that Gudrun's chicanery could eventually tarnish, even ruin, the work and reputation of the Glory Girls service organization of Glory Hallelujah Church.

As it was, even in death Gudrun had done the Glory Girls a bad turn. Edith Fay did not know the identity of Gudrun's killer, but she knew who was knowledgeable and clever enough to do the deed. It wasn't Buddy Lee, a crazed delivery man or a ticked-off church employee.

No. The culprit could be a Glory Girl.

Edith Fay theorized that the guilty Glory Girl wanted Gudrun gone because she, like Edith Fay, believed Gudrun's posturing cast skepticism on the Girls as individuals and as a group.

Edith Fay also held it possible that, as rumor had it, Gudrun had tricked her recipes out of home economics teacher Theodocia Price, thus drawing the outrage of Theodocia's family and friends. Considering Biddlebourne's twisted lineages, Edith Fay figured all the Glory Girls were in some way kith to Theodocia.

In a lull of the air conditioner fans, Edith listened for the return of the deputies but heard nothing. She considered Gudrun's recipes and reckoned that if Gudrun had been as protective with them as the Glory Girls and other cooks of Edith Fay's acquaintance were with their own recipes, she kept them close at hand—probably in her purse.

But even as Edith Fay ticked off reasons a Glory Girl could be Gudrun's killer, she lacked the feeling of certainty that accompanied her surest conclusions. She also felt a growing sense of unease for withholding from Dooley her suspicion about Glory Girl involvement in Gudrun's slaying.

After calling Dooley to confirm his receipt of her emails, Edith Fay told herself that the sheriff had asked nothing specific about the purse and recipes and she had no duty to speak of them. But as she wrote a note to Belle about the kitchen photos for Winona, Edith Fay sighed deeply.

Though Edith Fay was not convinced yet what role a Glory Girl might have had in Thursday's events, she was sure of one thing: Two crimes had been committed—the murder of Gudrun Wince and the theft of her recipes.

She had done it.

At 309 Muzzy Road, a redolent Chicken Cordon Bleu Casserole rested on the stove, a haggard Laverna Inys Wharton sprawled on a spindle-back chair, and a stack of typed pages lay on the kitchen table.

"What's for breakfast?" William called from the bathroom.

"How about toast?"

Wiping shave cream off his face, William entered the kitchen and sniffed the air. "Mmm. Did your mother bring over something for dinner?"

"No! I made it!" Laverna scarcely could contain herself. She had not slept since Wednesday night and had spent the previous fourteen hours salvaging what she could from Gudrun Wince's recipe box.

The task had been tedious. First she had separated the magazine, newspaper and cookbook recipes from the handwritten ones. She had placed the penned and penciled ones in a flat plastic bag and locked them into a tray of her jewelry box. Then she had sorted the published recipes by categories: entrees, side dishes, desserts and salads. The Glory Girls allowed cook-off contestants to use published recipes, of course, but encouraged adaptations to make the recipes "unique and personal."

Laverna had stayed up all night making the purloined recipes unique and personal—at least on paper. For example, onto the Country Lasagna recipe she scribbled "2 c. shredded cabbage." To

Peppermint Divinity she added "1 T. grated lemon rind," to Barbecued Ribs, "1 c. corn kernels." Then she had retyped each recipe on her desktop computer, given each one a new name and added the words *From the recipe files of Laverna Inys Wharton* at the top. After printing the product of her second consecutive sleepless night, she had 173 recipes for her own recipe box, which she had already ordered and received. She had fetched it from the laundry closet and happily filled it with her new recipes.

William edged closer to the stove to get a look at Laverna's creation. "Wow! That looks great, Honey," he said, choosing not to comment on his wife's tangled hair and stained clothing or the dribbles of undefinable ingredients on the floor.

He walked to a cabinet on the pretense of getting a drinking glass and glanced into the trash basket. He was puzzled when he failed to spot a Banquet or Stouffer's box, which was Laverna's standard cover-up for any meal that was actually edible.

What was going on? William Wharton had for years endured Laverna's cooking—or her non-cooking. Early in their marriage he had offered repeatedly to prepare their meals—he wasn't a bad cook—or even to hire a cook, but Laverna would have none of that.

No. Laverna Inys Wharton, who had a degree in business administration and efficiently ran her own consulting company from a room in the basement, could not get past, through or around the notion that every good woman could cook. She had learned business administration by reading books and was by-gosh certain she could learn to cook by reading books. Her womanhood was at stake, and no effort would go unmade.

William had his private opinion that their childlessness was the real reason for Laverna's culinary quest. However, he was as saddened as Laverna by their failure to conceive a child in their fifteen years of marriage and had no intention of sharpening his wife's pain with unlearned psychoanalysis.

But he was so concerned about Laverna this morning that his thoughts turned again to the possibility of professional counseling. She was disheveled head to toe. He was sure she had worn the same blouse last night at dinner, and her slacks were smeared with handprints and dollops of brown and yellow goo. She had Band-Aids on two fingers and a twist tie from a bread bag wrapped around her ragged ponytail.

He was mystified. If Laverna had made the dish that sat on the stove, she had achieved a breakthrough. But if so, at what cost? Come to think of it, Laverna had acted strangely all week. She'd been secretive and quiet, unlike her usual busy and talkative self. Had she gone over the edge? William vowed to pay closer attention to Laverna and to journal his observations—in case he needed to provide details for a therapist later.

"Well, I'm proud of you," he said, bending over Laverna and kissing her on the forehead, the only clean spot available. "Want to have lunch with me in town today? We can go to Fordyce's and have the garlic noodles."

"Oh, no. I mean, I can't. I have to . . . clean up here." She forced a chuckle and waved a hand around the kitchen, then got up and swatted flour from a pant leg. "Gotta get moving. I'll see you tonight. We'll have the casserole I made."

"Yes, we will," he said brightly. "I'll have breakfast at work, grab a bagel off the cart. I have an early meeting with the pastor."

Laverna alerted instantly. "Such sad news about Gudrun. I suppose you and Annie have to make plans for a big church funeral."

"Oh, no, nothing like that," he said. "I thought you might have heard. The Glory Girls are gonna be featured in some national magazine, and we have to coordinate the church calendar for, I guess, a whole week in August."

Laverna swallowed and tried to eject words from her dry throat. A national magazine. Coming to take pictures in Biddlebourne. Of the Glory Girls. And their food. If she timed it right, she herself could stand among the likes of Edith Fay Smith and Alwildia Louise Doak in that magazine layout. Her family, friends and neighbors would see her dazzling smile and her luscious entrees.

A warm glow overtook Laverna. She stood, gave William an especially amorous kiss goodbye and said, "Have a nice day, Dear."

Buoyed by her victory over Chicken Cordon Bleu Casserole and news of an upcoming magazine visit to Biddlebourne, Laverna decided to regroup her energies. She went to the spotless living room, threw herself onto the brocade settee and fell soundly asleep.

Waking refreshed and ready for more of what had refreshed her, Pearl Gay Osbourn turned to an empty pillow in the basement of her drive-through establishment.

"Jass, Baby, where are you?"

There was no answer. No toilet flushing, door slamming, coffeemaker perking or toaster popping.

Pearl Gay, who had spent close to thirty thousand dollars turning the basement into a studio apartment for her "comfort and convenience," as she had told the contractor from Parkersburg, regretted only one thing about the renovation. The floor, tiled with cheap vinyl because her bank account had been tapped by the time she chose the flooring, in every season of the year was as cold as tail waters in January.

She hated the first steps out of bed but took them anyway, which only heightened her impatience for Jass. Had he gone upstairs to fetch pastries? *That would be nice,* she thought, imagining them enjoying bear claws and each other.

Pearl Gay stepped lively to where her slippers lay and tucked her feet in. She walked to the bottom of the basement stairs and yelled, "Sweet cakes! Get those honey nut ones!"

Twenty-two miles away, Emerson Duty slapped his phone closed and punched the air with a fist.

"Confound that man!"

Turning from the coffeepot, Eleanor Duty said, "Who? What man?"

"The honorable mayor of Biddlebourne, that's who," he snarled. "He said this'd be a cinch. Easy money for a small favor. Now I'm in hot water and he's incommunicado."

The evening before, Eleanor had quit listening after Emerson explained that he was on paid administrative leave from his job. It was not the first time, and she supposed it would not be the last, for hubby had a quirky addiction to certain risky behaviors. As long as she could spend her days shopping, he could do what he wanted.

"What's the Biddlebourne mayor got to do with you?" she demanded with a yawn.

"My hearing's in eleven days and I need him to testify. This whole thing's out of hand."

Naturally, Emerson did not trouble himself to tell Eleanor either that he'd had a Plan B or that it had fallen through in the two minutes he'd just spent on the phone with his favorite shady lawyer.

Eleanor needed her coffee. As she tipped the cup to her lips, she said, "What thing?"

At seven Friday morning, Barry Dale Green had a line of work-bound customers at Biddlebourne Feed & Grain and no way to get into the cash register. He'd worked twelve years for Jass Pinbiddie and not once handled store money.

"I apologize, folks," he said. Barry Dale had just come from the back, where he was shelving fifty-pound sacks of dog food while customers grabbed goods and scuttled to the checkout.

"Where's Jass?" Virginia Rae Reams wanted her new hose coupler right now so she could water the cucumber patch after work. "I gotta go, Barry Dale. I'm just gonna put my money here on the table."

"Good idea, Virginia," said Larry Showalter.

Pretty soon, Barry Dale Green had five piles of money at the checkout and no idea what to do with it because he had never been permitted to manage the cash drawer of Biddlebourne Feed & Grain.

Barry Dale had already tried but failed to reach Jass at his home and at the city building. Neither could he reach Missy Johnson, Jass' *niece* who filled in for him occasionally at the register.

So Barry Dale did the only thing he could think to do, which was to hang a sign on the front door stating, "Closed until further notice."

Across the fair town of Biddlebourne, others were also waking to a Jass-less world. Pastor Annie Ido Scovill wanted to continue their debate on tax issues. Marthleen Lewis wanted to pass on a batch of phone messages. Doc Cecil Weber wanted to check on his patient. The forensic technician from the state police wanted his fingerprints. And the Garden Club social chairman wanted his meat selection for the annual awards dinner.

No one wanted to find Jass Pinbiddie more than Dooley Skiles. On his way to Glory Hallelujah Church, the sheriff called the mayor's private phone and got the message that Jass appreciated his call, truly wanted to talk with him and deeply regretted not being available at this moment.

Dooley swung by Biddlebourne Feed & Grain, took note of the hand-printed sign out front and banged on the door a good five minutes to no avail. He walked around the building to the dirt square that served as an employee parking lot. There, the absence of Jass' Blazer tire prints and the presence of Barry Dale Green's recent Toyota 4Runner tracks told him all he needed to know.

With the spire of Glory Hallelujah Church looming into sight, Sheriff Skiles got on his handset and ordered all his deputies to step up their watch for Jasper Eugene "Jass" Pinbiddie, age 52, height about 6-5, weight about 320, bald, brown eyes, probably driving a Chevy Blazer or Cadillac Escalade.

"Don't advertise it," he warned. "Just let me know if you see him."

Crimes are made secure by greater crimes. *Proverb*

CHAPTER THIRTEEN

"Hold on a minute, Emerson. I know why the Skyler County sheriff's lookin' for Jass Pinbiddie. Why do you need to contact him?"

Orville Powell and Emerson Duty held foam coffee cups in a hard booth at Joey's Luncheonette in Spartansville. Orville rubbed his shoulders as if he'd just chopped a cord of firewood. Emerson fidgeted because he'd been forced to come, once again, to his old school pal for help.

Fed up with Jass Pinbiddie's failure to respond to his phone calls, emails and text messages, Emerson had rooted through his card file for names of people to help him find the man to blame for his current woes.

Though Emerson had thus collected two names, Orville had just retired early from the Sklyer County Sheriff's Department and still knew all the guys there. Also, Orville owed Emerson big for tutoring him to C's in both trigonometry and chemistry in high school.

Actually, Orville Powell considered that debt long since paid. He'd helped Emerson and Eleanor switch residences not once but twice, had installed a new commode in their main bathroom—a back-breaking and disgusting job—and had once co-signed a loan so Eleanor could have her own car for shopping.

"I just told you, Orv. He tricked me into making a squirrelly inspection, and now I'm in trouble and I need to get in touch with him to set it straight."

Orville squinted as if to hear better. "Did you break the law, Emerson?" he asked.

"Well, uh, only technically. It was a trivial rule, really, but my new boss wants to make an example of me to keep the rest of the staff in line."

Orville was savvy to the ways of ambitious officials, but he also remembered Emerson's connivery, which had fetched them both into significant trouble four decades earlier in high school.

"Did he make you break the rules?"

"Not exactly. But he used his position to influence my decision."

"In what way?"

Emerson tapped the laminated tabletop arrhythmically. "Um, he telephoned in his capacity as mayor of Biddlebourne to lodge a complaint against a certain purveyor of food in that town. Naturally, I took his complaint seriously and acted on it immediately."

"I'm with you so far."

"But when I went there, I discovered the complaint to be generally unsupported, though there were incidental circumstances that led to my holding the, uh, establishment in violation of health laws."

"And you wrote up this establishment, and they complained to your new boss, and you got in trouble, and you want Jass Pinbiddie to shoulder the blame. That about right?"

"Well, my intention is not so base as that, but, yes, he could help me, as I said, explain why the inspection was necessary."

Orville had been gratified after his retirement to land a part-time gig as a security guard. But now he was taking double shifts because a lot of his fellow guards were catching extra duty on a murder case in Biddlebourne. He was exhausted, and his pain meds were useless, and he was done with Emerson's foolishness.

"Tell you what. It all sounds hinky to me. If you got caught in a dirty inspection, I think you'd be better off to admit it and face the music. I can't help you."

"Can't or won't?"

Orville looked at Emerson and said nothing.

Emerson rose stiffly and said, "I'm disappointed, Orv. I thought you were my friend."

"I'm still your friend, and as your friend I gave you my best advice. Take your lumps and move on. I've had to do that more than once in my own life. The truth isn't as bad as you think."

Emerson Duty was already considering Plan C, which had nothing to do with the truth. He turned and walked out.

The tardy backroom boys, having also found Biddlebourne Feed & Grain deserted, repaired to the Legion hall for a breakfast of peanuts and potato chips.

"Well?" said Bucky.

Everyone looked at Arnie Coker.

Arnie dropped a handful of nut shells and swigged a canned energy drink. "Sheriff's got the word out on Jass. Couldn't be helped. Sounds like he done run."

Just as Jass Pinbiddie supported many other clubs and coalitions in Biddlebourne, he also backed the American Legion. He was always ready with a donation here, a Pinbiddie amendment there, a bit of influence exerted anywhere it would do the vets some good.

The group grew silent as the men thought on this. For instance, though Jass was not a military veteran—a fact he did not like circulated—he'd had the town council build a solid granite monument on which were inscribed the names of Biddlebournians lost in battle.

Not only that, but the mayor had gone to a lot of trouble having Marthleen Lewis scour state archives so as to include on the monument the names of those who perished in wars all the way back to the American Revolution.

Therefore, almost every time a civil holiday swung round, a solemn ceremony occurred in the middle of town at the Heroes Memorial, as the monument had come to be called. Virtually every family in town thus reaped small annual rewards for their relatives' great sacrifices. Of course, the master of ceremonies was always the Honorable Jasper E. Pinbiddie.

In addition, Jass had for years sponsored the Legion's baseball, softball and soccer programs and, contrary to his usual practice, had not even had his name printed on team shirts. Instead, *God Bless America* was embroidered on the jerseys.

No doubt about it. Jasper Eugene Pinbiddie was a true-blue patriot.

Bucky thunked his Coke down on a stack of crates holding Christmas decorations. "Dad gum it, Arnie. We all heard what's goin' on. Don't mean he done it . . . necessarily. . . ."

Harley Baker, who had taken up landscaping in retirement and needed the mayor's referrals to keep the business going, said, "Yep. That's the truth. In the US of A, nobody's done it till it's said so in a court a law."

"Presumed innocent, that's the rule," Creed Fedderman concurred.

The men, individually and collectively, needed Jass Pinbiddie. But their loyalty went further than putting on a military uniform and flying the flag. They came from the raw-boned, hard-edged seam of humanity that knew how to fight and what to fight for.

They didn't fight because they were bellicose. They fought because they believed in what they held to be right.

"Well," said Arnie, "talkin' won't do us no good . . . if we don't even know where he is. . . ."

The Legion's head cook, Charlotte Powell, bumped into the storeroom carrying a washtub. "Hey, guys. 'Scuse me. I didn't know you all was in here. I'll just get those taters there in the corner and be outta your way."

"How ya' doin,' Charlotte?" Arnie asked. "And how's Orville gettin' along with that arthritis?"

Orville Powell had tried for a decade to quell the soreness in his arthritic knees. He'd used over-the-counter pills, prescription pills that inflamed his stomach, heating pads, cold packs and pain patches. Each yielded less relief as the years passed. Arthritis was the only reason he'd had to retire from the Skyler County Sheriff's Department.

"Not too bad today, Arnie," she said. "He's been pullin' double shifts at the plant 'cause of Gudrun's killing. He just called me from work and said he was runnin' late on account o' some guy he went to school with—a guy what works at the health department— was lookin' for Jass Pinbiddie."

"Really?" said Arnie, glancing toward Bucky. "He say anything else?"

"Nah, you know how he is. Says he don't like to weigh me down with the bad stuff."

"Bad stuff, huh?" Bucky said.

"Don't know how bad it was," she said. "Orville told the guy he couldn't help 'im."

"Let me help you with those taters," Bucky said. He carried them to the kitchen for Charlotte while the other guys chewed on her news.

"The hunt for Jass is sure heatin' up. Lotsa people lookin' fer him," opined Jeff Boyles. "First time I ever seen the feed store closed 'cept Christmas and the first day o' huntin' season."

"I reckon the health department guy lookin' for Jass is the one what come to the church yesterday and told them women to shut down the kitchen," said Charlie Simons.

"What's that?" said Jeff. "All I heard was Gudrun Wince got herself done in. You mean the health department locked the kitchen up 'cause somebody got killed there?"

Charlie, talking over a mouthful of barbecued chips, said, "Nah. Closed it 'cause some guy with a clipboard looked it all over and said it wasn't clean enough."

"I'm hornswoggled," said Creed. "That's hard to believe."

When Bucky returned, the backroom boys talked and cogitated some more.

And so, when push came to shove, as it often did for these people whose lives ebbed and flowed with the prices of coal or corn or hogs, they decided to do something. Yes, they would act as their flawed human souls led them to do, but they would act with the fervor that a thousand years of fighting had bred in them.

The pastor and the congregation's top leaders stood shocked and newly grieved in her office.

Dooley Skiles had just left the room, his belt, holster and polished boots rustling against his crisp uniform. Now Pastor Annie Scovill, Edith Fay Smith and William Wharton, chairman of the church council, tried to digest the sheriff's instructions.

Dooley had ordered the church closed. Not just the kitchen and its auxiliary areas, but the whole complex including the sanctuary, offices, classrooms, chapels, Hearth House, conference rooms, parlors, playground, parking lots, walkways, driveways, lawns, gardens, sheds and all other support facilities.

No one was to enter the area now being cordoned by Dooley's deputies until Dooley said so.

And, no, he had no idea when that would be because the murder of a Biddlebourne citizen inside a Biddlebourne institution would be solved no matter what it took. Also, anyone who disobeyed his orders would face charges of obstructing a homicide investigation.

The one concession Dooley had granted was a ninety-minute period in which church leaders could remove enough equipment and materials to operate the church from another location.

However, there were two provisos. One was that all the computers were to stay in the church. The second was that nothing more could be taken from the kitchen until the sheriff allowed the church to reopen.

In addition, Dooley told them, everything removed from the church would be inspected by deputies upon its exit. And persons thus entering and leaving the church would also be inspected.

"I'll ask Belle to sort what she needs from the office," the pastor said, one finger on the intercom button. "William, please contact the trustee chair, the worship chair and the finance chair and have them retrieve only those items absolutely essential for now. Make sure they print out the records we need for the tax dispute and bring any existing legal files as well."

"Certainly, Pastor," he said. "But for how long? It's impossible to know what we'll need without an end date."

"Let's say two weeks," Annie replied. "That will take us through two Sundays. Have people take worship supplies to Saint John's Church."

"Why Saint John's?" he asked.

"Father Bradley and I have an unofficial agreement about using each other's buildings in emergencies."

"I didn't know that," he said. "We can take the other necessities to my law firm if you like. We can spare a conference room for a couple weeks."

"Could you set Belle up with an office there as well?" the pastor asked.

"Probably. I'd have to consult with the facilities coordinator to be sure."

"We don't have time. Let's take everything but worship supplies to the parsonage. If a move to your office is doable—and necessary—we can move again," she said. "Have them put everything in the dining room. I'll call G.P. and tell him to stand by. And, oh, something else," she added. "Tell everyone we'll have an emergency council session at six tonight in the parsonage. I know a lot of folks have ball games, but it's crucial that we face this together."

William Wharton turned aside to make his contacts.

"What about Ladies Aid and the Glory Girls?" Annie inquired of Edith Fay. "Do you need help notifying everybody there?"

"I think not," Edith Fay said. "We did most of that yesterday when the kitchen was closed. I'll go to my office and email Ella Mae to start the phone tree and bring everyone up to date. Then I'll help Belle with the main office. I'll ask Ella Mae to come in too."

"Thank you, Edith Fay. I'm grateful for your steadfastness," Annie said.

"We'll get through this," Edith Fay said before picking up her bags and heading out the door.

William Wharton closed his phone. "I sent everyone text messages. I'll be going. I'm overdue at the courthouse."

"Thanks, William. Oh, that reminds me," Annie said. "Can you check around and see if any attorney around here handled a will for Gudrun?"

"Sure."

The Employment Subcommittee of the Glory Girls service organization of Glory Hallelujah Church, Biddlebourne, West Virginia, shall assist residents of Biddlebourne ages eighteen (18) years and better in locating, qualifying for, applying for and maintaining gainful employment. *Glory Girls Book of Bylaws,* adopted May 1959

CHAPTER FOURTEEN

Buddy Lee Delbert had one hellacious day on Friday. It was almost as bad as Thursday, he later told his Aunt Audra and Uncle Claude.

At nine in the morning, Buddy Lee shook and sweated in a cramped interrogation room at the sheriff's station. Buddy Lee wanted a Dr. Pepper, but Dooley said no.

"That can wait," Sheriff Skiles said. "For now, we gotta get straight what happened yesterday morning at Glory Hallelujah Church."

This was a Dooley previously unknown to Buddy Lee. The sheriff was wearing his hat indoors, which Aunt Audra called a *no-no*, and had his gun holstered where Buddy Lee could see it, gleaming and dangerous within inches of Dooley's hand.

Other times when Buddy Lee had been interviewed by Dooley, they'd said a few howdy-dos before getting down to business. But today, Dooley didn't even say hello—another *no-no*—and told Buddy Lee he could be charged with murder if he didn't tell Dooley everything that happened, and not be slow in doing it.

"Dooley, I ain't killed Gudrun," Buddy Lee said. "I liked her. She got me back on the straight 'n' narrow in school. She's the only reason I graduated."

"Be that as it may," Dooley said, "you found the body and, far as I know, you were the last person to see her alive."

"Geez, Dooley. How many times I gotta tell ya I didn't do it? Whaddaya want from me?"

"What do I want? What I want is for you to tell me everything you did, saw, heard and thought while you were at Glory Hallelujah Church yesterday morning."

Buddy Lee, who had been underrated and underappreciated all his life, swiped the sweat from his head and neck with his shirttail. Then he reached for his right pants pocket.

But the sheriff drew his gun and pointed it at Buddy Lee, saying, "What are ya doin'?"

"Just getting somethin' outta my pocket, Dooley. Geez." Sweat popped anew from Buddy Lee's forehead and armpits.

"Stand up. I'll get it."

"Okay, okay." Buddy Lee stood slowly and held his hands high while Dooley gingerly plucked a wad of folded notebook paper from the pocket.

The door opened and Sergeant Ike Henderson, who had been chief of police in Biddlebourne back when it had its own constabulary, poked his head in to say, "Sheriff, the fingerprint report's in. They rushed it."

"Thanks, Ike." The door closed softly. Dooley turned back to Buddy Lee and held up the paper mass. Without looking at it, he said, "What is this? Huh? I got no time for baloney from you today, Buddy Lee."

Buddy Lee, who had thought of Dooley as his friend, worked to compose himself. "Aunt Audra and Uncle Claude said I had to tell you about everything, so I put it down—to save you time. It's all writ out right there, Dooley."

"Well," said the sheriff, who suddenly felt himself unpuffing. "Sit back down then."

Dooley leaned on the wall, one eye on Buddy Lee and one eye on the papers as he unfolded them.

There were seven unnumbered pages filled solid, back and front, with hand-printed unparagraphed sentences:

I was doing chors for the Girls Thursday when I come up on Gudroon Wince in the church kichen. I went to the church about nine oclock becoz the glory girls said they would pay me. My job was to help the ladies cook. I wore my work close becoz I was goin to work. Miss Jo Clare said she would pay me seven dolars an our to work. I got to the church erly becoz a good worker is erly. . .

.

Someone tapped on the door, and Dooley yelled, "Come in, darn it."

It was Ike Henderson again. "Sorry, Sheriff. Ernie Blankenship's been callin'. Said your phone was off. He's mad as a hornet."

The sheriff stifled his irritation at the interruption and said, "All right, Ike. Tell Ernie I'll call him back soon as I get done in here." There weren't many folks Dooley felt obligated to call back, but Ernie Blankenship, president of the Biddlebourne Town Council, was one of them.

"Oh, and bring Buddy Lee here a cold Dr. Pepper . . . and an egg sandwich."

"You got it," Ike said before disappearing.

Dooley looked at Buddy Lee, then scanned the rest of Buddy Lee's statement.

"Just to get this straight," the sheriff said. "You write here . . . on page . . . never mind . . . that Miss Wince asked you to go to the Value Mart. What time was that?"

"Gosh, I don't know. I don't own no watch."

"Was it before or after the newspaper photographer came to the kitchen?"

"After."

"What did you get at the Value Mart for Miss Wince?"

Buddy Lee shut his eyes. "Uhhhh, it was butter. Said it had to be unsalted butter 'cause her recipe was special. I never heard o' unsalted butter before yesterday. I just thought butter was butter."

Once more somone knocked. "Dad blast it!" the sheriff shouted. "What now?" He threw Buddy Lee's statement on the desk.

Ike opened the door a fraction and said, "Sheriff, somebody said Jass' store's been closed. Thought you'd wanna know. And here's what you asked for."

"I already knew about the store," Dooley said evenly. "No more interruptions unless somebody's haulin' in Jass Pinbiddie's ass. Got it?"

"Yes, sir."

Dooley handed the sandwich and drink to his witness and said, "Never mind the butter, Buddy Lee. Tell me something else. Did anything really unusual happen at the cook-off? Anything at all?"

Now Buddy Lee was truly stumped. He cracked his knuckles and looked at the caged clock on the wall.

"All I can 'member is somebody spilled a whole bag o' sugar over by that big sink they got. What a mess. Sticky, ya know. I had to mop it three times 'fore Miss Mary Ellen said it wasn't sticky no more. I went to the store right after I mopped that up. I already had the money in my pocket 'cause Miss Wince just gave it to me."

Dooley stared at Buddy Lee. "Okay. How many times d'you leave the kitchen while you were workin' yesterday?"

"I tried to write all that down on the paper," he said, "but lemme think."

The intercom on Dooley's desk buzzed and the disembodied voice of secretary Lucy Jane Erskine said, "Boss, it's Ernie Blankenship on the phone again. Sounds serious."

Dooley glanced out the window and saw that the parking lot was already full of the vehicles of good citizens who wanted to help solve Gudrun Wince's slaying.

"Put Ernie on hold," he told Lucy Jane.

Rubbing his brow as he turned back to his witness, the sheriff said, "You did good, Buddy Lee. I'm gonna let you go for now. But don't leave town. You got that?"

"Yes, sir, Sheriff. I got it. Matter a fact, I got me a date tonight."

"Oh? Who with?"

"I'm goin' out with Miss Patty Leta."

The sheriff was impressed. "The secretary over to the high school?"

"Yes, sir."

"Didn't know you and Patty Leta was sweet on each other."

"Aw, Sheriff, it ain't like that. I went over there yesterday to say sorry Miss Wince got herself killed. Miss Patty Leta took it awful hard. Me and Miss Patty Leta liked Miss Wince. She done right by both o' us. So we just decided to . . . you know how it is . . . talk about it some more so we'd stop feelin' bad."

"Yeah, I know how it is, Buddy Lee. You got money for dinner tonight?"

"Yes, sir. Miss Jo Claire, she paid me for the whole day yesterday, just like I worked all day. Said it was only fair."

"I reckon she was right."

"Can I take my sandwich and Dr. Pepper with me?"

Buddy Lee was glad to get out of the sheriff's office, first because in Buddy Lee's opinion the sheriff hadn't been acting right, second because Buddy Lee had an appointment with one of his favorite people.

They met at the Mug, Buddy Lee's favorite restaurant, and his hostess encouraged him to order whatever he wanted. Having just consumed a breakfast sandwich and a soda pop, Buddy Lee turned to the lunch menu.

When his cheeseburger, fries and chocolate malt milkshake arrived, Edith Fay Smith said, "Buddy Lee, I want to thank you for meeting me today. I know you had a hard time of it yesterday."

"Yes, ma'am, I sure did. And you're welcome." Buddy Lee spoke only between mouthfuls and smiled often at Miss Edith Fay, observing the little "niceties" that Aunt Audra encouraged and which Miss Edith Fay seemed to like.

"I reckon I'm feelin' a lot better now," Buddy Lee allowed. "I can tell you all about what happened . . . that is, if you want me to."

"I'd be obliged if you would," she said. "Take your time, unless you have another appointment, of course."

"Doo told me to stay home, so that's where I'm goin'."

Edith Fay knew Buddy Lee had just come from the sheriff's office because a deputy at the church had told her so.

"Thank you, Buddy Lee. Just start at the beginning and tell me everything you remember. Don't worry if you don't remember everything. Nobody remembers everything."

This was good news to Buddy Lee, who smiled, swallowed his last French fry and began. "Well, like Miss Mary Ellen asked, I got to the church 'round seven. I brought me a peanut butter sandwich from home and I et that sittin' at one o' the tables in the big dining room."

"I often take my lunch in there too," Edith Fay said. "It's nice and cool in there."

"Yes, ma'am, like in here," he noted as he realized his shirt and pants were no longer stuck to his body with sweat.

When Buddy Lee finished his recollections and his meal, Edith Fay asked, "What about a piece of strawberry pie? I believe Gladys just made 'em. I'm going to have a piece."

The pie was warm and gooey and thick with berries from Crampton Orchards. Dooley was drinking milk and Edith Fay coffee when she asked, "How did Miss Gudrun pay for that butter you got for her?"

"Gave me a five."

"Did she have that big purse with the gold handle?"

Buddy Lee squeezed his eyes shut to remember. "Uh, I don't . . . I can't remember."

"Did you happen to see where she kept her purse in the kitchen?" Edith Fay asked as she smiled and placed a twenty-dollar bill on the table next to the lunch check.

Buddy Lee's face turned pink. "Maybe . . ."

Bertram Kimble wanted to bury Gudrun Wince.

Bertram the mortician wanted to bury her because Gudrun Wince, like all important persons in Biddlebourne, must be laid to eternal rest in a solid mahogany, hand-rubbed, velvet-lined coffin with three fully staffed viewings, the full photo and video tribute packages, the full memorial service package, the full cemetery package and the full obituary package. Not to mention the full escort package.

Bertram the father wanted to bury her because Gudrun Wince had cost him numerous nonproductive hours in her office discussing the behavior of Hiram and Byrom, his twin sons. The boys had only normal teenage playfulness, Bertram and his wife Laura agreed, but had nevertheless seemed special targets of Gudrun's patrols.

In addition, Gudrun had failed to address Bertram's complaints about the high schoolers who clung to the local Halloween night tradition of stowing away in his mortuary so as to scare the bejabbers out of his staff the next morning.

He had lost more than one good worker the day after Halloween because Gudrun insisted that students' comportment— oh, how he hated the word *comportment*—outside of school was a parental responsibility. Though Bertram, of course, knew who the delinquents were, he did not appeal to their parents for student discipline because that might imperil future business.

Now he could solve several ongoing problems—and beat out his archrival, Maximillian Kester—if only he could secure the consent of Gudrun's family to serve them in their time of need.

But the woman who answered the phone at the high school said she couldn't tell him anything because it was not her place to do so. His neighbors Jeff and Jackie Boyles belonged to Glory Hallelujah Church but knew nothing of Gudrun's next of kin. Even his contacts at the Biddlebourne Chamber of Commerce couldn't help.

Time was wasting, and wasted time in the funeral business was money out the window, so Bertram Kimble on Friday morning knew what he had to do. He donned a dark blue suit with nuanced pinstripes, a stiffly collared white shirt and a matte battleship-gray tie and left the building that housed his home and business.

Bertram was frisked at Glory Hallelujah Church and told by Deputy Arnie Coker to wait in the skylighted lobby. Something unusual seemed to be happening, more than he imagined might be occasioned by even a murder investigation. People were scurrying out of offices with boxes and bags. Belle Watkins, usually cordial and helpful, only nodded when she passed him in the lobby.

And when Annie Scovill came to the lobby, she did not take one of the high-backed upholstered chairs. So neither could he.

"Bertram, there's nothing I can tell you," she said when he had inquired politely about Gudrun's relatives. The fullest truth was that Annie had confirmed the evening before that Gudrun Wince had been born in Wetzel County, West Virginia, in 1951, relinquished by her birth mother at age two, lived with various foster parents and attended various schools until, at age fifteen, she ran away to a location unknown by county officers. The social worker who provided this information noted that Gudrun's case had been closed in 1969 when Gudrun would have turned 18.

"Surely the lady brought relatives with her to church from time to time," Bertram insisted.

"Perhaps one of your staff could go back through the visitor cards and locate a name and address."

Pastor Annie, who knew an ambulance-chaser when she saw one, nevertheless felt compelled to speak civilly. Smiling to gain a fraction of time in which to formulate such an answer, she said, "I am sorry, Bert, but as you see we've been caught off guard here. I apologize, but I must ask you to excuse me now, as Sheriff Skiles has asked us to vacate the building—only temporarily, of course. We're pushed for time."

As Bertram Kimble walked away dejectedly, church treasurer Shirl Burrows approached Annie and said, "I wasn't eavesdropping, Pastor, but I was takin' files out to the car when I overheard a little of what you and Bert were saying."

"That's all right, Shirl. It wasn't a private conversation."

"That's not exactly what I'm gettin' at. I can fill you in a little on Good Time Goldilocks. That's what they called her back in the day."

Annie looked at Shirl for a long moment while she considered the rightness of listening to hearsay. One reason Annie's work at Glory Hallelujah Church had succeeded was her unyielding respect for the power of words—all words.

"All right, Shirl. Can you ride along with me while I go to Saint John's Church? I want to hear what you have to say, but I want *that* conversation to be private."

Far from home, near thy harm. *Proverb*

CHAPTER FIFTEEN

Two hundred miles away in Cleveland, Ohio, a large, bald, middle-aged man sat with a laptop computer in the business center of the Lafayette Hotel.

His charcoal gray Brooks Brothers suit bore a subtle glen plaid weave, his Avanti dress shirt the color of first light and his silk Hermes tie the muted sheen of personal wealth. His black, tasseled Johnston & Murphy shoes had never touched snow or mud, and his manicure had been finished with a coat of clear enamel followed by a swabbing with cotton.

He pounded the keyboard as if life depended on it, though he frequently peered out the double windows and drank deep from a tall glass containing Mountain Dew and a flotilla of maraschinos.

All that marred his appearance was the trickle of sweat slipping down the side of his face nearer the windows. Only one other guest was in the business center, and she seemed engrossed in a spread sheet laid out on a coffee table.

"That should do it," he mumbled as he closed the computer and rose. Now he could rest easy for a while.

The woman looked up and smiled. As she straightened on the sofa, he noticed her big breasts and low-cut blouse. "You've been working hard," she said, placing extra emphasis on *hard*. "Are you here alone?"

The man had wanted to avoid the truth, the truth being that he was very much alone. He thought about the mess he'd left behind. About the bigger mess that lay ahead. About nights in the regional prison. About the rumpus sure to be raised by Pearl Gay Osbourn and other women of his affectionate acquaintance. And about his bank accounts in Luxembourg and the Cayman Islands.

The woman stifled a yawn and stretched.

"My name's Ja . . . ck. What's yours?"

Dooley called it the double blitz because he had two ways to attack an investigation.

One was the official *public* method, which entailed due diligence interviews, inspections, orderly evidence collection, established forensics methods, inter-agency coordination, media updates, Mirandizing suspects, note-taking, meetings and painstaking research.

The public method required logic, professional language, tidy uniforms, a lot of useless input, enough paperwork to sink a johnboat in the Ohio River, and more legwork than any West Virginia sheriff's department could reasonably devote to a case.

The other way—the unofficial, *unpublic* way—comprised bull collected at bars, motels and parking lots; hearsay provided by cousins, baseball buddies and mistresses; dubious wiretaps and searches; misdirection to suspects, media and victims; and cover-ups as necessary.

The unpublic method required more luck than logic, but more often than not it sifted out the grains of truth that enabled Dooley and his boys to clear most cases simply and swiftly.

But the Wince murder probe needed the double blitz.

Sheriff Skiles hunched over a kitchen counter in Glory Hallelujah Church studying some of his official weapons: a timeline of events on Thursday, June 14; copies of church blueprints marked into ten-square-foot grids; his own meticulous drawing of the area where Gudrun's body was found, and his notes as first officer on the scene.

Next to those lay the two sets of photos he had collected: those taken by Winona Wilcox shortly before Gudrun's slaying, and those taken afterward by forensic techs and emailed to him Thursday night.

In the file case beside him were the summaries of the Girls' interviews by his staff, summaries that gave him only one piece of useful info, which was that the summaries were uneven, incomplete and unhelpful.

Though Dooley had never needed to clear a true homicide, he'd taken seriously the courses and clinics he'd attended through the years. So he had also developed a chart with the headings *who, what, when, where, why* and *how*, and another page titled *conclusions*.

Dooley's staff—regular and auxiliary—worked elsewhere. Some searched the church, grid by grid, for any sign of a murder weapon, a hiding place, a hurried escape or any of Gudrun's personal belongings, especially a purse. The men had been instructed to take their time, look everywhere and move every item in and around the church—including those in the garbage, gardens and garages. They were to look into ducts, subfloors and the crevices that held hardware for folding doors.

A smaller detail of deputies, people who'd been by Dooley's side the longest, were spraying Luminol on every sharp or bladed object in the church to seek traces of blood.

Still more deputies, including those lent by the sheriffs of Doddridge and Wetzel counties, were questioning, or requestioning, the long list of persons supplied by Dooley: the ten Glory Girls besides Edith Fay Smith, the eight surviving cook-off contestants, the delivery people, the *Sentinel* people, the church staff, Boyd Eddy, Doc Weber, Marthleen Lewis and staff at Biddlebourne High School.

Those persons were to be asked, in addition to any other queries the deputies might come up with, the same five questions: Were you in Glory Hallelujah Church on Thursday, June 14? What was your relationship with Gudrun Wince? Where were you, exactly, between 10 a.m. and 12:30 p.m. on Thursday, June 14? What did you take in and/or out of the church? Did you see, hear, smell or otherwise sense anything out of the ordinary inside or outside the church?

Everyone had been provided with new notebooks and copies of Dooley's timeline and grid map. They were told to put on paper all information gleaned no matter how trivial it might seem.

Trumpets blared the West Virginia University fight song on Dooley's phone, signaling it was time to activate the unofficial investigation into the mysterious death of Gudrun Wince.

"Yeah," he said to the caller. "We need to see where those guys were Thursday morning. Yeah, everyone who testified against Wince at that board hearing in . . . '09, I think."

"Right," said Arnie Coker, "that'd be Aubrey Wise, Jess Wheeler, Dessel Beatty . . ."

"And Sterling Rowley," the sheriff said. "Hit 'em hard. Scare the crap out of 'em if you have to. If none of them did it, they know someone who does."

"Okay. What about Jass? Me and the boys was gonna sit in at the feed store this morning and see what we could see, but it wasn't open,"

"I know," Dooley said. "I went there too. You and the boys just keep your eyes and ears open. Stop in at the Drinkin' Depot and the hardware store. Have the boys check every fishin' cabin in the county. And the gas stations. He had to gas up that tank of his somewhere if he left town."

"Got it."

"Above all, do not make it sound like he's a suspect. He's just a person of interest at this point. Don't wanna give him a heads-up if he's only thinking of vamoosing."

"Sure, Sheriff, but I gotta tell ya, people are talking about Jass already. Ain't nobody seen him since he left the church yesterday afternoon."

"We'll find him. Just keep it on the down-low for now."

Dooley didn't mention that he'd been the one who foolishly let Jass slip out of view and possibly out of state.

The Clothing Subcommittee of the Glory Girls service organization of Glory Hallelujah Church, Biddlebourne, West Virginia, shall provide new or used clothing for qualified residents of Biddlebourne, and shall purposefully recycle unwearable clothing. *Glory Girls Book of Bylaws,* adopted May 1959

CHAPTER SIXTEEN

When Chief Deputy Stan Neiswonder politely booted Edith Fay Smith out of Glory Hallelujah Church, she had two hours in which to wash up, interview Buddy Lee at the Mug, get home and prepare a Glory Girl-worthy lunch.

The Girls' lunch consisted of individual heirloom tomato and Gruyere cheese pies, chilled fennel and cucumber soup, iced fruit tea and the rest of the strawberry scones and apple turnovers.

The women consumed everything set before them except the scones and turnovers, which they asked to be packaged for later.

While Edith Fay wrapped the desserts, the other Girls cleared the table, placed plates and utensils in the dishwasher, took the tablecloth to the laundry room, wiped the counters, swept the floor and carried the iced tea and glasses to the sunroom.

There they talked quietly until Edith Fay entered, took a seat near the large bird's nest fern and said, "Ladies, our topics today are the next kitchen inspection, the church closing, the rescheduled cook-off, the photo shoot and the investigation of Gudrun's death."

The Girls turned off their cell phones and reached into their purses for calendars and notebooks.

"In that order, Edith Fay?" asked Fonda Renee as she discreetly adjusted her bra to accommodate the hearty lunch.

"Yes."

A small whisper rippled around the room. The Glory Girls, who had been overhearing gossip and asking each other the last twenty-four hours who had killed Gudrun, were notoriously restless over unanswered questions.

"Patience, ladies," Edith Fay said. "Let's attend first to our ministries." Edith Fay knew the Girls would attend swiftly to the first matters in order to move to the more interesting final matter.

"I can recap the kitchen situation," Edith Fay said. "Depending on when Dooley lets us back in, there still will be a lag of one or two days before the new inspection."

"Why two days?" Zula Ruby asked.

"It takes that long for the health department to set up a full kitchen inspection."

"Wait a minute," Alwildia Louise said. "I thought the health department didn't know when they could reschedule."

"Apparently that changed overnight," Edith Fay said, "because I received a call from Mr. Duty's supervisor this morning. She advises she will expedite our re-inspection."

"Hmm," the Girls said.

While that news sank in, Edith Fay misted the bird's nest fern.

With a nod to her second-in-command, she continued, "Thanks to Ella Mae and Mary Ellen, we have the kitchen cleanup chores assigned.

Ella Mae explained. "Lloyda Ruth and Mary Ellen will sanitize the floors. Shari Odell and Ella Mae, walls. Zula Ruby, counters and cabinets. Alwildia Louise, sinks, refrigerators and freezers. Fonda Renee, stoves and dishwasher. Jo Claire, toasters, mixers and other small appliances. Ula Maude, cookware, serving ware, dishware and tableware. Bida June, food and disposable supplies."

The women had already known this, but the information had to be made part of the Girls' official minutes. Minutes had spared the Girls much time and many squabbles.

"I estimate the cleaning will take us twelve hours if we hit no major problems," Edith Fay noted.

"What do you think?"

A low babble erupted as the women took calculators from their purses and swatted numbers.

"More like sixteen hours," Mary Ellen said.

"Closer to eighteen," Ula Maude offered.

"All right," said Edith Fay. "Let's go with eighteen hours to be safe. Since we'll need to move right away, we'd better gather our cleaning supplies and equipment ahead of time."

"Right," the women chimed.

"What about the light fixtures?" It was Bida June, whose family operated a cleaning service that employed thirty-three men and women.

"I'll ask the trustees to lend us Charlie Simons for the lights, doors, windows, receiving desk and foldout doors."

"He's the new custodian?" Fonda Renee asked.

"Right."

Ella Mae interjected, "We'll figure out the rest of the cleanup details by email, if that's okay with you, Edith Fay."

"Of course," Edith Fay replied. "Also, we'll obviously need to redo our budget after all this is over, but we'll take that up at another meeting.

"As for Family Ministry Day," Edith Fay continued, "I've asked the newspapers and radio stations to announce that the regular activities are cancelled for next Tuesday."

Pained expressions greeted that statement, but Edith Fay moved on. "But we're also announcing that all the Glory Girls will be at Saint John's Church Tuesday for anyone who wants to come in for lunch. The auxiliary at Saint John's will serve the lunch.

"As far as the rest of the church calendar is concerned, including the cook-off and the photo shoot, I'll know more after the council meeting tonight."

"Does *Home Cookin'* know about the closing?" Jo Claire queried.

"I've been communicating with our contact editor about the particulars," Edith Fay said. "I think we can stick with the dates we have . . . for now. If for reasons beyond our control we must change our shoot dates, the magazine can do that if we give them two weeks' notice."

Smiles emerged around the room.

"Speaking of notice," Edith Fay said, "Ella Mae has sent each cook-off contestant a letter outlining the issues in broad terms and explaining that we'll give one week's notice before they will compete again."

Fonda Renee spoke. "Ivajean Hardman—she's my third cousin twice removed, as you know—is supposed to play piano at a wedding in Grafton, July fourteenth, and hopes the cook-off won't be then."

"I understand," Edith Fay said. "We'll have to do our best to make it fair for all the contestants. Emmy Rae Newsome defends her doctoral dissertation July twelfth in Huntington, and Penny Kay Gorby's daughter-in-law is due to deliver at the end of June."

It had taken the Girls nearly three weeks to arrive at their original date for the cook-off. They knew that as summer wore on it would be even more difficult to get the candidates together.

Edith Fay had given much thought to what she would say next. If it wasn't the entire truth, it was close enough.

"Ladies, on another topic, we have an opportunity to assist the sheriff with the investigation."

"How?" they chimed. Nobody wanted to prolong the probe because, first, they wanted to know who'd done in Gudrun and, second, they wanted to hurry back to Glory Girls business, especially the photo shoot.

"To start with, we can make a little diagram and show where all of us were when Buddy Lee . . . sounded the alarm."

Edith Fay observed carefully as the Girls digested her suggestion. There was no need to tell them she suspected a Glory Girl had killed Gudrun.

"I've got a blank sheet of paper here in my bag," Bida June volunteered.

"I can draw a simple sketch of the kitchen," said Jo Claire.

It took Jo Claire only a few minutes to pencil in the kitchen walls, doors, cooking audition stations, refrigerators and other large equipment and furniture. Several Girls looked over her shoulder and offered minor corrections until they all agreed the sketch would do. Jo Claire handed the paper to Edith Fay.

"Thank you. This looks excellent," Edith Fay said. "I'll just pass this around and ask each of you to place your name at your location when Gudrun was discovered by Buddy Lee."

The women nodded as Edith Fay passed the sketch left to Ella Mae.

"Meanwhile," Edith Fay said, "let's brainstorm ways we might further aid the sheriff's inquiry—without interfering where we shouldn't, of course."

Alwildia Louise raised her hand. "I was thinking about that, Edith Fay," she said. "We need to know why Gudrun really entered the cook-off and how in the world she expected to get away with it."

The sketch of the church kitchen, which had already been handed off to three Girls, fell soundlessly into the lap of Zula Ruby Hissom. The women put down their pens and looked left and right to check their own instincts against those of the others.

This was because the Glory Girls of Glory Hallelujah Church, who as a point of principle and purpose did not speak ill of others, had reluctantly been talking among themselves and members of the Ladies Aid Society about Gudrun.

When in February, Gudrun Cassandra Wince had announced her intention to compete in the June cook-off, the Glory Girls to a woman knew immediately that some sort of chicanery lay behind her move.

They knew this for many reasons: first, that Gudrun Wince had obtained her job as high school principal by improper means;

second, that Gudrun Wince had cheated on her taxes for at least twenty years; third, that Gudrun Wince had engaged in amorous affairs with no fewer than eight *gentlemen* of the community; fourth, that Gudrun Wince did not keep a bank account in Biddlebourne, a fact which alone pointed to skullduggery.

And, fifth, but by no means the least of her duplicitous ways, Gudrun Wince persistently and petulantly avoided actual work. She would not help in the toddler room, where running to catch preschoolers was necessary. She would not help set up for the numerous meals served by the Ladies Aid and the Glory Girls, telling one and all she had a back ailment, which Doc Weber hinted privately was not so. She would not distribute fliers about events, make telephone calls for the prayer chain, bake bread to be given to first-time church visitors, or wash by hand the hundreds of communion cups used on any Sunday.

Further—and this was the most egregious of her lazy habits— Gudrun Wince refused to participate in the church's All-Clean Days, the special events organized by the Girls to fight the indoor and outdoor clutter, litter, grime and dust that accumulated despite the best custodial efforts.

No, Gudrun Wince had not labored in the ministries of her church, let alone toil extra long and extra hard, as all Glory Girls must do. She had shamelessly stretched her report of volunteer labors to qualify for the cook-off, and the Girls had allowed her to compete on the unstated assumption that she could not possibly win the contest.

Therefore, each Glory Girl had already quietly surmised, since Gudrun apparently had gone to great effort to qualify as a cook-off contestant, that her motives must be as hinky as her known methods. It could be no other way.

Edith Fay had feared something like this might happen, something that would get the Girls off their pledged course of service and sacrifice. She considered the options, realizing as she did so that the Girls would ask their questions about Gudrun whether or not Edith Fay approved.

"All right, ladies," she said quietly. "Because the ministries of the Glory Girls and of the church as a whole are at stake, I agree that we should look into Gudrun's reasons for participating in the cook-off despite her, um, aversion to certain activities.

"But let's remember," she continued, "that everything we say and do reflects on the church . . . and on Christ himself. Let us be respectful and focus on obtaining only the information that seems based on facts. Mere hearsay will not do us, or anyone, any good."

The women signaled their agreement, and the sketch of the church kitchen moved from Zula Ruby to Shari Odell. Edith Fay watched carefully but saw no hesitation by any Glory Girl in penning her name on the drawing.

When the sketch arrived back at Edith Fay's seat, she drew a circle alongside the kitchen and printed *Edith Fay Smith, in GOB office.*

"What else can we do for the investigation?" asked Zula Ruby, a known watcher of numerous TV crime shows. "The boys are searching the church. Maybe we can . . ."

At that moment the door chime sounded.

"Excuse me, ladies," Edith Fay said, but Shari Odell spoke up. "I'll get it, Edith Fay. You've done so much today."

A minute later, Shari Odell was back in the sunroom with a shocked expression on her face and Laverna Inys Wharton on her heels.

"I heard there was a Glory Girl opening, and I heard you were meeting today, and I made a casserole this morning, and, can you sample it and if you like it let me be in the cook-off, whenever you have it, that is, and I brought plates and forks and napkins, and where can I set it down?"

Having announced herself, Laverna Inys Wharton gulped air and pulled a hot pad from an IKEA bag.

Feather by feather, the goose is cooked. *Proverb*

CHAPTER SEVENTEEN

"Gudrun was a . . . a hootchy-kootchy dancer," Shirl Burrows said as she fondled a pack of cigarettes.

"Oh my!" said the pastor, only a little surprised.

"Yep. It's true. She was a showgirl, a dancer, a *stripper*," said Shirl, who had gained her bookkeeping experience at a low-rent Cincinnati furniture outlet that stood amid several adult establishments.

Shirl told Pastor Annie she had often watched passersby from the front window after tallying the furniture man's meager receipts.

"Yeah, I saw all the showgirls coming and going," she said. "A couple of 'em traveled with bodyguards—or maybe they were pimps—but most of 'em walked past the store around the middle of the morning. I guess the bars opened at eleven."

Annie said, "You're positive you saw Gudrun walking to a . . . a show bar?"

"Absolutely. She was younger then, of course, and wore different clothes and all. But it was her. I musta seen her go past a coupla hundred times. In warm weather she wore tank tops and cutoff shorts."

"Oh dear."

"At first I wasn't gonna say anything," Shirl replied. "I've done a few things myself that I'm not so proud of."

Annie nodded and said, "Haven't we all?"

"But I know the truth has gotta come out," Shirl continued, "because Dooley ain't gonna leave nobody alone until it does."

They sat silent for a moment. Then Annie asked, "Can you remember the name of the place where Gudrun worked?"

"The Glass Slipper. The Glass Slipper Saloon. The girls dressed up like, um, naughty fairy tale characters. Place still there, according to my brother. He lives in Cincinnati, ya know."

"Hmm," said Annie. "And you're positive that the woman you saw was Gudrun?"

"Yeah, I know it seems hard to believe, her bein' a school principal and all. But my boss, Butch Leasure, he saw her too. Like I said, business wasn't exactly booming at the furniture place. He sold mainly junky bedroom sets and crummy lamps. The cheap motels around there would come and buy the stuff by the truckload. Anyway, Butch had a lot of free time. He'd say he was going out to lunch and then head for the Glass Slipper."

"I'm beginning to see where this is going." Annie pulled into the Saint John's Church lot and turned off the engine.

"Yep. Butch would come back after two or three hours at that joint. He'd be half-drunk and when some of those motel owners came in, he'd talk about Good Time Goldilocks—that's what Gudrun called herself—and another one o' his favorites, Little Red Riding Hood. I didn't realize it was her when she first came to Biddlebourne. I got my job and the church stuff and my bingo and a house to keep up, and all the kids I know are long outta high school. I guess I just wasn't payin' attention. Heh heh."

Annie pushed a button to lower the windows.

"But when Good Time Goldilocks, I mean Gudrun, began showing up at church I put it together. Wasn't anything to be proved talking about her past, so I didn't tell nobody about her and the Glass Slipper till today. Well, I did mention her to my brother, but like I said, he's still in Cincinnati. She wouldn't have recognized me, ya know, because I was always inside the store looking out at her."

"Shirl, you are the soul of discretion. But I'm wondering something. Did Gudrun work at the Glass Slipper all the time you were at the furniture store?"

"Let me think." Shirl put a hand to her chin and mused. "Come to think of it, Butch stopped talking about Goldilocks maybe a year or so before I left. Coulda been because that's when he got married. Coulda been because Gudrun left the Glass Slipper. Hard to tell which. Heh heh."

"And you left Cincinnati in what year? I know you've mentioned it, but I'm just not recalling it at this moment," Annie said.

"I know what you mean. Sometimes I can't remember what I did yesterday. Yep, I came to Biddlebourne in '81. Been workin' part time at Biddle Banking & Trust ever since."

"Biddlebourne's gain and Cincinnati's loss," Annie said with a smile. "But tell me, Shirl. Did you see Gudrun leaving the Glass Slipper every day? I mean she arrived around ten in the morning. When did she leave?"

"Funny you should mention that," Shirl said. "Most o' the girls musta worked till the wee hours o' the morning. Wanted to catch guys after work, ya know. But Gudrun was out of there every day by, oh, I'd say three in the afternoon. I never did figure out why she worked short shifts like that. But I guess it wasn't a coincidence that Butch would come back from lunch, heh heh, around the time she left. That's why I noticed it at first."

"Hmm. So you're saying that Gudrun worked at the show bar from around ten in the morning to three in the afternoon?"

"Seemed that way to me," Shirl confirmed.

"Look, Shirl, I really appreciate your taking time to fill me in on this. It might help with . . . what we need to get done. I'm sorry to hurry away like this, but . . . "

"No problem," Shirl said. "I think I'll get me a cuppa coffee at the Hoot 'n' Scoot and bum a ride back to the church to pick up my car."

"Oh, my goodness. I'm sorry," Annie said. "I didn't even think about that. Please let me take you back to Glory Hallelujah."

"Nah, that's okay. I'll go in and say hey to Pearl Gay until somebody drives by. I don't mind."

"Thank you, Shirl. Thank you for everything, and I promise to keep what you told me as confidential as I can."

Shirl opened the door. "Maybe it doesn't matter now, but I hope it was the right thing to do—to tell you, I mean."

"I think you did the right thing, Shirl, when you didn't talk about Gudrun before and when you did talk about her today."

As Shirl turned toward the Hoot 'n' Scoot, Annie picked up her phone to make two calls, the first to fill in Sheriff Skiles about Gudrun's early career, the second to ask Belle Watkins to take the visitor records with her when she left the church.

"Did you hear about Mayor Pinbiddie?" Thelma Blivins demanded.

"What about him?" replied Hazel Simons. She and Thelma talked by phone every day, sometimes three or four times depending on what was happening in Biddlebourne.

"Well," said Thelma. "I heard from Arnie Coker that the sheriff put out a BOLO on Jass."

"BOLO?"

"You know. Like on *Law and Order*. Be on the lookout!"

"Oh, right. Wait a minute here. You're saying Dooley BOLO'd Jass just because he acted up at the church when Gudrun got herself killed? I think Dooley overdid it, don't you?"

"No, no, there's more," Thelma said. "Jass didn't show up at the feed store or his office today. That's why Dooley BOLO'd him. What do you think of that?"

Jass Pinbiddie was many things to the people of Biddlebourne. He was seller of farm and home goods, top elected official, backer of charitable causes, teller of tales true and untrue, instigator of projects and owner of a finger in almost every pot of trouble that bubbled up in Biddlebourne.

But above all, Jass was a person who was present in Biddlebourne. Except for his *official* Thursday absences, he did not skip council meetings, constituent conferences, public hearings, budget sessions, development debates or meet-and-greets.

Nor at Biddlebourne Feed & Grain did he miss any opportunity to sit at the counter, ring up a purchase, jaw with a customer, sell an extra bag of lawn seed, joke with a youngster or compliment a female on her good looks.

So when Thelma Blivins reported Jass' absence to Hazel Simons, whose husband Charlie had just started his new job at Glory Hallelujah Church but who was home under her feet today because the sheriff had closed down the church, Hazel put two and two together and came up with five.

Hazel reckoned that if the church was closed, there must be a lot of evidence there for the sheriff's deputies to collect in secret. And if Jass had hightailed and the sheriff had BOLO'd Jass and only Jass—of this Hazel was sure because if the sheriff was going after other people, Thelma would have said so—the mayor must have killed Gudrun Wince. It made perfect sense.

In the split second it took Hazel Simons to arrive at this conclusion, she took a deep breath and sat up straight. "Lordie, Thelma! He done it!"

"It sure looks like it. I mean, nobody's seen Jass since Doc Weber took him home from the church yesterday. Barry Dale says Jass didn't show up at the feed store this morning. And he can't get him on the phone. Ain't nobody seen him. I know 'cause I put out my own BOLO and asked around. Ha."

"Wait a minute," Hazel said. "Doesn't Jass go on those buying trips of his sometimes?"

"Yes, that's true," Thelma allowed. "But Marthleen Lewis says he usually tells her at least a week ahead so she can make his reservations and tell him what clothes to pack. He didn't do any of that this week."

"Where could he have got to?"

"Beats me," Thelma said. "Arnie says the sheriff told the boys to keep it on the hush-hush. So don't breathe a word of it to anyone."

"Yes, yes. But I heard something else about Jass," Hazel confided. She looked toward the kitchen to see if Charlie was eavesdropping. But she didn't see him and figured he'd gone out back to fix the holes in the porch screens.

Thelma, who kept herself busy during phone calls by filing her nails, put down her file and said, "What did you hear?"

"Well, I heard that Pearl Gay Osbourn dumped him when she heard he killed Gudrun!"

"Oh my!"

"You know why?!" Thelma crowed.

"I 'spect it's 'cause she don't wanna hang around with a killer."

"No, no. It's 'cause Jass was messin' around with Gudrun and now everybody knows it after he set up a big ruckus at the church over her dead body. He was cryin' and blubberin' and Doc Weber had to give him somethin' to settle him down."

"You don't say," Hazel replied in sincere surprise.

At Hoot 'n' Scoot, Shirl Burrows and Pearl Gay Osbourn shared a lunch of bologna sandwiches from plastic packages, chips from the outdated-goods box and Buds straight from the bottles.

"You still seein' Truman Dent?" Pearl Gay wanted to know.

"Yeah, I guess."

"Sounds like you're not sure," said Pearl Gay, who had dated Truman before that rat Jass Pinbiddie started showing up with shiny jewelry and skimpy lingerie.

"Aw, he wants to get married. I ain't the marryin' kind, know what I mean?" Shirl said. "I like to do things my own way. I got my own income, and I sure as hell don't wanna start pickin' up after a feller at my age."

Pearl Gay, who could not have agreed more, wiped her lips and said, "Verl used to drop his skivvies wherever he took 'em off. One day I started trashin' 'em instead of washin' 'em. Made him real mad. You know how cheap he was. But he got the point after a while and started puttin' 'em in the hamper."

"How long did that take you, to train him to pick up his drawers?" Shirl asked.

"Oh, about fifteen years from the day we were married to the day I actually saw him pick up a pair o' tighty-whities."

"That's just what I mean," Shirl said. "I don't wanna spend the next fifteen years trainin' Truman. It ain't my style. You want him back?"

Pearl Gay, who indeed was considering taking Truman back—but only if Shirl was done with him—said, "I'll think about it."

Shirl, who knew full well that Pearl Gay and Jass had been more than friends since the Valentine's Day dance at the American Legion where Pearl Gay had sung a couple torch songs while wearing black tights and a clinging low-cut sweater, thought carefully before she spoke.

"Uh, does that mean you're . . . lookin'?" she said tactfully.

"You could say that," Pearl Gay replied with a sour expression.

"Oh?"

"He's a no-good bum. Ran out on me . . . and was foolin' around on me to boot," Pearl Gay admitted.

"Whaddaya mean, he ran out on you?" Shirl was more than curious now because she had heard, as had at least ninety percent of the Biddlebourne population, about Jass Pinbiddie's lunatic behavior after Gudrun's death.

"Aw, he was here last night but bolted out this morning without even a goodbye. Just left me a yellow-belly note."

"What'd he say in the note, if you don't mind my askin'," Shirl said.

"Nah, I don't mind. I got no good reason to look out for his precious reputation now. Like his reputation was more precious than mine. I'm a businesswoman, ya know." Pearl Gay gulped the last of her Bud and belched involuntarily. "'Scuse me," she said, shaking her head.

"That's right," Shirl said, emptying her own bottle and slamming it to the table.

"Anyhow, here's his note, that jerk." Pearl Gay withdrew a creased piece of lined paper from her jeans pocket. "You can read it for yourself."

Shirl gingerly opened the note and read: "Pearly girl. I got things to do out of town. I don't know when I'll be back. Look after Ralphie for me. He needs two cups of Sam's Best dog food, three treats and two walks a day. We had fun while it lasted. Your lover boy."

"I notice he didn't put his name on it," Shirl said drily. "Or a date."

"Yeah. Prob'ly no accident there."

"You gonna take care o' his dog?"

"That would make me an ever bigger fool," Pearl Gay said. "I already called animal control. Jass Pinbiddie has had his last good deed from Pearl Gay Osbourn."

"You think he had anything to do with killin' Gudrun? That why he's runnin'?"

"How would I know what that old skunk is up to?" said Pearl Gay. "All I know is I ain't gonna lie for him if it comes to that."

"Right!"

So Pearl Gay fetched two more Buds and they drank to not picking up dirty underwear.

"Stan, I got your message. What happened?" Dooley said, breaking department policy by using a cell phone while driving.

Chief Deputy Stan Neiswonder said, "Aw, boss, it's hit the fan. It's all over town that you put out a BOLO on Jass Pinbiddie. The town council president is crawling all over me, and there's a list as long as your arm o' people wantin' to know where Jass is—Barry Dale at the store, the forensic guys who want his prints, some inspector from the health department who says it's urgent. . . ."

Sheriff Skiles muttered some words that failed to assuage his anger, then said, "All I wanted was a low-key watch for Pinbiddie. He ran out on me at his place, but I figured he had some kinda official business to tend to."

"Boss, it's worse than you think. Pearl Gay Osbourn called. Jass gave her a dumb note. Said she got it this morning. Just brought it over here to the church. Said you didn't answer her call."

"I was busy. What kinda note?"

"Sorta like a Dear John letter. Here, I'll read it to you."

Stan read the note to Dooley, who groaned at its conclusion. "Shoot. He's on the run. Now I am putting out that BOLO. Get on it. I'm on my way back to the church right now."

"I'm on it, boss."

"One more thing," Dooley said.

"Yeah?"

"You guys turn up anything coulda been the murder weapon?"

"Nah," said Stan. "Place was clean as Aunt Millie's parlor."

"You had the guys look through the trash too?"

"Sure did. Nothin' there but food wrappers and corn cobs."

"All right. Talk to you when I get there," the sheriff said.

Dooley pulled up to Glory Hallelujah Church, where he was met by Winona Wilcox and Wilford Nicklin.

"Where you been, Sheriff?" Winona asked as she took the lens cap off her camera. "I been waitin' here nearly half an hour."

"I was unavoidably detained, Winona. Sorry. And I got more bad news for you. We didn't find the murder weapon yet."

"You puttin' me on?" Winona said with a glare. "I gave you my pictures in good faith. . . ."

Standing next to Winona, Wilford Nicklin said, "I'll take it from here, Winona."

The photographer transferred her glare to Wilford, but Wilford had already begun his interview.

"Sheriff, I've heard that Mayor Jass Pinbiddie killed Gudrun Wince and left town yesterday afternoon. Do you care to comment?"

Two hours later, Pearl Gay Osbourn, in a pink sequined top and cheek-high cutoffs, stood squarely in front of the sheriff's office door and began talking.

"I know you gotta talk to me about that note, but for the record I wish I'd a killed her but I didn't."

Dooley waved her in, and she came toward him holding out a roll of faintly inked paper. "Here's the cash register tape from yesterday. I know 'bout everyone who came by, and they know me, and I wrote down all their names on the receipts in case you wanna check anything. The time's stamped on the receipts, case you gotta know what time they come by."

"Have a seat," he said. The sheriff rubbed his eyes as he sat in the rickety swivel chair. Pearl Gay sat, crossed her knees and bounced her left foot.

"I'm sorry, Dooley, but I gotta get back to the store quick as I can. I got the *Back in 30 Minutes* sign up, but people can't wait. It's Friday and they got plans. I'da called Janie in to handle the register, but she didn't answer her phone either."

Dooley, who felt an uncharacteristic wave of fatigue, only nodded. He had pictures of the crime scene to examine more thoroughly, more interviews to review, his time line to organize if he had any hope of figuring out who could have been close enough to Gudrun to kill her, the videos from Value Mart to check, another call to make to an irate town council president—and a burning desire to talk with Edith Fay Smith.

"Sheriff, you with me?" Pearl Gay was slapping the top of the desk. "I thought you went to sleep on me," she said as Dooley's eyes popped open and his right hand instinctively moved toward his weapon.

"Yegads, man! I can come back another time. I ain't goin' nowhere 'cept the store."

Dooley caught his breath and throttled back on his gun hand. "Pearl Gay, I already checked and I know where you were when Gudrun was killed. What I wanna know is where you think Jass might have got to. Stan read me that note Jass left you."

"I been thinkin' about that all day. That son of a hounddog. Me and him never traveled much together, 'cept once he took me over to Marietta to buy a coupla bushels o' tomatoes. Wanted me to can 'em so he could have his homemade chili in the winter. After he told me why he took me I told him to go to hell and can his own tomatoes. That was the last trip we took together."

"I see," Dooley said. "Do you know where Jass might have traveled previously on his own?"

Pearl Gay, who was realizing how little she knew about Jass Pinbiddie after all their years together, said, "Well, Sheriff, he'd tell me he was goin' to scout John Deere equipment or size up his competition. I never knew exactly where he went, now I think 'bout it."

"Did he ever call you while he was on a trip?"

Now Pearl Gay was getting angrier with Jass, if that was possible. "He'd call me once in a great long while when he was outta town. He'd say he was 'in the bar' or 'at the race track,' but that rat never named a city that I can recall."

Dooley looked out the barred window that faced west. It was nearly dinnertime. He wished he had dinner plans with Edith Fay. At her house.

"Dooley! Darn it, I'm leavin' now. You're not payin' the least mind to anything I say."

"Just one more question, Pearl Gay."

She looked skeptical but stayed seated.

"How long was Jass gone on these trips of his?"

"Well, now that I know what a two-timer he was, he couldda been back in town a long time before he got in touch with me, but, generally, he'd leave on a Thursday after he, uh, visited me. Said he couldn't leave the store too long or Barry Dale would forget to open the door in the morning."

"I take it he spent last night at your place," the sheriff said.

"Yeah," she said. Her nostrils flared. "He did. I can tell you it was the last time."

"How did he get over to your place? The Blazer or the Caddie?"

"Neither one. He walked all the way from his place to mine. Least, that's what the skunk said. First time I ever heard o' him walkin' more'n a block."

"Okay, Pearl Gay. Stay in touch and let me know if you hear from him. Thanks for comin' in."

"Yeah, that's okay. You know where I am if you need anything else."

The Food Subcommittee of the Glory Girls service organization of Glory Hallelujah Church, Biddlebourne, West Virginia, shall obtain, prepare and serve food in support of all other ministries of the congregation. *Glory Girls Book of Bylaws,* adopted May 1959

CHAPTER EIGHTEEN

"His name is Jasper Pinbody, but he told me it was Jack Pemberton, and I think he's a con man."

Maria Angelica Ogden sat uneasily in the unmarked police car in an abandoned industrial district. She wore large plastic sunglasses and a floppy beach hat over her platinum-blond hair, in contrast to the mocha silk suit, peep-toe alligator pumps and Gucci shoulder bag she'd worn in the hotel.

Cleveland Detective Jimmy Campanella sniffed. He had to sift everything she said because she had a habit of feeding him bad information as well as good. On a few occasions, though, her tips had led to high-profile busts.

So, having nothing much better to do and needing to boost his collars so he could advance a pay grade, Jimmy said, "Yeah? Why you think he's a con?"

Maria Angelica glanced out the windows in all four directions, pulled the visor mirror down to check her lipstick and touched up the corners of her mouth with a pinkie.

"C'mon, I haven't got all day."

"I met him in the business center at the Lafayette," she said.

"Yeah, you being a businesswoman and all."

"Look, Jimmy, I have to make a living like everyone else. I'll tell you what happened but cut out the hassle, okay?"

The detective smirked and settled back in his seat.

Maria Angelica continued. "As I was saying, I was in the business center at the Lafayette pretending to work on a spread sheet. Actually, it was a spread sheet. My brother Giorgio gave it to me. It's from his company."

Detective Campanella rolled his eyes. Giorgio Ogden's company bought knockoff electronics and sold them at prices so ridiculously low that anyone with half a brain should have known the goods were either stolen or assembled in a bootleg basement. Apparently, the entire Ogden family went for quantity over quality.

"Yeah?" he said, hoping to keep Maria Angelica on track.

"This guy was working on his computer, but I saw him looking at me but trying not to let on. You know?"

He nodded.

"And so when he shut his computer down, I said a word or two to him, and he said a word or two to me, and soon, you know, we were at the hotel bar."

"Just like that," Jimmy said in mock surprise.

"Yes, just like that," she said, running a hand along the front of her blouse to remind him how good she looked in her work clothes. "And pretty soon, well, you know how it goes, we were in his room."

"Here comes the good part," Jimmy said.

"I told him it would be a thousand dollars for two hours," she said, "and he acted indignant, as if he was surprised that I am a . . . professional woman. However, I, um . . . convinced him that he would enjoy his time with me, and he asked if he could pay with a credit card. That was no problem, but when I took his payment I noticed the name on his credit card was not the name he gave me."

"That all you got?" Jimmy asked, ready to start the engine and get Maria Angelica back to the city.

"No, no. I didn't ask him about his name before we, uh, proceeded. But while we were in bed he called me Cassie. I thought he couldn't remember my name, so I told it to him again. I said maybe Cassie was his own little term of endearment, you know, to give him an out for speaking the name of another woman while with me. But he said no, no, it was the name of his lady love."

"You're bringin' me to tears here."

"Quit interrupting! But then he told me she died recently and the people in his town thought he killed her, but he didn't, and would I please forget he said her name."

"Just like I thought. You got nothin'." Jimmy turned the key and put the car in gear.

"You are so thick in the head!"

"So far you haven't said a thing to convince me this guy's anything other than a businessman who gave you an alias because he didn't want his wife to know he'd been with a . . . professional woman, as you conveniently call yourself."

"I should not tell you the rest because you are so rude," she said quietly.

Jimmy Campanella wanted a kiss from his wife, he wanted a half-hour of soccer with his boys, he wanted his dinner, he wanted to take out the trash and walk his terrier Shorty, and then he wanted to watch television peaceably until bedtime.

But he wanted that pay raise more, to support all those activities he enjoyed so much. He killed the engine.

"While he went into the bathroom, I took the liberty of . . . checking his briefcase, which he had left open."

"I'm sure."

"Please. In his briefcase I found many securities. You know, stock certificates, bearer bonds, insurance policies, things like that. They were all made out to this Jasper Eugene Pinbody. Hmm. Or Pinbotty. Or some such. I can't help but think he's a man on the run. He may have killed this Cassie person. You know?"

Jimmy stayed quiet.

"And underneath all those documents there was a . . . you know . . . a hidden apartment."

"Compartment. Which was also open, I suppose?"

"Not exactly. But it fell open when I just touched it lightly with the tip of my knife."

All the Cleveland detectives knew about Maria Angelica's Swiss knife, which she claimed to employ only for snipping tags off new clothes. They let her get away with it because she had never actually used it on anyone—that they knew of—and now and then provided a decent tip. Jimmy suspected she occasionally supplied other favors to a couple of the guys, but that was their business.

"Yes, yes, the knife. What did you find?"

"Diamonds. Like this one."

She opened her left hand, which Jimmy realized had been closed during their discussion. Jimmy held out his hand, and she dropped the gem into it.

He examined it up close and then, reaching into the backseat for an old newspaper, laid the diamond face down on the newsprint. He could not read the print through the stone. Then he held the diamond close to his mouth, breathed on it and checked to see if retained any fog.

"It ain't illegal to have diamonds," he said while he tried to remember what warrants he'd seen lately for jewel thieves.

"Of course not, but these were many diamonds, maybe one hundred, and he told me a made-up story, and he told me his woman was dead, and he . . . ah, couldn't do . . . what he wanted to do with me. That meant he was nervous, very nervous, about something."

Jimmy was silent, thinking.

"One more thing," Maria Angelica said. "I asked if I could use his cell phone to call for a cab, and he wouldn't let me."

"Why, do you think?"

"It's obvious. He was afraid I would listen to his messages. This man is hiding something, maybe more than one something. I'm sure."

Jimmy considered the possibilities. Maria Angelica had no reason, or none he could think of at that moment, to make up such a story. And even if she had made up the story, she had not made up the diamond.

"You notice a name like Cassie on any of the insurance policies?"

"I did not read them through," she said. "He could've come back in at any moment."

"Okay. You see an address on the documents?"

"Yes, but, as I just said, I was in a hurry. Some town I never heard of. Maybe West Virginia. Maybe Washington. It started with a *W*."

"How many times I gotta tell ya details make a difference?" Jimmy scolded. "Maybe you're just leadin' me on to keep me busy lookin' for something doesn't exist."

"I see what you think. I have brought you valuable information, and your response is to complain it is not tied up in a box with shining ribbon. Never mind. I'll take my information to Earl. He is more appreciative."

Maria Angelica put her hand on the door handle.

Of all Jimmy's colleagues in the detective division, Earl G. McGlade was the one he most envied. Earl G. seemed able to take the tiniest factotum and spin it into a stickable arrest.

Jimmy needed only an instant to consider the value of nabbing a con artist, possibly an international jewel thief, who dealt in baubles like the four-carat diamond he had just seen.

"You think he's still at the Lafayette?"

"I left him there a couple of hours ago. I don't know where he is now."

"All right, gimme his description."

"I shall. But first please give back my diamond."

There had been no natural reason for Laverna Inys Wharton to perspire so profusely in the sunroom, which Edith Fay maintained at a constant seventy-two degrees and fifty percent humidity for the comfort of people and plants.

Therefore, as the Glory Girls pecked at Laverna's casserole, they looked on in wonder as perspiration pooled on her upper lip, bare arms and décolletage. But they became alarmed when the serving spoon slid from Laverna's moist hand to the floor and she sneezed five times.

"How do you like my Chicken Cordon Bleu Casserole, ladies?"

Everyone looked to Edith Fay, the Girls hoping their leader could frame a noncommittal answer and Laverna hoping Edith Fay would bypass rules on the spot and declare her eligible for the coming cook-off.

"It has a taste all its own," Edith Fay said with a kind smile.

"Oh, thank you, Edith Fay," Laverna said. "I so hoped y'all would like it."

"Yes, it is certainly distinctive," Jo Claire agreed.

Dead calm reigned. Laverna dared not breathe for fear something else—or perhaps she herself—would fall to the floor. The Girls, save Edith Fay, feared showing any emotion, making any move or speaking any word that might further abet Laverna's culinary confusion.

Ella Mae Pugh stood. "Well, ladies, all of us have work to do."

She spoke in such a tone that the Glory Girls understood her to mean, *We are leaving immediately. Our leader's job is to deal with Laverna and her dreadful food. Our job is to answer the question of why Gudrun Wince really wanted to become a Glory Girl.*

The other Glory Girls, save Edith Fay, stood as one, gathered their materials and decamped within sixty seconds of thanking their hostess and her uninvited guest.

Though Edith Fay felt perfectly comfortable, she said, "Laverna, let's have some iced tea with lemon. It appears the room has grown warm."

The tea reduced but did not halt Laverna's perspiring, though it did limit her sneezing to only two more outbursts. They sat away from the windows and chatted a few minutes before Edith Fay smiled and asked, "What ingredients did you use in your casserole? I thought I tasted something unusual."

"Oh, the seasonings? Let me see. I wrote everything down on this card here. Thyme, garlic, Dijon mustard, cayenne pepper and celery seed."

The wheels in Edith Fay's head spun like cattails in the wind behind Cletus Houston's moonshine factory. She called from memory Chicken Cordon Bleu Casserole recipes she'd tried; recipes other Girls had tried; recipes she'd seen in magazines, newspapers and cookbooks; private recipes she'd received from her mother, neighbors and friends; and recipes that came on jars, boxes and new oven mitts.

But she could not recall an original, legitimate recipe for Chicken Cordon Bleu containing celery seed, either whole or ground.

This was a predicament, as the origination of a recipe was as essential to the Glory Girls' culinary archives as were its ingredients, instructions, photo and popularity rating. Sometimes the Girls' culinary historian had to conduct a rigorous, years-long investigation to learn just who had developed a recipe.

"Um, Laverna, I'm interested in where you obtained the recipe," she said.

"Oh my, you're right, it is very warm in here," Laverna declared as she tapped a dishtowel on her forearms. But sweat kept emerging from her pores like dew on the grass of a summer morn.

When Edith Fay did not respond, Laverna went on. "Well, I had some recipes from my younger days that I collected before I met William. I'm afraid I can't begin to remember where any of them came from."

That didn't matter, because Edith Fay knew exactly who had originated the unique combination of thyme, garlic, Dijon mustard, cayenne pepper and celery seed in Chicken Cordon Bleu Casserole.

That person was Theodocia Price, the late and beloved teacher of home economics at Biddlebourne High School. Theodocia had brought her Chicken Cordon Bleu Casserole to numerous Glory Hallelujah Church potlucks, and it had been roundly favored until the day she added celery seed to the recipe.

On that particular afternoon, when the congregation was marking Super Bowl Sunday with a grand brunch after the third worship service, the comments of several eaters led Theodocia to understand that celery seed did not belong in her casserole.

"Lordie, Lordie, I thought celery seed would perk it up," she'd told fellow members of the Ladies Aid Society, "but I missed my guess this time."

Theodocia had laughed heartily about it, "I'll just pop this recipe into my exam file so I can use it for a test question."

"May I see the recipe?" Edith Fay said to her guest.

"Of course." Laverna retrieved a bright yellow card from her purse and handed it over.

Edith Fay paled as she took the card and instantly recognized its distinctive hue. Theodocia Price had always used saffron-colored cards—for classroom and personal recipes.

That was how Edith Fay Smith learned that Laverna Inys Wharton had possession of Theodocia Price's original, errant recipe for Chicken Cordon Bleu Casserole, in which celery seed was an ingredient.

"We need to talk about this," Edith Fay said.

"How 'bout some dinner, pal? My treat."

Andy Brewster had one hand on the door of Dooley's office and the other on a super big takeout bag from Li Chu's Chinese Eat Now, the only locally owned Asian restaurant between Biddlebourne and the Troop One state police command in Shinnston.

Dooley walked to a table decorated by Lucy Jane, who said the room needed a touch of color other than gray. With one sweep of an arm, he cleared off a puffy arrangement of fake pink carnations.

"Nothin' I'd like better," he said. "Put 'er down right here."

State Police Captain Andy Brewster, who'd done his share of policing alongside Dooley Skiles before signing on with the state cops, glanced at the toppled flowers and said, "Lucy Jane do that?"

"Yeah, I couldn't bring myself to tell her *no*," the sheriff said with a grin. "She's just so darned useful otherwise around here."

"I remember," Andy agreed as he parked his size 16's on the table. "You still a fiend for kung pao steak?"

Dooley laughed. "Worse 'n ever."

Three pounds of Chinese food later, Dooley and Andy leaned back on the ancient flowered couch, a donation from Arnie Coker's grandmother. Telephones jangled and voices filtered in from the squad room.

"What about the interviews with the . . . whadda they call themselves . . . the Good Women?" Andy said with a snicker.

Dooley chuckled. "The Glory Girls. And don't underestimate 'em. They're behind a lot of projects around here. They help so many people it kinda makes me wanna go to church myself."

Andy laughed but Dooley didn't.

"Are you serious?" the captain asked the sheriff.

"Maybe. I don't know. One thing I can tell ya, Andy, is that those women know how to talk a lot and say nada. My guys spent hours talkin' to 'em and didn't get a thing that helps."

Andy's eyebrows lifted. "You think one of them did it?"

"Jeez, I highly doubt it, but I gotta be sure."

"Want me to grill 'em?" Andy volunteered.

"That won't work either. There's only way to get 'em to talk, and it's not a way I'm used to."

"Whatcha mean by that?"

"Never mind. I'm still thinking about her . . . I mean it."

"We're getting off track," Andy said. "What about that kid who found the body—Buddy somethin'?"

"Buddy Lee Delbert," Dooley said. "I interviewed him here a couple hours ago. Gave me a written statement about everything that happened. Doesn't sound like he did it. Frankly, he's too dumb to pull off a murder in broad daylight with a couple dozen people within earshot."

"Or maybe he's too dumb not to know that'd be a bad plan," Andy conjectured.

They sat and thought a minute on that conundrum before Dooley said dejectedly, "We haven't found anything looks like a murder weapon yet. Nothin' in or around the church or in the garbage cans."

"Friend, I'd like to tell you I have good news from what our guys did yesterday, but it isn't so, at least not yet. You got the pictures they took, didn't you?"

"Yeah. I'm gonna compare those photos to shots the Biddlebourne newspeople took before the contest. The body's gotta go to Charleston for the state M.E. to see. All the local guy says is that the deceased had at least two stab wounds to her torso that apparently caused her death."

Andy shook his head. "Man, this is frustrating. What else ya got?"

Dooley rubbed the back of his neck and said, "I'm pinning my hopes on what we might find in Gudrun's house. I'm takin' a crew over there tonight."

"What ya lookin' for in particular?"

"Oh, everything, I guess. But I suspect we could run across something, uh, off the books."

"She was dirty?" Andy asked with renewed interest.

"Lot o' talk goin' around about her. My gut tells me she had some, shall we say, bad habits. Trouble is, we only got one guy can do computer forensics—Denzil Westover. Met him at that forensics class in Beckley—and I got him workin' already on Jass Pinbiddie's home computer."

"I saw the BOLO on Jass," Andy said. "D'ya think he skipped 'cause he did it?"

"Don't see how he coulda done it. He was in his office—with the pastor of the church—when it happened. But he mighta had somebody else do it. But I searched his house right after he skedaddled, though I didn't know at the time he was gonna leave town, and spotted some computer discs."

"You searched the mayor's house and took computer files without a warrant?" Andy let out a long, low whistle. "Man, you got balls."

"It wasn't an official search," Dooley allowed. "The report will say I was looking for Jass because I was concerned for his health after he became ill at the crime scene."

"Good luck with that," Andy said. "Listen, I got some official stops to make while I'm out this way. But let's keep in touch. I'm stayin' at the Microtel in Spartansville. Here's a card I picked up at the desk. Gimme a call if you need me."

"Yeah, sure, Andy. I appreciate it. And thanks for the kung pao."

Dooley waited until he heard Andy bantering in the squad room to set the flowers back on the table and call Edith Fay.

Detective Jimmy Campanella rapped on the car window just as Biddlebourne's first citizen hit the accelerator.

Jimmy jumped back and shouted, "Stop! Police!"

Jass Pinbiddie hated split-second decisions. He liked to gnaw on a decision like a dog chomped on a bone, dragging it around for days, burying it occasionally, keeping his eye on it while pursuing other pastimes, and leaving it a nub drained of any potential for benefit to himself.

What Jass did next reflected neither his decision-making philosophy nor a lick of common sense. He kicked the car into reverse, backed into a *Yield to Pedestrians* sign, changed gears again and entered traffic without looking right or left.

By the grace of the angel who sometimes sits on the shoulder of a fool, Jass struck no human object with his rental, a brand-new Lincoln Town Car. He sailed into a westbound local lane, through a green light, into and out of four more intersections and straight onto U.S. Route 6, where he settled into a steady sixty-two miles an hour and a healthier respiration rate.

"No, damn it, I didn't get the plate number," Jimmy Campanella shouted into the phone. "He nearly hit me with the car. He turned west. Alert units in the vicinity. It's a black Lincoln Town Car. Driver's a Caucasian male, late fifties, brown, bald, about 6 feet, maybe three-fifty. May be armed."

"Name of the driver?" said the dispatcher.

"Jasper Pinbody. P-I-N-B-O-D-Y. Subject is suspected of felony theft, fraud . . . and flight to avoid prosecution." Jimmy's palms suddenly felt sticky.

The dispatcher pecked on her computer keyboard. "Is it a rental car or a personal car?"

"Mandy, for God's sake, I'm not on the stand. It's probably a rental. Now put out the word."

"All right. I mean *roger*."

Jimmy had to wait at the curb three full minutes before a hole in traffic opened. He screeched left and pointed the unmarked sedan at Cleveland Hopkins International Airport, cursing dispatchers, commuters and international borders.

The Persons Ages 17 and Under Subcommittee of the Glory Girls service organization of Glory Hallelujah Church, Biddlebourne, West Virginia, shall assist families in nutrition, social and physical development, safety, custody and nurture of children from birth through age seventeen (17) years. *Glory Girls Book of Bylaws,* adopted May 1959

CHAPTER NINETEEN

Annie Scovill and William Wharton sat in her dining room, each digesting yet another inexplicable revelation about Gudrun Wince.

"Are you certain that's what it says?" Annie asked.

William twirled a pen through his fingers.

"I'm sorry, William," she said. "Of course you're sure. It's just . . . I'm flabbergasted that Gudrun made Edith Fay her primary beneficiary."

"You can't be any more surprised than I am. I didn't even know she'd come to our firm to have it done. I thought I'd have to call around to find out who put it together. But when I mentioned it to Ted, he took it out of the safe and handed it to me."

Ted Cavotte was William's law partner. They'd both graduated from the Duquesne University Law School, but Ted had founded the practice and was the senior partner.

"When did Gudrun make the will?"

"Twelve years ago, according to Ted, before I joined the firm, and before you came to Biddlebourne, if I remember correctly."

Annie nodded. "I take it no confidentiality is breached by your obtaining a copy of the will."

William's face reddened. "Well, we don't actually have a death certificate in hand, but I think we can reliably expect to receive one. Anyway, there's a stipulation in the will that it is to be *disseminated*—that's the exact word she used—immediately upon her death."

"Tell me the details again, please," Annie said. "I fear I became so rattled by the first sentence that the rest flew right past me."

William picked up the copy of Gudrun's will from the table, quickly read several paragraphs and put it down.

"In essence, Gudrun left all her tangible personal property, digital assets and residual estate to Edith Fay Buckingham Smith."

"Buckingham?"

"That's what it says. Edith Fay Buckingham Smith."

"Are we sure that's our Edith Fay?" Annie asked.

"The will gives our Edith Fay's home address, birth date and even a Social Security number, though that is irregular," he said with a trace of concern.

"I've never heard Edith Fay use the name Buckingham, and I'm pretty sure she's never been married," Annie mused.

"We can check the Social Security number and birth date with Edith Fay, of course, but I doubt Ted would have used that information if he thought it was inaccurate."

"Makes sense."

"What else do we know about Gudrun?" William asked.

Annie filled him in, from Gudrun's troubled childhood in Wetzel County to her dancing days in Youngstown and Cincinnati, her studies at the University of Cincinnati and her early teaching career.

"Gudrun is a woman of mystery in death as well as life," William noted.

"I'll follow through with Edith Fay," Annie said. "Thank you, William, for seeing to this so promptly. I imagine we can agree to keep this confidential for now."

"Of course. I need to get back to the office. We can talk tonight after the council meeting if we need to. I'm not distributing a printed agenda. We'll focus on temporary worship arrangements and Family Ministry Day projects."

"Yes," the pastor said. "We'll get a new financial projection too, one that takes dinner cancellations into account, and start more publicity to let folks know what's going on."

"See you at six then."

"I'm stunned," Edith Fay said, unable to do anything but drop to a seat and stare at the document on the table in the dining room of the church parsonage.

"I'm sorry, Edith Fay," Annie Scovill said. "I didn't mean to shock you. Are you all right?"

"I think I'm okay. But I don't understand. Why would Gudrun do that? She was always, uh . . . I would have to say, antagonistic toward me. Every conversation I ever had with her was strained. I can think of no earthly reason for her to have left her estate to me."

Belle Watkins came in with tea and oatmeal cookies. Belle, who never let her weight exceed one hundred pounds, declined their invitation to join them, so Annie and Edith Fay helped themselves and quietly considered Gudrun Wince's inexplicable last will and testament.

Edith Fay picked up the will and paged through it. "Does Gudrun give any explanations in the will?" she asked.

"Ted Cavotte told William Wharton that he drew it up virtually verbatim from Gudrun's notes, that she was quite clear about her intention, and that he didn't leave out anything."

"Hmm. It's dated November tenth, 2000."

"Twelve years ago," Annie said. "Did anything special happen between you two around that time?"

"I can look back through my journals, but offhand I can't remember any special connections with Gudrun around that time."

They sipped the last of their tea and petted Fannie, the Scovills' venerable cat, as she meandered around the chair legs. Three sets of church bells—Presbyterian, Lutheran and Glory Hallelujah—chimed five o'clock from the center of Biddlebourne, the jangling notes carried to the parsonage on a strong easterly breeze.

"Edith Fay, this may be none of my business, but may I inquire whether you . . . have you ever used the name Buckingham?"

"Never. I'm just as mystified by that as by everything else."

"I thought Buckingham might be an old family name," the pastor offered.

"I can't remember Mother or Dad ever mentioning that name. I don't have family around here. I was an only child, as you know, and my parents' people died or moved away over the years."

"Are there any records . . . old documents . . . or anything like that you can check?"

"Maybe. I'll have to go through Mother and Dad's papers again. I thought all of that was behind me."

"I'm sorry, Edith Fay. Would it help if I looked up your baptismal record in the church archives—when I can get to them, that is?"

"Maybe. Thank you for offering." Edith Fay fingered the edge of the paper and closed her eyes. After a long moment she said, "I'll confer with Ted Cavotte about this. I can't say I'm altogether comfortable with receiving what belonged to Gudrun. Perhaps . . . no, never mind. I will see to it. Thank you, Annie, for bringing it to my attention."

"William wanted me to give you that copy of the will, of course. I dislike bringing up the topic, but the last page outlines Gudrun's wishes for her funeral, and the will states that you, as the executor of her estate, are to carry out those plans."

Edith Fay closed her eyes and recalled the funerals of both her parents, at which she had stood anguished for hours beside their caskets and greeted hundreds of friends and neighbors who came to pay their respects.

To perform that deeply personal duty for Gudrun Wince would be painful—and strange. As she placed the document in her tote bag, she tried to quell her concerns about discussing the unexplainable with the many persons who would pay their last respects to the late principal of Biddlebourne High School.

No Biddlebournian had a normal dinner the day after Gudrun Wince's death.

By six o'clock, the church council was convening; Sheriff Skiles and his deputies were burrowing through Gudrun's home, office and car; Laverna Inys Wharton was selecting a dress to wear to the *Home Cookin'* shoot; Buddy Lee Delbert was trying to plant a kiss on Patty Leta Keys; the Legion boys were buying drinks in various bars; and ten of the Glory Girls were igniting the phone lines with uncharacteristically pointed questions about the deceased.

Nor did the mayor have a normal dinner on Friday.

In fact, he had no dinner on Friday. His stomach was too upset from the fried pig's ears, fried potatoes, fried sausage and fried pickles he'd consumed at the Cedar Point amusement park before taking a ride on the Wicked Twister, which had turned him—and his digestive system—upside down.

Now, wearing plaid shorts, a new Cedar Point T-shirt and a fresh sunburn, he sat quietly on a bench beside his Worksman Cruiser bicycle, swallowed Pepcid pills and surveyed the choppy waters of Sandusky Bay.

Jass wondered whether it would be wise to take the twenty-two-mile ferry ride while feeling so full and nauseated. The wind blew light and cool across his pinked face and arms, but he was no sailor, a fact he'd demonstrated on every boat excursion he'd ever taken.

Behind him, the sounds and smells of lakefront Sandusky, Ohio, churned nonstop, as did his stomach. The movements of the waves and vessels, to which he had an unspoiled view from West

Shoreline Drive, dizzied him if he locked his gaze on them for even a few seconds.

Jasper Eugene Pinbiddie checked his phone again for a new text message. There were plenty of old ones, from Dooley Skiles and Barry Dale Green and Marthleen Lewis and Annie Ido Scovill and—blast him—Emerson Duty. There was even one from Pearl Gay Osbourn, in which she excoriated him for bailing out of her town and her life.

However, these were not people with whom Mayor Pinbiddie wanted to communicate at the moment. He desperately hoped to hear from Arnie Coker, son of his late best friend Gerald Coker and Jass' private eyes and ears at the Skyler County Sheriff's Department.

Arnie's last hurried and garbled update had let Jass know there was a BOLO out on him and that serious questions were being asked in Biddlebourne and beyond about his possible involvement in Gudrun's slaying. Some guy from the health department was carrying on about what happened at Glory Hallelujah Church. And, worst of all, longtime Jass supporters were saying nasty things about him for abandoning his dog.

Ernie Blankenship, president of the Biddlebourne Town Council, had texted Jass early on to say he wanted one hundred thousand dollars to keep his trap shut about the mayor's financial finaglings. Jass had wired Ernie the money and blocked his phone from further messages from the turncoat.

As his stomach burbled and he expelled a blast of intestinal gas, Jass considered the realities before him. Yes, he was sought in Biddlebourne, West Virginia, for a crime he had not committed. And he was sought in Cleveland, Ohio, for slightly lesser but nevertheless chargeable offenses that he had committed.

However, he was not sought yet for other offenses, these of a non-homicidal nature. And he had in his possession the partial proceeds of a black-market career so profitable that he need never work again and which he might enjoy, if he made a clean getaway, in the planet's sunniest climes with its most beautiful women.

So he secured the bike to the bench and walked a block to the Water Street Bar & Grille, where he entered the men's room, poked two fingers down his throat and vomited until he had a headache but no stomachache.

The bartender, who'd hurriedly departed the restroom while Jass retched, gave him the stink-eye when he walked out without buying a drink.

Jass squared his backpack on his shoulders and patted his shorts pocket to make sure his wallet and keys had stayed put while he puked up his guts, then sauntered to the dock where the Pelee Island Ferry would carry him across Lake Erie to a country that had never heard of Jasper Eugene Pinbiddie.

Family Ministry Day shall be organized and conducted by the Glory Girls service organization of Glory Hallelujah Church, Biddlebourne, West Virginia, each Tuesday of the year, including holidays and election days, according to goals and guidelines set forth in the Seven Paths of Discipleship™ program to be inaugurated at Glory Hallelujah Church July 1, 2001. *Glory Girls Book of Bylaws,* adopted May 2001

CHAPTER TWENTY

Dooley Skiles had fired grenade launchers, wielded battering rams, tracked fugitives in swamps and coaxed an angry cougar out of a coal pit where it had fallen. But now his courage faltered when Edith Fay Smith asked why he'd needed so urgently to speak with her.

"Well, uh . . . " Dooley fixed his gaze on the salt shaker.

There was only one facet of the investigation that Dooley could rightly share with Edith Fay. He couldn't tell her that his top suspect was Jass Pinbiddie, that Jass apparently had disappeared, that Gudrun Wince had uncountable enemies and probably for good reason, or that he was sublimely distracted from this important inquiry by the person and presence of the formidable Ms. Edith Fay Smith.

"I imagine you need to keep up with all facets of the investigation," she suggested as she placed a ham sandwich beside the German potato salad on Dooley's plate. "I had that emergency meeting at the parsonage and missed my dinner. I hope you don't mind joining me for a little something while we talk."

A platter near Dooley's elbow held grape clusters, cantaloupe slices and cheese wedges. The scent of cinnamon wafted from an apple pie in the oven.

"I appreciate it, Edith Fay. I've been awful busy today too. I am sorry about the inconvenience for the church . . . despite the way it may have looked."

"We understand. We'll worship at Saint John's Church on Sunday . . . as long as we need to. I don't suppose you have any idea yet how long that might be?"

Dooley swallowed fruity iced tea from a chilled glass. "Some of the guys are still at the church looking for the weapon," he said, hoping Edith Fay didn't notice the huskiness in his voice.

She nodded, well aware that deputies remained at the church.

On familiar ground now, he went on. "One thing I'm curious about is how there's not even a speck of chicken or beef blood on the cooking knives. I'd thought that would be our biggest problem in identifying a murder weapon."

"I can help with that," Edith Fay said. "We soak our cooking knives in bleach solution after every meal, and that's before we put them through the commercial dishwasher. There's not much chance of any leftover blood."

"Yeah, I saw the dishwasher. That's a doozy," he said. "So I guess that's a bust. And we've searched everywhere a knife—or anything like a knife—could have been stashed in that church and haven't found a thing of any use."

"I see." Edith Fay held her breath. *Had she put everything back in place after her own hunt that morning?* She hadn't worn gloves and mentally kicked herself for that oversight.

"I'm starting to think the murder weapon was carried out of the building shortly after the crime," Dooley said.

"Oh?"

"Yes. You said you had your ladies stay with the crime scene until I got there, right?"

"That's right." Edith Fay's throat constricted.

"Which ladies were they?"

Edith Fay fought to stay calm. It took a lot to overwhelm her, but she was getting there fast. Four more dinner cancellations had come in, though the organizers of the homecoming dinner were hanging tough and hadn't called yet. *Home Cookin'* had barraged her with messages about the photo shoot. People who had left various containers in the church kitchen suddenly, desperately, inexplicably needed to retrieve them.

But worst of all, the Glory Girls, themselves normally rocks of perseverance in times of uncertainty, were showing signs of frustration because their personal visits, emails, phone calls and assorted texts had so far yielded no information they could use to nail Gudrun's killer or the reasons behind her run for the Glory Girls.

And now Dooley may have connected the missing murder weapon to something or somebody who had left the church soon after it happened—somebody like a Glory Girl.

Edith Fay had that very day counted the families and individuals aided by the church through the ministries of the Glory Girls in one year. The numbers staggered even her, for the Glory Girls had helped 231 individuals and 347 families with matters including groceries and cooking instruction, utilities, rent, transportation, child care and elder care, job training and placement, home management, anger management, marriage enrichment, addiction recovery and faith development.

And Edith Fay Smith felt personally responsible for every one of those persons and programs.

In her mind, it followed that she was to blame for the church closure—and the kitchen closure before that. She should have established better security standards for the cook-off. She should have required more diligence from the Glory Girls who monitored the cook-off. She should have been present in the kitchen during every minute of the cook-off. She should not have allowed anyone to enter or leave the kitchen once Gudrun's body had been found. She should have . . .

"Edith Fay?" Dooley said

"I'm not sure I remember who they were," Edith Fay lied. "Things were happening so fast. She gulped tea, glad for a reason to look away from Dooley because she felt tears stinging the back of her eyes.

Then Dooley did something he had never done before.

The sheriff was a just man. He might have ridden his family's reputation to the sheriff's post in his first election, but every four years afterward, he had earned his votes the hard way, spending endless hours at work and exercising a dogged determination to hear everybody's side in a conflict.

His fair-mindedness kept him on the job, but it also kept him single. He could never love a woman as much as he loved law enforcement and would not subject a woman to his constant preoccupation with crime-fighting. There had been no home and hearth for Dooley.

But now Edith Fay sat before him, protective of her Girls because she too was fair-minded, unwilling to bask in the public admiration she deserved, as devoted to her calling as he had ever been to his own, personally responsible for the improved welfare of many souls in Biddlebourne, serving him the best food he'd ever tasted, sole keeper of this comfortable but huge home, improbably beautiful with her mussed hair and bare feet and, for some reason he could not discern, apparently near tears.

Dooley rose from his chair, walked around the counter and took Edith Fay's hands into his own. He pulled her hands to his lips and gently kissed them.

"It will be all right," he said.

Denzil Westover was up to his big, blue eyeballs in computer files.

In an untidy conference room at the rear of the Skyler County Sheriff's Office he hacked into the hottest digital records of the hour—and possibly of the century—in Biddlebourne.

For this task he had been born and bred. At age three he had played Pac-Man on his dad's IBM PS/2 desktop computer. At seven he had taught himself to type so he could email his grandparents, netting their admiration as well as cash gifts for his hobby. When he was a high school freshman he had built an IBM-compatible computer and used it to do his advanced-placement physics homework and calculate betting odds on professional football games.

His gray T-shirt was soiled at the neck from sweat and spilled sloopies from the sub shop. His jeans, from college days, bore greasy streaks on the thighs where he had wiped his hands after consuming pork-rind pizzas ordered in from Deserio's Pizzerio and charged to the sheriff's personal tab.

Denzil felt he was on the brink of cracking yet another password on Mayor Jass Pinbiddie's records. Fort Knox could use Jass, Denzil thought, as he put his feet up to wait while his secret password-busting program spun through the billions of bits and bytes that concealed the mayor's doings.

Waiting was all right with Denzil, who had all the time in the world to crack these files because he was racking up $45 an hour for the job. The amount was an unheard-of wage in Biddlebourne, West Virginia, where in a year the best teachers hauled home $33,000 and the owner of the town's only gas station cleared $29,000 and two tired vehicles abandoned by their owners.

So, while his paycheck swelled and he waited to receive the computers of Gudrun Wince, the scourge of his adolescence, Denzil turned aside to check the results of his latest bets.

"Ernie, I can't thank you enough for your help."

Pastor Annie Ido Scovill breathed a prayer of gratitude while the president of the Biddlebourne Town Council nibbled nervously at a cookie and explained that he had opposed the mayor's plan all along.

"I told him, I said, 'Jass, friend, that's not right. No way will a tax on church dinners stand up in court,' but he insisted we keep it on the council agenda."

Annie waited for him to say more.

Ernie Blankenship really did not want to say more. He had gone to the Progress Bank in Wheeling that afternoon and cashed Jass Pinbiddie's cashier's check for one hundred thousand dollars. He had then driven to Morgantown and placed the cash and a printout of his text conversations with Jass in a safe deposit box at the High Mountain Bank.

All that thinking and driving had fatigued Ernie but had also buoyed him with the hope that Jasper Eugene Pinbiddie, who had bullied the town council long enough, was gone forever from Biddlebourne.

But, however much Ernie Blankenship deplored Jass Pinbiddie's specious brand of politics, Ernie was also a politician at heart. And he was a politician sitting at this very minute in the parlor of one of Biddlebourne's most influential citizens.

"Yes, ma'am," he continued. "Why, even the budget committee refused to consider it. Cy Merrill, he's the chair of the budget committee since Glenn Twyman moved to Weirton you know, he told me so himself."

Ernie did not mention that he planned to lampoon every last piece of pending legislation advanced by Jasper Pinbiddie and propose his own measures, or that he planned to get this done before everyone else realized Jass had forsaken Biddlebourne.

"Are you saying the issue is off the council agenda for good?" Annie asked.

"I promise you, Reverend Scovill, as long as I have anything to do with the Biddlebourne Town Council, no tax will be levied on Glory Hallelujah Church."

It was obvious to Annie that Ernie Blankenship intended to run for mayor if Jass Pinbiddie had truly cleared out—which she figured he had—and that Ernie would like her endorsement, or at least her tolerance, of his candidacy.

Annie considered her words carefully. "Ernie, the members of Glory Hallelujah Church are grateful for justice in all its forms."

"Mr. Duty, my name is Cecil Weber, and I am a physician in Biddlebourne."

Emerson Duty had been minding his own business at the Spartansville Dairy Queen when the stocky man in a rumpled brown suit stopped at his table, slid a chair back with his foot and sat.

Dr. Weber was well known to Emerson Duty because Doc consulted routinely with the health department on matters ranging from polio shots for prisoners to condom distributions in the schools, neither of which practices Emerson favored.

Doc Weber bulldogged an issue until he was satisfied it had been dealt with fully and properly. Emerson had logged plenty of extra legwork and paperwork because of the doctor, causing him to regard Doc with a mixture of reluctant respect and muted hostility.

"Actually, we've met. At the county fair, in '96, I think," Emerson said.

"Yes."

Emerson crossed and uncrossed his feet under the tiny table.

"What brings you to Spartansville?" he finally asked.

"Your inspection of the kitchen at Glory Hallelujah Church brings me here, I regret to say."

"That inspection met every specification of department guidelines," Emerson said. But his face reddened.

"I think not." Doc dropped his chin and looked up through his eyebrows.

"What do you mean?"

"Sir, I will not take time to cavil with you. I want to know who paid you to inspect that kitchen on that particular day. Either you answer my question now or I will put it to the cabinet secretary of the state health department. I doubt your personnel record can withstand much scrutiny."

"I don't know what you're talking about," Emerson said.

Doc Weber clamped a steady gaze on Emerson's twitching left eye. The counter server yelled, "Number 598! Yer order's ready." Emerson fumbled for his register receipt and felt his stomach rumble.

"I remember the county fair in '96," the doctor said. "Eleven people went to the hospital because you forgot to check the oil temperature at the chicken booth."

"How did you know . . . ?" Emerson blurted.

"You would be mightily surprised to learn what I know about you."

Doc Weber rose to leave.

"Wait, wait," Emerson said, pulling an envelope from his shirt pocket. "Here's the information I received about the church."

Bertram Kimble hummed *Amazing Grace* as he checked off items on his deluxe inventory list that would be needed to bury Miss Gudrun Wince in a style commensurate with her importance and her budget.

Bertram had just come from the American Legion hall, where he lunched every Friday on deep-fried fish and potato cakes. It didn't hurt that the Legion lunch usually yielded a useful tidbit or two of scuttlebutt.

For instance, Bertram learned over a recent lunch that Willie McQuaid had come into money. This fact led to Bertram's kind offer to serve Willie in his time of need upon the untimely passing of his dear wife, Gertrude McQuaid.

Then there was the time Boyd Eddy came into the Legion for a drink—or four—after completing a run to the Huth farm when Seldon Huth had taken a fatal fall from a hay mow. What a tragedy, everyone said, and Mariah Huth ordered up a fine funeral from Bertram to underscore that very circumstance.

But today's news was the best yet. Bertram had sat thunderstruck while eavesdropping on the conversation between a file clerk and her boyfriend at a table beside his. While her companion finished off a stack of beef burritos and a large side of hash browns, the young woman rambled on about the will of Gudrun Wince.

"Left it all to Miss Edith Fay," the clerk reported. "Who'd a known that would happen? I mean, why would she give everything to somebody who wasn't even her kin?"

Bertram had held his breath until the clerk came to the important part. "And, oh, the funeral. Wooee! Miss Wince planned everything out, down to what kind of casket and stuff like that. She wrote it down in the will. She told Miss Edith Fay exactly what to do, and it's gonna be a wingdinger!"

"Damn, damn, damn!"

Detective Jimmy Campanella pummeled a tiled wall at Cleveland's airport and chanted his frustration.

A preschooler walked up to him and asked what was wrong, then waited for an answer until her mother screamed, "Tilda, get back here!" and pulled her away.

Jimmy's little tirade barely drew a glance, however, from other passersby, especially the business people who knew from grievous experience that flying elicited the harshest human emotions.

Jimmy's phone buzzed.

"What?!" he yelled at the caller.

His partner, Amelia Houghenberg, ignored his mood. She was used to it.

"I take it the guy didn't show at Hopkins," she said.

Jimmy had busted his butt the better part of Friday hunting a man whose name might or might not be Jack Pemberton or Jasper Pinbody, who might or might not be a major jewel thief, and who might or might not still be in the United States.

Jimmy's last stop had been the Air Canada desk at Cleveland Hopkins International Airport. He reasoned that if his quarry had headed to Canada he would have booked a seat on Air Canada, Hopkins' only commercial airline offering nonstop service to Toronto. The Air Canada clerk had quickly accommodated Jimmy's request, pulling up passenger lists for flights two hours back and twenty-hours forward.

But no passenger was listed under *Pemberton* or *Pinbody.*

"No. What'd you dig up?"

"We checked trains, buses, taxis and private airports. Nobody listed under either name."

"Damnation."

"Why are we wastin' time on this?" Amelia asked. "We got no real evidence except some nonsense Maria Angelica dreamed up. What we do have is plenty of other cases we oughtta be workin'."

"I told you I got a feeling about this one," Jimmy said with a disappointed edge to his voice. "The guy maybe stole a bunch of diamonds and . . . besides that . . . he mighta killed somebody named Cassie."

"You're wacko, ya know that, Campanella?"

The detective, who was crazy like a mountain lion stalking a doe on Thunder Ridge, slapped his phone shut and stomped back to his car, stopping only to purchase an extra-large coffee and a box of chocolate-frosted donuts.

CHAPTER TWENTY-ONE

Biddlebourne Educator Slain in Church Kitchen
Murder weapon sought by Skyler sheriff
by Wilford Nicklin
Sentinel Staff Writer
Friday, June 15, 2012

Longtime Biddlebourne High School Principal Gudrun Cassandra Wince was stabbed to death Thursday while competing in a cooking contest at Glory Hallelujah Church.

Miss Wince's lifeless body was discovered around noon in the kitchen of the church complex, which occupies the 700 block of Bailey Street in Biddlebourne.

Known by townspeople for her firm supervision of restless teenagers, Miss Wince was one of nine contestants in a cook-off organized by the Glory Girls, a women's service group at the church.

The winner of the cooking contest was to have become the twelfth member of the Glory Girls, which works through twelve subcommittees involving community economic, educational and health needs.

Friends and neighbors gathered outside the church as emergency personnel responded to the report called in to the Skyler County Sheriff's Department at 11:53 a.m. by Edith Fay Smith, of Biddlebourne, leader of the Glory Girls.

Smith was unavailable for comment Thursday.

Dr. Cecil Weber, a consultant to the county medical examiner, pronounced Miss Wince dead at 12:40 p.m. He declined comment on her cause of death.

By all reports, at least fifteen people were in the kitchen when Miss Wince's body was discovered, including contestants, cook-off monitors and a kitchen helper. All were questioned Thursday by sheriff's deputies.

"I was shocked," said Garrison McKee, who was among bystanders at the church after emergency responders arrived. "She was killed with a whole bunch of people right there in the kitchen. How could that happen?"

Members of the Glory Girls had arrived at the church at 7 a.m., and the contestants arrived around 8 a.m. The body was discovered about 3½ hours later by Buddy Lee Delbert, 27, of Biddlebourne, who had been hired by the organization for the day to assist the entrants.

"Nobody saw it happen," said Ella Mae Pugh, a member of the Glory Girls. "One minute everything was going along just fine, and the next thing you know, Buddy Lee was hollering for help."

Asked whether Delbert is a suspect in the slaying, Sheriff Dooley Skiles said Thursday afternoon that his department was conducting a detailed investigation and that no one had been charged yet in the case.

Although no official cause of death was announced, witnesses in the kitchen said Miss Wince's body was bloody and that she appeared to have been stabbed. They said they didn't see a knife or other potential murder weapon in the confusion following the discovery of the body.

"Miss Edith Fay had the area closed off, so I only got a peek, but Miss Gudrun's blouse was all covered with blood. It was awful," said Eulalah Bee Pritchard, a contestant. "Of course, everybody was running this way and that, so I guess the killer got away good."

Though Skiles at press time Friday morning denied any suspects had been identified, it was reported by several reliable sources that Biddlebourne Mayor Jasper Eugene "Jass" Pinbiddie had left town unexpectedly shortly after the slaying and had not been seen or heard from as of press time Friday.

A spokeswoman with the West Virginia State Police confirmed Friday morning that a lookout order to regional law enforcement agencies had been posted by the Skyler sheriff's office for Pinbiddie.

The body of Miss Wince was removed to the office of the Skyler County medical examiner. An autopsy is scheduled for Monday in Charleston.

According to Bertram Kimble, funeral arrangements for Miss Wince are pending at the Kimble Funeral Home in Biddlebourne.

Glory Girls Pledge of Service—"I (full name including maiden and married names) do solemnly swear that I have truthfully met all qualifications for membership in the Glory Girls service organization of Glory Hallelujah Church, Biddlebourne, West Virginia, in that I have no outstanding financial debts, have committed no felonies, am a true-born woman at least forty (40) years of age, have served the requisite tenure in the Ladies Aid Society of Glory Hallelujah Church (or its approved affiliates), that no person depends solely upon me for care and/or sustenance, that I am able-bodied, that I own a motor vehicle and am able to drive a motor vehicle, that I am not a smoker of tobacco or user of illegal drugs, and that I hereby pledge my time, talent, gifts and labors to the service of our Lord and our community for the duration of my eligibility. *Glory Girls Book of Bylaws,* adopted May 1958

CHAPTER TWENTY-TWO

"They're gonna name the high school after Gudrun, and she's gonna have the biggest funeral ever in Skyler County, and it's gonna cost over twenty thousand dollars, and the dinner's not gonna be at Glory Hallelujah Church!"

Thelma Blivins stopped talking, out of breath but not yet out of information.

Hazel Simons, who was making peanut butter fudge for her nephew in the Army, wiped steam off her glasses and hitched up a stool to the stove, phone in one hand and stir spoon in the other.

"I heard," she said.

Disappointed, Thelma put out another morsel. "Well, did you also hear that she left everything, and I mean everything, to Edith Fay Smith?"

"Really? Strange. Why'd she do that?" asked Hazel, who had long since learned that Thelma had answers to most questions.

"You got me there," Thelma admitted.

After a stunned silence, Hazel suggested, "Maybe she wanted Edith Fay to use her money on charity."

A low, gritty laugh greeted the notion. "Oh, you think so? Far as I ever heard, Gudrun never helped nobody but herself—at least when it came to money."

"I thought she held those benefits at the high school for needy students and such," Hazel countered.

"Mebbe she did. I heard she did. But Genevieve Crimmons told me at card club that they only got about seventy-five dollars outta that shindig Gudrun threw for little Everett, God rest his soul."

"Half the town attended that," Hazel noted.

"More like the whole town," Thelma corrected, "and the admission tickets was $10 apiece, and the refreshments cost three dollars for a hot dog and two dollars for a cuppa coffee."

"I remember. You sayin' Gudrun took the money for her'n ?"

"Listen, Hazel," Thelma said, "I been hearin' about this kinda stuff since Gudrun come here. From the fire department. From the prom moms. From kids raising money to go on trips and such. Where there's smoke, there's gotta be fire, know what I mean?"

Hazel nodded agreement. "Jass hasn't turned up either. Maybe he and Gudrun had more goin' on than hanky-panky, if you know what I mean."

"Sheriff's been askin' questions 'round town like he thinks so," Thelma offered.

"What a shame to think that big funeral's gonna be financed with money she stole off the town," Hazel said.

"Which brings up another point," Thelma replied. "Doesn't seem likely Gudrun wanted her money put to charity at that church 'cause she put it in the will that the funeral dinner ain't gonna be there like regular."

"I saw her lookin' daggers at Edith Fay more times than I can count," Hazel supplied. "It's got me wonderin' why she'd go and give her the money. This don't sound like anythin' good to me."

"Me neither. I'm gonna check 'round and get to the bottom of it," Thelma promised.

The thermometer in the fudge pot showed it had reached soft-ball stage, and Hazel turned off the fire.

"Gotta get after this fudge," Hazel said.

But Thelma had already clicked off.

Dooley wanted to pour himself into Edith Fay—to comfort her, to relieve her fears, to lighten her burden. But, sensing her hesitation, he released her hands and stood back while apologies and explanations rushed through his head.

Edith Fay held his gaze a long while, then smiled so faintly he feared he'd imagined it.

"Excuse me, Edith Fay. I was out of line," he said, turning away.

But she put a hand on his sleeve and said, "Dooley."

He faced her. She took a deep breath and spoke slowly. "So much rests on the work of the Glory Girls. Some people think it's just cooking and serving dinners, but it's much more than that."

"I understand." He placed his right hand over hers on his arm and gave it a squeeze.

"Dooley, I think we can help each other. . . ."

"I think you're right."

Edith Fay rose from the stool and faced him. He bent to rest his head on her shoulder. Her heart beat faster than she ever thought it could, and for the first time in twenty-five years she wrapped her arms around a man and kissed him.

"There's so much I want to say to you," Dooley said. "But everybody's counting on me to solve this case."

"Yes. I'm among those who need you to solve this case—perhaps more than anybody else."

"What do you mean?" he asked.

"Come with me," she said.

Nineteen birders trooped off the MV Pelee Islander onto the marina dock at Leamington, Ontario. The caps on their heads and binoculars around their necks marked them as clearly as if they were pileated woodpeckers.

Thirteen women and five of the men quickly split into groups and headed on foot for Hillman Marsh, Seacliff Park or Point Pelee National Park.

But the last man with binocs on a strap and maps in his pockets unchained a bicycle, thanked the crew, rolled onto the pavement and pedaled nonstop to the Enterprise Rent-A-Car lot.

A sinewy young woman gave the man a weekend deal on a Chrysler Town and Country.

"Thank you for your business, Mr. Bachand," she said, handing back his driver's license and credit card.

"You can call me Gregory," he said with a warm smile. She blushed and, pointing to her badge, said, "Janine."

Gregory Bachand was sorry, momentarily, that he would not be returning to Leamington. He tossed the bicycle into the back of the minivan, put the vehicle in gear and hit Highway 3 for the half-hour trip to Windsor, Ontario.

"Mr. Bachand, may I take your luggage up?"

"Just the suitcases. I'll take the rest," he told the bellman. After a shower, Gregory Bachand spread out his new identity on the bed and reviewed everything: the passport, the driver's license, the credit cards, the snapshots of his *family*, the prescription pills, and the initials sewn into his luggage.

The crossing from Ohio to Canada had been smoother than he expected, and Jass felt the agreeable growl of an empty stomach. It had been many hours since he'd had a meal, but part of that time was especially well spent burning his old ID at a roadside park, donning designer jeans and a smart golf shirt in the restroom of a busy gas station, and finding just the right dumpster in which to chuck the clothes of his old life.

Now Gregory Bachand put on gray slacks, a pale yellow dress shirt open at the neck and a navy blazer, complete with a monogrammed handkerchief in the breast pocket. He smiled approvingly in the full-length mirror before descending to the hotel restaurant, where he ordered the finest steak and wine.

The meal was lovely, as were a full night's sleep in a king-size bed, a room-service breakfast of eggs Florentine, fresh croissants and coffee, and a scenic train ride from Windsor to Toronto.

The Saving and Investment Subcommittee of the Glory Girls service organization of Glory Hallelujah church, Biddlebourne, West Virginia, shall invest and administer funds collected by the organization and designated in official minutes as "above and beyond operating expenses." The subcommittee shall be accountable to the Executive Board of the Glory Girls service organization and to the Board of Ministry of Glory Hallelujah Church. *Glory Girls Book of Bylaws,* adopted May 1959

CHAPTER TWENTY-THREE

Edith Fay took Dooley's hand and led him through the dining room and sitting room to the grand mahogany staircase that had been timbered from trees less than a mile from the Smith family homestead.

She put her arm through his and took the first step up.

But Dooley didn't move.

"Edith Fay, I don't know. . . ."

She threw her head back and laughed, the movement accentuating the laugh lines of her brow and mouth.

"Oh, my goodness," she said. "It's not what you're thinking. Is that what you're thinking?"

Dooley dropped his head and said, "I guess I was. Maybe it's what I was hoping, too, but . . ."

"It's okay," she said. "I just want to show you something."

Dooley loosed a guffaw that filled the room and bounced off the walls before he leaned in and gave her a noisy smooch on the cheek.

In a heartbeat they were both laughing and gabbling, Edith Fay repeating that she merely had some papers for Dooley to see and Dooley declaring that he would love to see whatever it was.

"Grab a chair," she said upstairs in her study, and Dooley pulled up a simple Danish chair to join her at the desk.

She handed him a thin stack of papers. "This is Gudrun's will."

"Edith Fay, I already heard about it," he confessed. "If you have this, the rumors must be true that you are her main beneficiary."

"Yes, it's true," she said. "Look at the name Gudrun used for me in her will." She pointed to the paragraph that contained the name Edith Fay Buckingham Smith.

"I don't understand," he said. "Is Buckingham a second middle name your parents gave you—maybe your mother's maiden name?"

"My mother's maiden name was Stealey," Edith Fay said.

She opened a deep drawer on the left side of the desk, withdrew a single sheet of paper and placed it on top of Gudrun's will.

"I found this today. I . . . I thought I'd collected all of Mother and Dad's papers after they died, but this was in a box of my baby things."

Dooley peered at Edith Fay with a sudden surge of awareness. He picked up the page and scanned it.

"You were adopted," he said. "I never knew it either, but then it wouldn't a been any of my business."

Edith Fay pulled a tissue from a box and blew her nose.

"I didn't know about my adoption until today."

"Is that why you were . . . upset . . . because you were adopted?"

"Not exactly," she said. "It's the rest of it. Gudrun knew my birth name. Look. There at the top."

Dooley studied the adoption document until he spied the block marked *infant's name.*

There, written more than fifty years earlier in the precise hand of a county clerk, was the name given Edith Fay before her adoption by Malcolm and Julia Smith.

Emily Elaine Buckingham.

The large, gracefully designed home of William and Laverna Inys Wharton had until this week served as a haven of solace and tranquility, its shaded lot commanding its own cul de sac and the sycamores and elms thereon sheltering warblers and wrens that sang as sweetly as Gussie Rae Harper at the annual town homecoming.

William and Laverna had heretofore agreed on almost everything important, including what TV shows to watch, how much to spend on vacations and renovations and, most important, how and when to enjoy their bedroom time.

But now, in light of Laverna's recent behavior and what William had heard in the church parking lot after the council session, he had no choice but to find out why all that had changed so suddenly and so peculiarly.

He must tread lightly, he realized, not just because he loved Laverna with every iota of his being but also because she had possibly—no, probably—broken the law.

Neither he nor his law firm, of course, should be held responsible for the misbehavior of a partner's spouse. But that rule, if it was a rule, did not pertain in Biddlebourne, West Virginia. In this town where William Wharton had grown up and where he would live until he died, what one's husband or wife did affected a person socially, politically and sometimes economically.

For instance, when Mansfield McAdoo's wife Suzette embezzled cash from the Spartansville Kmart, he lost his job as Biddlebourne town treasurer because the town council figured that the McAdoos' finances were so awry and Mansfield so henpecked that Suzette would next cause him to steal community funds.

Throwing off thoughts of the possibilities should Laverna not level with him, William went in through the back door and found the love of his life in their bedroom preening before a long mirror.

Laverna caught his reflection and offered a cheek for his kiss.

"What do you think of it?" she asked, twirling in a rustle of pink, red and purple fabric.

"It's gorgeous. You're gorgeous," he said, slipping an arm around her waist to pull her into a warm hug.

"Mmm," she murmured. Laverna wrapped her arms around William's neck and nestled on his chest.

"Did you eat?" he asked.

"Huh-uh. I was too busy shopping. How about you?"

"I was busy all day . . . and I was thinking about that terrific casserole you made this morning."

Laverna stood back suddenly. "Oh, about that," she said. "I'm afraid it's all gone. I, uh, shared it with some friends."

William had already heard all about it. How Laverna had showed up at Edith Fay Smith's home. How she had practically force-fed her casserole to the Glory Girls. How she had been quizzed about her casserole ingredients.

And how she had apparently failed that quiz. And how all of the Girls knew that she had managed to acquire the original recipes of Theodocia Price, the late, legendary home economics teacher.

And how the Glory Girls, for all those stated reasons and a bundle of additional unstated but nevertheless convincing reasons, knew with certainty that Laverna Inys Wharton was guilty of theft.

And how, to William's utter and soul-shaking dismay, several of the Glory Girls had stated quietly among themselves—and also to William but only as a courtesy because of his church leadership—that Laverna had somehow killed Gudrun Wince.

William Wharton couldn't eat dinner now if a 16-ounce T-bone, grilled to perfection and accompanied by a triple-stuffed potato and an ear of Silver Queen corn new from the garden materialized before him.

"Baby, it's too late for dinner now," he whispered into Laverna's ear. "Can we just go to bed?"

She raised her head, brushed his neck with her lips and turned for him to unzip the dress.

Detective Jimmy Campanella of the Cleveland Division of Police sank his teeth into the case like a wildcat clamping fangs to the haunches of a flailing rabbit.

Jimmy walked and talked, threatened and pleaded, lied and whined, braced informants old and new, smiled and scowled, and generally misled his partner and captain all day about the purpose of his fervent inquiries.

But he could not take a bite out of Jass Pinbiddie.

The trouble was that Jimmy did not know the name of his quarry. Or his background. Or his plans. Or his habits. Or his skills. Or his current description.

All he had was the scent of crime. It was a stink he recognized from twenty-seven long, dangerous, underpaid and overworked years as a cop in a tough and gritty city.

He'd be damned if he'd let a few knots untie his golden thread to a promotion. He arose at 4 a.m. Saturday and went to the station five hours before his shift was to start, there to comb reports based on the thin, very thin, evidence provided by Maria Angelica Ogden.

He plugged the surnames Pemberton and Pinbody into every regional and national database he knew of that listed persons wanted for jewelry theft.

Nothing.

He performed the same search for persons wanted in murder cases.

Nothing.

He trolled blogs, entered offbeat search terms and tried every spelling for Pemberton and Pinbody that he could imagine.

Still nothing.

He gave special attention to states and cities that began with W, including Wisconsin, Wyoming, West Virginia, Washington state, Washington D.C., Winnipeg, Winston-Salem, Waterloo and Wilkes-Barre.

Less than nothing. Except for residents of the nation's capital, citizens of those W-locales apparently spent little time killing each other.

When he learned from an overseas contact that Interpol wanted so badly to catch the Pink Panther gang of jewel bandits that other, lesser thieves were less likely to be named on wanted lists, he pounded his desk and inadvertently knocked his framed photo of Luann and the kids to the floor in a scatter of glass.

He soothed himself by feeding five dollars to the vending machine and wolfing down four Twinkies and a chocolate bar.

At 8:38 a.m., when he knew his partner would show up in exactly twenty-two minutes with two large coffees and an extra-large serving of criticism for his ongoing search for a nonexistent perpetrator, he punched into his computer the search terms *homicide victims* and *June 2012.*

A newspaper article from some backwater in West Virginia popped up.

Bingo.

"Ow!"

"Burn yourself?" Dooley asked.

"It's nothing." Edith Fay set the hot pie on the stove.

Dooley walked her to the sink and held her injured fingers under cool water with one hand while he rummaged in drawers with the other.

"What are you looking for?"

"Your first aid kit. Where is it?"

"Really, I'll be all right. I must have been distracted."

"I take responsibility for that," he said. "I want gauze and salve."

"Third drawer down. I feel the same way about . . . responsibilities."

"I know."

The grandfather clock in the hall bonged.

"Eleven-thirty!" she said. "Maybe it's too late for pie."

Dooley's answer was scotched by the doorbell. Edith Fay went to the door and found Doc Weber standing on the porch. He chuckled when Edith Fay held up her hand and said, "Cecil, it's only a little burn. You didn't have to make a house call."

Nevertheless, the doctor walked with her to the kitchen, where he greeted Dooley and checked Edith Fay's hand. He agreed with the sheriff's plan to paint the burn with ointment and wrap it lightly with the gauze.

"You're always welcome, Cecil, but you've not come this late without a reason," Edith Fay said. He nodded, and the room went quiet as they ate pie and drank cold milk.

"I saw Dooley's truck and have information both of you need to know." Doc seemed to muse a while and finally added, "That is, unless I should, um, come back later?"

Edith Fay blushed. "Please stay, Cecil. What is it?"

A breeze riffled the curtains. An owl hooted from the spot where the original Smith barn had stood. Clouds scrimmed the waning moon as it hung over Edith Fay's solar collectors.

"It's about the kitchen inspection yesterday," the doctor said. "I think Jass and Gudrun set it up."

Edith Fay gasped, but Dooley just clenched his jaws.

"What proof do you have?" the sheriff asked.

The doctor took a cell phone from his jacket and opened a text display. Edith Fay and Dooley leaned over his shoulders to read the incriminating words *just shut the place down and I'll take care of the rest.*

Edith Fay studied the message, her heart hammering and her breath suspended because the words held implications far beyond the temporary inconvenience of a kitchen closure.

Dooley scratched the shadow on his chin. "That was sent from Jass' phone all right. Remember the dust he raised to get those zeroes for his last four numbers?"

Edith Fay had just enough wind to say, "Yes."

"But it's not exactly ironclad proof," the sheriff went on. "He could claim somebody else used his phone. Whose phone you got in your hand there, Doc?"

"Emerson Duty's," Doc said.

"The health inspector?" said Dooley.

"Exactly."

"I don't want to know how you obtained that phone," the sheriff cautioned the physician.

"I have no intention of telling you."

Edith Fay allowed herself to breathe but put her hands up to support her head, which had suddenly become heavy. She bumped her burned finger and inadvertently exhaled a low moan.

"You okay?" Dooley asked her.

"Oh my, yes, very much so," Edith Fay said with a troubled smile. "But why did Jass want to do that? And why did Mr. Duty agree?"

"I have some ideas about that," the good doctor replied.

The eye that sees all sees not itself. *Proverb*

SATURDAY, JUNE 16

CHAPTER TWENTY-FOUR

Biddlebourne was awake past midnight for the second day.

The backroom boys, already drunk as a surfeit of skunks imbibing moonshine runoff, reconnoitered at the Legion hall after a day of looking out for the affairs of Jass Pinbiddie, their best buddy ever.

But even the Legion waitresses refused to serve them more beer, and after a brief, and loud, conference at the bar they staggered as one to the parking lot. The majority, who unfortunately were so sotted they could not see straight, vomited on or around the prized trucks and SUVs of several other Legion members as they hunted their own vehicles.

The few Legion boys who still had some piss and vinegar in them decided to stir up a little more fun, so they boosted each other into the double dumpster near the kitchen door and proceeded, with much cheering and whooping, to toss its contents onto the asphalt, into the shrubbery that Navy vet Gary Shelby had installed with his own hands and equipment, and upon the roof of the Legion building.

It was true that Barry Dale Green had never touched the cash register at Biddlebourne Feed & Grain because Jass handled the money when he was there and Missy Johnson did when Jass was absent.

But Barry Dale Green had dealt with everything else at Jass' store. He'd carried the hundred-pound feed bags. Stacked the agricultural chemicals. Rolled out the bins and troughs. Sorted the tractor parts. Coiled the hydraulic hoses. Binned the hitch pins. Cleaned the spilled motor oil. Shaken fleas out of the jeans. Drawn the signs and printed the fliers. Shoveled the snow. Painted the walls. Mopped the floors. Scoured the toilets.

As he was the only full-time employee of Biddlebourne Feed & Grain, he had done these things seven days a week for twelve years with only Thursday afternoons and *legal* holidays off, had received the minimum wage for every one of his sixty-six weekly hours, had been required to eat his lunch cold from a paper bag every day, had worn out nineteen pairs of sneakers, and had driven hundreds of unreimbursed miles in his own vehicle to make deliveries and pick up returns.

Naturally, there was no discussion of health insurance at Biddlebourne Feed & Grain, with the consequence that Barry Dale's knees now ached nonstop and his back creaked when he sat on the toilet during one of his rare breaks.

Therefore, Barry Dale Green earlier that day had quietly boxed up his and his mother Ida Jean's essential possessions, placed them in the back of and on the top of his 4Runner, helped Ida Jean into the front seat, driven to Biddlebourne Feed & Grain and left the motor and air conditioning on while he went inside.

Now, holding a flashlight between his lips, he expertly twirled the knob of the old Brush Punnett safe in the mop closet next to the restroom. The night breeze blew and the ancient wooden building keened. Barry Dale stilled to listen for footfalls. But there were no noises he had not heard hundreds of times before.

Finally, he reached the last number in the combination. He stopped only to wipe away drool and sweat before he turned the lock a sixteenth of an inch and heard the tumblers click sweetly.

In Spartansville Emerson Duty sweated too.

The day had been one of the worst of his life, worse than when he'd left his personal diary in the break room at work, worse than the day eighth-grade bully Fallon Fuchs had beaten him senseless on the school playground, and certainly worse than the time his boot-camp drill sergeant had marched alongside him screaming, "If you can't learn your left from your right, soldier, I'm gonna staple signs to your worthless ass."

Beside him, Eleanor lay in a sheer garment of a kind Emerson had not seen before. Nevertheless, he knew its purpose.

And he knew his part in its purpose.

For years, Eleanor had accepted Emerson's excuses. He had hemorrhoids. He had colds. He had early shifts. He had late shifts. He had toothaches, and stomachaches, and headaches, and earaches. He had meetings to attend. He had friends to see. He had trips to make. He had grass to mow, snow to shovel, leaves to rake, porches to paint.

But now, as his retirement loomed, Eleanor made it clear she would hear no more excuses, brook no more delays, accept no more avoidance, believe no more made-up stories of any stripe.

Tonight, Emerson had an honest reason not to make love. His soul was crushed. No, not from guilt over what he had done to the congregation of Glory Hallelujah Church. But rather for what his actions had done to himself.

He would be lucky to keep his job, he realized. But, in addition, Dr. Cecil Weber could easily turn Emerson's very name to mud in the media and minds of everyone he knew. Why, he could even go to jail or, worse, be required to pay back all the bribes he had taken over the years.

Eleanor rolled to face him, closed her eyes and waited for Emerson to begin.

On the steps of the front porch at 351 Flair Avenue, two young people talked earnestly.

"She gave me a chance. I had a . . . rough time at home, and she knew it," Buddy Lee Delbert said.

Patty Leta Keys took his hand and looked into his eyes. "What do you mean?"

"I don't like to talk about it much."

She squeezed his hand and smiled at him.

Crickets squawked and mosquitoes sizzled on the bright bulb over the door, though no light shone inside the house.

"I got poison ivy on my behind," Buddy Lee divulged suddenly.

Patty Leta, taking a deep breath and a high leap over convention and cool-headedness, leaned toward Buddy Lee and whispered in his ear.

Doc Weber put down his fork and said, "What I'm about to tell you must remain within these walls."

Edith Fay nodded thoughtfully.

But Dooley shook his head. "Doc, I have reservations about a thing like that. First, if I hear about anything criminal I'm duty bound to act on it. Second, I'm in the middle of a murder investigation, and I'm gonna get that job done no matter what it takes."

Doc gazed at the cold fireplace while the big old clock in the hall chimed the quarter hour.

"Sheriff," he said, "this information came to me in a doctor-patient relationship, and I am just as bound by my oath as you are by yours. Will you at least not mention my name if you have to use the information I have?"

Dooley had been made privy to lots of secrets, many of which he had acted upon. But he had let just as many secrets lie where he found them. He said, "Okay, Doc, you got it. I won't mention your name if I need to use the information you give me."

The doctor folded his hands on the table and said, "I have good reason to believe Jass trades in black market diamonds."

Edith Fay gasped. "You don't mean black diamonds as in coal, do you?"

Dooley, who had been studying Doc Weber's expression, said, "No, Edith Fay. That's not what he means. He means Jass deals with conflict diamonds. Some people call them blood diamonds. Am I right, Doc?"

"You are, Sheriff." Turning to Edith Fay, the doctor said, "They call them conflict diamonds because they're mined in an African war zone and used to fund insurgencies."

"How do you know about blood diamonds?" Edith Fay asked. "I have to admit I thought they were merely a fiction for movies."

"I read up on them on the Internet," Doc said. "Diamonds for import and export are supposed to be certified through a convention called the Kimberley Process. But a lot of individuals—and some governments—have found ways around it."

"And you believe Jass is involved in that?" Edith Fay said slowly.

"I'll get right to the point about why I think so," the doctor responded. "As you may know, I performed a surgical hernia repair for Jass in March. He tried to pay my bill with diamonds."

Dooley said, "Whew, that's crazy even for Jass. I've heard he has cash flow problems though. What happened?"

"He was in my office for a post-op exam when he asked how much the operation cost," Doc explained. "I had to ask the account manager because, frankly, I don't keep track of the statements. When I came back with his bill, Jass took an envelope out of his shirt pocket and handed it to me. 'Open it,' he said. And when I did, half a dozen small, rough diamonds fell out."

"Are you sure they were diamonds?" Dooley inquired.

"Not at that point, but I soon became convinced."

"Go on," Dooley said.

"Jass didn't seem fazed when I refused to accept the diamonds as payment. He probably knew it was a long shot to begin with. But then he took the diamonds, held them out in his palm and asked if I wanted to make an investment—a *side venture*, he called it. When I asked for more information, he said, 'There's plenty more where these came from. They come cheap and sell for plenty. You won't be sorry.'"

The coffee pot on the counter beeped and Edith Fay rose to pour a cupful for each of them. She put cream and sugar on the table and sat.

"Did you and he discuss the source of these diamonds?" Dooley asked.

"I pressed Jass for details on where the diamonds came from and where they would be sold. All he would say was that he was only a middle man and didn't know everything that happened up and down the line. But he promised me a big payday if I'd go in with him on the business."

"You know as well as I do that Jass is full of grand schemes, most of which are pure baloney," Dooley said. "Why would this be any different? Jass could simply have bought six fake diamonds and tried to rip you off. He's not above it. Besides, he'd need international contacts to pull off the kind of diamond deals you're talkin' about."

"I agree," Doc said, "but as long as I'm revealing patient information I'll tell you I've written Jass prescriptions for meds to take on trips abroad, and my nurse has given him immunizations he'd need for places like Africa or South America. Further, you two may not remember it, but Jass went to a trade show in Zimbabwe in 2010," Doc added.

Dooley and Edith Fay exchanged a long glance. Dooley said to Doc, "That could have been where he made his initial contacts. Do you think Jass brings the diamonds back with him from these trips?"

The doctor pondered a moment. "This is conjecture, but I doubt he could take large numbers of diamonds through customs undetected. His appearance draws attention. I suspect he goes abroad to cut his deals and then has the diamonds smuggled to him inside goods that are shipped to the feed store."

Dooley let out a low whistle.

"You've given this a lot of thought," Edith Fay observed.

"Yes, and I wouldn't have said a word about it to anybody if Gudrun had not been murdered."

"So you see a connection between Gudrun and the diamonds?" the sheriff said.

"Let me put it this way," Doc said. "I see a connection between Jass and the diamonds, and another connection between Jass and Gudrun, so it doesn't seem much of a jump that the two of them were working together."

"Be that as it may," Edith Fay commented, "I still don't see what that has to do with Mr. Duty's spurious inspection of the church kitchen."

"That's why I'm talking to both of you right now," the doctor said. "When I talked with the health inspector, he said Jass was worked up about some group of women in Biddlebourne who were thwarting his aims."

"Couldn't have been any group but the Glory Girls," Dooley said.

"Agreed," Doc Weber said. "This Duty fellow got an impression the mayor intended to 'kill two birds with one stone' by engineering a bogus kitchen inspection during the Glory Girls' cook-off."

"What do you mean?" Edith Fay asked with a steely gaze in the doctor's direction.

"My opinion?"

"Yes," she said.

"My opinion is that Jass set up that inspection—and paid Emerson Duty handsomely for it—to help his girlfriend get into the Glory Girls."

"Cecil, I do not follow your logic," Edith Fay said.

"Your mind doesn't work like Gudrun's," Doc Weber said. "Gudrun was a horrible cook. She could never have won that cook-off without cheating, so I figure Jass orchestrated Emerson Duty's visit as a distraction so she could pull some kind of shenanigan to put her entry on top."

"I'll be darned," Dooley said softly.

"But how does that tie in with the diamond business?" Edith Fay persisted.

"I have an impression Jass and Gudrun wanted to use Glory Girls projects to move the diamonds," Doc Weber replied.

"Move the diamonds!?" Edith Fay exclaimed.

The sheriff's office was abuzz when Dooley returned shortly before midnight. "What's up, boys?" he said. "Any response to the BOLO on Jass?"

"Nah, not exactly," said Arnie Coker, "but this just came in." He handed the sheriff a long handwritten message.

"Summarize it for me."

"Detective name of Campanella from Cleveland called 11:05 p.m. Said he had information about Jass. His description sounded just like Jass. Said Jass was dressed like Diamond Jim Brady and flashing cash and a case full of financial documents and gave a lady of the night a diamond for her efforts. Said Jass almost for sure has left the country. Got the guy's contact information right here."

Dooley tossed his notebook to his desk. "Everybody, pay attention!" he shouted.

His command brought the room to an instant standstill. "Listen up," he said. "I'm not gonna say this twice."

They put down their soda pop and and phones and took up paper and pens.

"We need to find Jass and bring him back here."

"You think he did Gudrun?" Deputy Lou Shilky asked.

"He's a person of interest in Miss Wince's death, and don't interrupt me again," the sheriff instructed.

"Yes, sir."

The office phone rang. Dooley motioned for Deputy Tag Moffett to answer it and continued, "Lou, get the FBI field office in Wheeling for me."

"Right now?"

"When do you think, Lou? Next week?"

"Sorry, Boss."

Addressing Chief Deputy Stan Neiswonder, Dooley said, "Stan, go and wake up Judge Lincoln and get me a search warrant for Jass' house, his office in the city building and his store. Have him call me for details."

Stan adjusted his gun belt, jingled his keys and left the squad room.

"Lucy Jane, call Andy Brewster at this number and ask him to come on over and meet me here," Dooley said as he handed over Andy's business card.

Deputy Moffett, looking fearful, said, "Dooley, sorry to butt in, but this here is Denzil on the phone. Says he has the results of those, uh, files you asked him to run."

"Everybody dismissed," Dooley said. "I don't mean dismissed to go home. I mean dismissed to get whatever else you got goin' outta the way so you can stand by to look for Jass."

The men wandered away, some to their desks and some to the back stoop to smoke and call their girlfriends. Lucy Jane picked up the phone at her desk. Tag held up two fingers to indicate Denzil Westover was holding on line two.

"Denzil, whattaya got?" Dooley said as he shut his office door and began rummaging through the mail piled on his desk.

"Took me a while to break his passwords," Denzil offered.

Dooley tore open an envelope containing complimentary tickets to an outdoor concert and threw them into the wastebasket.

"Denzil, I appreciate all that. Did you find anything substantive?" Dooley plucked the tickets from the wastebasket and reached into his pocket to put them in his wallet instead.

"I think so. Lots of spreadsheets with dollar figures."

"Can you make out where the money came from?"

"Some of it looks like regular income from the feed store."

"Right. But what else?" the sheriff asked.

"The other spreadsheets aren't labeled, but the figures on them are bigger."

"How much bigger?"

"In the thousands at first and later in the hundreds of thousands."

The sheriff mused. "Denzil, how far back do those records go?"

"Sheriff, that's the thing. They start in '99 and continue through this month. The total's probably in the millions of dollars."

Lucy Jane knocked on Dooley's door and opened it partly. "Boss, Andy Brewster's on his way, and I got a special agent of the FBI holding on line five."

Dooley nodded his thanks to Lucy Jane and said to Denzil, "Okay, come on back to the office and make printouts of everything. Just one set. Then lock down the computer and lock the room behind you and bring me back the printouts and the key I gave you. Got that?"

"Sure do," Denzil said. "Take me about twenty minutes to git over there."

The noblest revenge is to forgive. *Proverb*

CHAPTER TWENTY-FIVE

Edith Fay covertly checked her watch while Doc Weber finished his apple pie and followed it with the last of the coffee.

Not that she wanted the doctor to hurry, but Edith Fay was drained and longed to unwind with a bath and a spot of meditation.

Dooley had already left for his office but only after they heard the finer points of Doc Weber's suspicions. Now, however, Cecil gave no sign of impending departure. Trained from childhood to show every courtesy to a guest, Edith Fay made small talk while Doc sipped and stalled.

Edith Fay breathed deeply to avoid yawning. Mentally listed the morrow's duties. Swallowed. Blinked her eyes fast.

Finally, when Doc could drain not one more drop from the cup, he noisily cleared his throat. "Edith Fay, there's something else."

"Cecil, I must ask you to forgive me. I fear I cannot take in much more today. Perhaps we can chat tomorrow?"

The clock struck twelve. They peered across the table at each other. Physician and patient. Community workers. Neighbors. And friends.

Doc Weber took Edith Fay's hands and said, gently, "This will not take long, and I believe it best—for your sake—to inform you now."

"Inform me of what, Cecil?" Her stomach turned as if she were in high school again and riding the roller coaster at Kennywood Amusement Park.

"My dear lady, I have information that will be helpful to you in coming days. I want to tell you about your birth."

Edith Fay had heard the story of her birth from her mother dozens, if not hundreds, of times, of how Julia had gone into early labor while she and Malcolm were visiting friends in Philadelphia, how Julia had been rushed to the Hospital of the University of Pennsylvania, how Julia had delivered a perfect baby girl after eleven hours of labor and then remained hospitalized for three more days, and how there were no birth pictures of Edith Fay because Malcolm and Julia had been surprised by her early arrival.

"Cecil, I was born in Philadelphia. What would you know about my birth?"

"I was there, dear lady. I delivered you into this world. But it was not in Philadelphia."

Cecil Weber had been close to the Smiths as long as Edith Fay could remember. He had seen her through measles, mumps, adolescence and migraines. Edith Fay trusted him implicitly, but she wondered at this moment whether he had lost his perspective or his mind.

But Cecil Weber, M.D., was of sane mind and keen eye. "Julia and Malcolm trusted me with their most precious secret and their most valuable achievement. That's you."

Edith Fay struggled to sift the possibilities through a haze of fatigue and mental overload. She gently pulled her hands from his and folded the dishcloth into a six-inch square. Silently, she wiped the table.

"When your parents had been married eight years and failed to conceive a child, they asked me to help them. I used my contacts to locate a young woman who was pregnant and planned to give up her child for adoption.

"It so happened I had privileges at the hospital where the young woman gave birth—it was in Wetzel County—and I had the honor of delivering you and handing you over to your parents. It was a memorable day."

Edith Fay stopped wiping. Quietly refolded the cloth and put it back into the apron pocket. Checked her watch, saw that it was a tick or two slow, carefully corrected the gap.

Finally she spoke. "I'm not totally surprised by all this. I went through Mother and Dad's papers today, or yesterday, and found a birth certificate with the name Emily Elaine Buckingham on it."

Doc smiled with relief. "I should have known you would get to the bottom of this on your own. So you know the rest of it then?"

"The rest of it?"

"Dear lady, the name of the woman who gave birth to you was Felkin Wince."

Edith Fay gasped. Put a hand to her head in sudden, awful understanding.

"And I had a sister named Gudrun Wince."

The flatness of Edith Fay's voice concerned Doc Weber. Would she be able to comprehend the motives of the woman who had given her up at birth? Would she be forever wounded by the falsehoods that Julia and Malcolm Smith had fabricated to protect her?

The exterior lights around Edith Fay's home turned on automatically, as did electric candles in all the windows. For a moment, Edith Fay and Doc stared at the trio of lights on the sill over the sink.

"Cecil," she said.

"Yes?"

"I'll be all right. It will take a while. But I need to understand it all."

"Ask anything you like."

"I should tell you I suspected for years I'd been adopted. But Mother and Dad were so good to me, gave me everything, saw to it that I had the experiences and education that made me who I am today."

"But you still had questions?"

"Not at first," she said, "but as I grew up I noticed little things. Relatives at family reunions would make odd comments. The parents of my friends in school would ask too many questions about my name and my parents' supposed trip to Philadelphia just before my birth."

"I understand," he said. "It must have been hard on you."

"No, actually, it wasn't," Edith Fay said. "In the back of my mind I knew I was different, but I loved Mother and Dad and accepted their judgment. I decided—I guess it was around the time I turned fifteen or sixteen—that I would not pursue the matter out of respect for my parents. They were my parents, my real parents, in my mind."

"You're satisfied then?"

"Almost. I have only one question for you."

"I'm ready," Doc said.

"Why is my birth name Buckingham if my birth mother's name was Wince?"

He smiled because the answer was simple and straightforward.

"Your birth mother was Felkin Wince and your birth father was Archer Buckingham."

"In that case, may I clarify one more point?" she said.

"Of course."

"Was Archer Buckingham also Gudrun's father?"

"He was."

"In that case, was her birth name Gudrun Buckingham?"

"Her birth name was Gudrun Cassandra Buckingham, and she kept that name throughout her childhood and young adulthood."

"Thank you, Cecil. You have given me understanding, and I'm grateful."

Emerson Duty was a complex man.

He was an only child, his father a chemical engineer and his mother the first female executive chef in Wetzel County. Emerson was small for his age but nimble in games and witty in speech. As a child he played dolls with girls and marbles with boys. As a preteen it was video games with his buddies and board games with the neighborhood girls. In his teen years he happily dated those same girls and shared stories of his sexual adventures with those boys.

Soon after entering the nursing program at Panhandle Community College, he met the quietly beautiful Joann McCoy in an anatomy class and fell in love with her. Eighteen months later she accepted his marriage proposal. But when they shared their hopes for a large family, she asked him to switch to pre-med studies.

A natural caregiver but also a natural follower, Emerson acceded to Joann's request, adding to his course load, his debt load and his stress load. He earned a bachelor's degree in biology and was admitted to the West Virginia University School of Medicine, where he managed B's while working full time as an oncology nurse.

But when he entered his medical internship and had virtually no free time to spend with Joann, she dumped him and within six months married Cullen Sawyers, a fire captain who worked four days on and three days off every week and got free use of a department car.

Emerson imploded. He quit medical school, lost his nursing job because he was too heartsick to go to work, and had to move back in with his parents, who welcomed him with the kind of smothering love most likely to stymie his emotional recovery.

When he met Eleanor Purdy, he was so grateful for her cool demeanor, minimal expectations and well-appointed home that he hastened to wed her before she realized how broken he really was.

Now, as he lay beside this woman who had—at least initially—supported him and encouraged him and healed him and treasured him, Emerson felt stirrings that reminded him of their earliest days together. The tugging in his loins and the tightness in his chest made him want her as he had not done for years.

But he had amends to make. Though Eleanor's eyes were closed, he knew she was awake. "Ellie, Honey," he said, "I want to tell you some things first."

"What?" she said with suspicion and disappointment.

"I . . . I love you. I know it's been a long time since I said that. Things have gotten away from me. I've messed up badly at work, and I'm scared to death of what might happen to me . . . to us. I need your help."

Tentatively, he cupped her face and kissed it again and again, from forehead to nose to cheeks to chin. Eleanor locked her wrists behind his neck and pressed her body to him. "It's about time you admitted it," she said.

"You knew?"

"Of course, I knew. But I was selfish too. I wanted to spend my time shopping and reading. I thought if I ignored the problem it would go away like it did before. But it isn't going away this time, is it?"

"No, Ellie. It's not."

They embraced each other with arms and legs and let their feelings and tears flow. He poured out a confession that pained and humiliated him. She poured out a love that, for the second time in their marriage, freed him from the torment of his errors and infused him with hope.

They spent all their words and all their essence and all night throwing off what had divided them and embracing what in days to come would unite them.

The Fundraising Subcommittee of the Glory Girls service organization of Glory Hallelujah Church, Biddlebourne, West Virginia, is charged with the financial administration of all projects of the organization. *Glory Girls Book of Bylaws,* adopted May 1959

CHAPTER TWENTY-SIX

Saturday dawned warm and humid in Biddlebourne. Farmers looked to the sky and hurried to do chores before the rain came. Housewives closed windows and turned on air conditioning. Kids headed to fishing holes, skateboard parks and tree houses.

Ernie Blankenship hastened to the Biddlebourne Municipal Center, where he met Marthleen Lewis, whom he had called in on her day off. He told her to contact the other members of the Biddlebourne City Council and bid them attend an emergency meeting at noon in council chambers.

Council members initially resisted Ernie's summons, telling Marthleen variously that they had fields to till, hogs to castrate, accounts to balance or—in the case of Junior Woodburn—a wedding to go to, since he and Marilee Hoover were tying the knot at high noon after living together seventeen years.

But Marthleen, following Ernie's adamant instructions, told Junior, "Look, I planned to come to your wedding, but Ernie's got something stuck in his craw. Best if you tell Marilee you'll be there as soon as you can."

In the end, all the council members except Junior said they'd show up for the special session, and when the dust in the conference room settled at 11:59 a.m. seven men and one woman were sitting around the table with frowns on their faces and printed agendas in their hands.

"Ernie, you got a lotta nerve makin' us come over here while Jass is on vacation," said Rosaphone Ashe.

A murmur rose from the others. Wayland Carse turned to her and said, "Rosie, we all know he ain't on vacation."

"Well, I don't believe he did anything wrong," Rosaphone said hotly.

"Nobody said he did," Wayland replied, "but he's been gone two days and canceled the regular Thursday night meeting for personal reasons. He's not been in touch with anyone in town that I heard of, and we can't put business on hold indefinitely. As you recall, we had a couple must-votes on the Thursday agenda."

Rosaphone cleared her throat. "All right. We're all here now so we may as well get on with it. But I'm warnin' you, Ernie Blankenship, you better make this quick so's we can all git over to Junior and Marilee's weddin'. I hear there's gonna be a chocolate fountain with strawberries at the reception."

Nods of appreciation greeted this fact, which fit perfectly into Ernie's plan.

That was how and why, on Saturday, June 16, 2012, the Biddlebourne Town Council in quick succession passed several controversial measures, including the purchase of a $150,000 police boat, the introduction of a town service fee for each household and business, and the placement of a tribute to garbage-truck drivers in the town square.

Thus, though pro-tem Mayor Ernie Blankenship declared that those measures advanced the welfare of the people of Biddlebourne, they would coincidentally advance the purposes of Ernie relative to Bud Hinchee's Sea and Shore Inc., the mayor's discretionary fund, and Ernie's sister Judy Ray, who was the mother of a garbage-truck driver.

Neither was it an accident that council members axed—at 12:49 p.m. just as the *I do*'s were being said at the Baptist church—on third and final reading the Pinbiddie amendment to tax churches on meals served.

By 1:15 p.m., Rosaphone, Marthleen, Ernie and many other town luminaries, the most notable exception being erstwhile mayor Jass Pinbiddie, were drinking cheap champagne and eating bacon-wrapped wienies at the Lions Club.

Ernie Blankenship, much to Annie Scovill's surprise, winked at her on his way to the chocolate fountain, causing her to rejoice silently and send text messages to Edith Fay Smith and William Wharton.

Dooley Skiles, whose work most often involved drunks and speeders, had no time for weddings because he was busy hunting a murderer and an international jewel swindler.

He made a quick trip home at 4 a.m. Saturday to feed Corndog and take a shower. He napped for an hour, ate a bagel loaded with peanut butter and buckled the pooch into the front passenger seat of his squad car for the ride back to his office.

Dooley liked maps. He liked them because they were a black-and-white way to approach a shades-of-gray criminal case. Accordingly, he had State Police Captain Andy Brewster combing West Virginia's fifty-four other counties for leads to Jass Pinbiddie's whereabouts, and FBI Special Agent Miles McCullough working the world beyond the Mountain State, starting with Cleveland Detective Jimmy Campanella and a woman who called herself Maria Angelica Ogden.

Those arrangements not only covered the appropriate geography but also got Andy and Miles out of Dooley's office and let Dooley stay focused on Jass' home turf.

When he arrived back at the station Saturday morning, Dooley hollered, "Obey, come on and run Corndog for me." The youngest deputy on the force came out of the break room with an egg biscuit in one hand and a report form in the other.

"You bet, Boss," he said, glad to ditch the paperwork.

Humidity hung in the air like laundered long johns on a clothesline, so Dooley added, "Don't push him too hard. It's awful muggy already."

Then Dooley sent his unofficial, unsworn investigators home from the drunk tank, where they'd landed after their foolery in the American Legion parking lot, with stern orders to forgo all further efforts to help him solve Gudrun's murder.

"You boys are plumb lucky Gary Shelby didn't feather into you himself after what you did to that landscapin'," the sheriff said as they meekly trooped out.

Next he dispatched six of his official, sworn guys to turn the screws even harder on the usual snitches, gossips and blabbermouths, plus every bartender, fast-food worker and poker player in the county.

"You think they got even a hint of an idea where Jass is, push 'em," he instructed. "Push 'em hard."

Lucy Jane knocked on Dooley's door to tell him Judge Lincoln had weighed Dooley's summary of events and signed the search warrant for Jass Pinbiddie's home, city office and business office.

"Lucy Jane, hold up," Dooley said as she turned to go.

Haggard from long hours at work and long nights away from her hot boyfriend, she said, "What ya want, boss? I got three calls on hold."

Dooley felt bad, but not very bad, for pressing his staff so hard. But he appreciated their loyalty and hard work.

"Call up Gladys at the Mug and ask her to send over two dozen subs and four pies around lunch time. My treat."

Weak applause emanated from the squad room.

"Everybody get back to work," Dooley said.

Stan Neiswonder and Arnie Coker hadn't been assigned yet. "What about us?" Stan said.

"You two go and do another set of interviews on Pearl Gay Osbourn, Barry Dale Green and Marthleen Lewis. Take your time. Get all the details. I mean everything."

"Anything in particular you want we should bear down on?" Arnie asked.

"Yeah," said the sheriff. "I wanna know how often Jass traveled outta town, where he went and how long he stayed. Now git."

Jass Pinbiddie/Gregory Bachand had never before moved so quickly. He stashed two changes of clothes into his carry-on along with the documents and gems. He threw the rest of his clothes and toiletries down the trash chute across from his room on the hotel's penthouse floor.

He retrieved Gregory Bachand's passport from the front desk, paid his bill with a clean credit card and went to an automated teller machine to withdraw the maximum cash allowed from three other credit cards, all bearing the name Mingo Varrick.

He taxied to Toronto's Pearson International Airport, Canada's busiest air hub, and used one of six tickets he had purchased online the day before.

When his cell phone buzzed, he pressed the green button and said, "Arnie, I got your text message. Thanks for warning me. I owe you. . . ."

"Jass," Arnie said, "Never mind that. It's worse than I thought. The boss got a warrant to search your place official like. And I heard Dooley talkin' with an FBI guy in his office. They were talkin' 'bout numbers they found on computer files. Big numbers. The agent, McCullough's his name, you know him?"

"No," Gregory replied.

"This guy McCullough said the Feds could trace the money and find you if you use any o' your credit cards. Holy cow, man, you're in the soup."

"It's all right," he said. "I've taken . . . precautions. Gotta go now. Don't call me again. I'll call you."

Arnie had no chance to reply before the former Jass Pinbiddie ended the call and walked toward a departure gate operated by the official airline of the United Arab Emirates.

"Sonny, I think I'll enjoy this," Ida Jean Green said from the comfort of a chaise longue beside the pool of a Holiday Inn Express in Lexington, Kentucky. She removed her brogans and socks and carefully began applying Hold Me Close, a deep rose polish, to her toenails.

Barry Dale rubbed sunscreen on his arms and legs, then opened his new laptop computer to check the Facebook news out of Biddlebourne.

"Hmm," he said.

"What's wrong, Sonny? Are you ailin'?"

"No, Mom. Not at all," he said. "I'm just enjoying our time in my own way."

"What do you mean?"

Barry Dale Green, whose lifelong pool time totaled about six hours, smiled. "I mean my life doesn't revolve around Jass Pinbiddie anymore. I don't have to work when he says work, eat when he says eat, shut up when he says shut up."

"My boy, I know you had it bad with him," Ida Jean commented. "You did it for me, I reckon. Now I'm gonna let you in on a little secret I been keepin'."

"Mom! What secret have you been harboring?" Barry Dale exclaimed in alarm.

"Settle down, Sonny. You'll like it," she promised.

Emerson Duty scored a hat trick at 7:48 Saturday morning when he telephoned his boss, Blaize Luzader, since she disliked being awakened before 8 a.m., hated speaking to human beings before 8 a.m. and abhorred hearing a telephone ring before 8 a.m.

When Ms. Luzader explained, in patient but ascending tones, how she felt about his early call, Emerson said, "I apologize, ma'am. I'll make this short."

"Yes, you will," she agreed.

He swallowed. "Ma'am, I . . . um . . ."

"Speak up," she commanded. "Time's a ticking!"

"Ma'am, I have information for you. It goes back . . . um . . . several years. I'd like to speak privately with you if I may."

Truth's best ornament is nakedness. *Proverb*

CHAPTER TWENTY-SEVEN

"I'm sorry. I'm so, so sorry," Laverna Inys Wharton said between sobs.

"Respectfully, Laverna, I don't know what you're sorry about," Dooley said. He glanced at William Wharton entreatingly but received no response.

They were seated in Dooley's office with the sheriff on a folding chair and William and Laverna Inys Wharton occupying the couch. Corndog the Coonhound lay at Laverna's feet with his chin resting on her right shoe. Corndog preferred women's shoes.

Laverna reached for the tissue box on the end table. William tightened his arm around her shoulders. "Sheriff," he said, "my wife has done something of which she is not proud. Her motives were perhaps confused, but she is a person of integrity and a community servant, as you know."

Dooley nodded and pointed to the plastic grocery bag she had carried in. "May I open that?" he said.

"Yes," she said, her tone barely above a whisper.

The sheriff upended the sack, and out fell an oversize ochre-colored leather purse with a gold chain strap. He put it on the coffee table and waited.

"It's . . . Gudrun's," she said.

"Did she lend it to you?" Dooley asked.

"No, sir."

The sheriff paused. Mused. "Was this the purse she had on the day she . . . died?"

"Yes," Laverna wailed.

William shifted in his seat, crossed his right knee over the left, then the left over the right. He handed Laverna another tissue and waited for the storm to subside.

"Lucy Jane," Dooley bawled through the closed door.

"What?!"

"Coffee all around," he ordered.

"Comin' up."

"Sheriff, as you see, my wife is quite upset," William noted. "May I take Laverna home now and come back with her after she's . . . rested?"

"Hold up now, William," Dooley said. "I need to ask Laverna a few more questions."

The coffee helped. After her first few gulps, Laverna blew her nose and sat up broomstick straight with her ankles locked. Corndog whimpered. "Go ahead, Sheriff, I'm ready," she said. William took a starched white handkerchief from his pocket and wiped his brow.

"I'll start with the obvious, I guess," the sheriff said. "How'd you come by Miss Wince's pocketbook?"

"I got it at the Value Mart."

Dooley waited for Laverna to go on, but she maintained her prim posture and stared at him unblinkingly.

"Did you buy it there?"

"No, sir. They don't sell purses at the Value Mart."

"You get it from Miss Wince herself?" Dooley said, realizing that Laverna had no intention of telling him more than exactly what he asked.

"No, sir," she said.

"From who then?"

"Not from who. From where. I got it out back of the store, from that little shed where Bill Roy keeps his rakes and such."

"You have any idea how the purse got in that shed to begin with?" Dooley asked.

"I'm not at liberty to say," Laverna replied.

"You don't know, or you don't wanna say?"

William Wharton butted in. "Sheriff, I've advised my wife to speak with you only about the purse itself . . . at this time."

Dooley knew as soon as he dumped the purse out of the grocery bag that it had something to do with Gudrun's murder. But he couldn't begin to guess what the upright Laverna Inys Wharton might have done that had her blubbering and dodging his questions. William Wharton knew all about it, but the sheriff's chances of getting the facts out of either of his visitors were as slim as the willow sapling outside his window.

"Did you arrange for Miss Wince to be killed?"

"I most certainly did not!" Laverna retorted.

"Did you have anything at all to do with Miss Wince's death?"

"Of course not!"

"Then you'll need to tell me how you arranged to get her purse."

William rose and pulled Laverna up gently from the couch. "We're done here for now, Dooley," he said. "My wife is stressed and needs to see her physician before she becomes ill with anxiety. If I personally promise that she will answer all your questions Monday morning, will you allow her to go home with me for now?"

"You promise you'll be with her all the time?" Dooley asked.

"I do," William said with a tender look in Laverna's direction.

"I reckon that'll be all right, you bein' an officer of the court and all," Dooley said. "I have one more question for today, though."

"What is it?" William inquired.

"Did anyone else besides you two handle the purse since you . . . uh . . . received it?"

"No," Laverna said.

"Okay. You two can go. But don't leave town. And I mean it!"

William took Laverna's hand and they left the office.

"Stan, pick up Buddy Lee Delbert and bring him in," Dooley said into his phone thirty seconds later.

"It's good to see you," Ted Cavotte said as he extended a hand to Edith Fay.

"You too, Ted. Thanks for seeing me on such short notice."

The offices Ted shared with William Wharton stood in the western shadow of the Skyler County Courthouse and had been built in the same era. The lamps were from Tiffany and the leather chairs from Ted's great-great grandfather, who had bought the building in 1901 when an oil boom brought big money to county landowners and the lawyers who represented them.

"That's no problem," he said. "I intended to spend the day here anyway. Melva's got a crew at the house cleaning carpets and scrubbing walls."

Edith Fay smiled, remembering her mother's seasonal cleaning binges, and said, "Dad always left too when Mother went after the walls."

"May God rest their souls in peace."

"Yes," she agreed.

"So, Edith Fay, how may I help you?"

She folded her hands in her lap and spoke calmly. "Ted, I understand that you drew up Gudrun's will."

He nodded and placed a file folder and a legal pad on the desk in front of him. "Yes. I trust you have read it by now."

"I have. The provisions are spelled out clearly, though I cannot pretend to understand Gudrun's reasoning. Can you shed light on her motives for naming me her beneficiary?"

He opened the file and pulled out a handwritten page. He reached into his shirt pocket for a pair of glasses and settled them on his nose. He looked up at her over the lenses.

Edith Fay gave him a slight nod, and Ted began to read:

"I, Gudrun Cassandra Wince, have on this date, Dec. 10, 2000, signed my last will and testament and assigned it to the keeping of my attorney, Mr. Theodore Cavotte. In this statement I wish to reflect on the experiences and circumstances that led to my decisions regarding my estate.

"I have prepared this statement for the edification of my sister, Edith Fay Smith, nee Emily Elaine Buckingham, although I herewith grant permission, should it be needed, for Mr. Theodore Cavotte and/or Ms. Edith Fay Smith to share it with individuals of their choosing.

"As may be known by my sister Edith Fay Smith by the time she reads this document, she and I are daughters of the same mother and father, namely, Felkin Wince and Archer Buckingham.

"I was born May 14, 1951, in Wetzel County, West Virginia, and at the age of one week was placed in foster care because my mother was addicted to heroin and my father was unemployed and unable to care for me. My father and mother were not married, and my mother relinquished her parental rights to me when I was two years old. I have never known where my father was or had any contact with him.

"I spent the first fourteen years of my life with foster families. I changed schools nine times during that period and at twelve years of age was prescribed medication for what my foster parents called 'mental health issues.'

"The medicine made me sick and unable to do my school work, which I desperately desired to do because I saw school as my only way out of poverty. But when I stopped taking my medication so that I could function in school, the social workers threatened to move me to another family if I did not resume taking the pills.

"Shortly thereafter, when I turned fifteen years old, I ran away from my foster home. I put my past behind me and supported myself in ways that others disapproved of. By hard work and persistence I graduated from college and became a licensed teacher and, eventually, high school principal in Biddlebourne, West Virginia.

"When I was seventeen years old, I was informed by a reliable source that my parents, Felkin Wince and Archer Buckingham, had become parents of another daughter. For years I searched for my sister, who I understood to be my only sibling.

"Eventually I learned that my sister had been placed at birth with adoptive parents, Julia and Malcolm Smith, in Skyler County, West Virginia. I tracked my sister's activities through newspaper reports and eventually moved to Skyler County with the hope of establishing a relationship with her.

"However, upon arriving in Skyler County I observed that my sister and I lived quite differently and held opposing views on many issues. I found it necessary to expend my time and energy in advancing my professional career.

"I also observed that my sister held positions of public influence, first at Skyler County General Hospital and later at Glory Hallelujah Church in Biddlebourne. Though I had no interest in religion, and indeed am an atheist, I joined the church with the hope and intention of making my identity known to my sister and forming a familial relationship with her.

"However, as time passed I saw that my sister and I had received vastly different upbringings. I learned that Emily Elaine, named Edith Fay by her adoptive parents, had been given every advantage by her parents while I had struggled as a foster child to cope with disinterest and discontinuity.

"My sister received an appropriate and timely education, whereas I was forced to work two menial jobs to attend a junior college. She became the top executive of a community hospital. As a high school dropout I labored in venues of questionable character and came late into my life's calling.

"I eventually decided not to reveal my true identity to my sister or to others, as I believed I thereafter would have been compared unfavorably with Edith Fay and thusly constrained in my professional and social relationships.

"On this date I have named Edith Fay Smith, née Emily Elaine Buckingham, sole beneficiary of my personal and real holdings in recognition of the blood ties we share and in regret for having blamed her for the circumstances that separated us throughout our lives. She is not to blame for those circumstances."

The Art and Music Subcommittee of the Glory Girls service organization of Glory Hallelujah Church, Biddlebourne, West Virginia, shall present and promote visual, audio and performing arts in the church and the community at large. *Glory Girls Book of Bylaws,* adopted May 1959

CHAPTER TWENTY-EIGHT

"Boss, Boss!"

"I can hear you; ya don't hafta shout," the sheriff said. He had Jass Pinbiddie's computer printouts on the desk and needed to concentrate.

A kerfuffle in the squad room signaled that Gladys Swan's delivery boy Missouri "Mizz" Sole had brought the lunch order from the Mug. If Dooley didn't get out there fast, nothing would be left.

"And make it quick, would ya?" Dooley added.

"Boss, Buddy Lee's gone!" Stan Neiswonder hollered.

"Aw, phooey," said the sheriff while a knot in his gut canceled his interest in lunch.

"Same thing I said," the chief deputy reported.

"Well, what else did you learn?"

"Landlady—you know her, Innie Grimm—said she went up this morning to collect his rent and he wasn't here. Said he never failed to pay his rent before. Said he never left the place before breakfast either. He has a room-and-board deal with Innie."

"Stan, that doesn't mean he's gone. He's probably fishin' over at the backwaters."

"No, he ain't. I had the boys check the holes he favors, even under Muddy Creek Bridge there at the bend and by the old Wiley place. Thing is, Boss, Buddy Lee don't have a vehicle. He can't have got too far but he's nowhere around here. We asked all over before I told you."

"Innie didn't see him leave, I take it," the sheriff stated.

"She didn't. But she said she heard a car idling outside the house real early—she was up makin' bread for the boarders—but figured it was only Johnny Ferrebee leavin' eggs on the porch. But when she went out to git 'em later, there wasn't no eggs there. Maybe we got an egg thief on the loose."

"I wouldn't worry 'bout that," Dooley said. He figured he knew exactly what Buddy Lee had done. He couldn't share his guess with Stan and had a hard time getting him to stand down from the search for Buddy Lee. At any rate, the arrival of Shirl Burrows cut their conversation short.

Dooley thanked Shirl for coming in, swore her to secrecy and showed her the printouts from Jass' computer files.

Shirl studied the pages, shuffled them into several piles, then collated those piles into one stack with the most recently dated documents on top.

"You got an addin' machine, sheriff?" she asked.

He opened the middle desk drawer and took out a calculator. While Dooley gave Corndog fresh water, checked his text messages and studied his notebook, Shirl keyed the calculator, tore strips of paper from it and tossed them into the wastebasket, all while humming a tune resembling *Somewhere Over the Rainbow.*

After about fifteen minutes, Dooley opened the office door and yelled, "Lucy Jane, you got any sandwiches left in there?"

"Sure do, Sheriff."

"Well, bring one on in here for Miss Shirl, would ya?"

"Many thanks, Dooley. Iced tea too, if you got it," Shirl said without looking up from the calculator. She was tapping it with one hand and with the other making a long list of numbers on the back of an envelope she'd plucked from the wastebasket.

"I heard," Lucy Jane said as she went to the break room and poured.

Shirl finished her numbering but ate a meatball sub before picking up the envelope. Dooley closed the office door and drew up a chair.

"Dooley, if I hadn't seen these documents with my own eyes, I wouldn't a guessed Jass was up to anything o' this magnitude. Good God, the man's a millionaire several times over. My guess? These papers are just the tip o' the financial iceberg, know what I mean?"

Sweet little Cassie sat on his lap and laughed at an old joke, throwing her head back and brushing a lock of hair from her forehead. She twisted to face him and nuzzled her cheek against his, inviting a kiss. He put a hand to the small of her back and breathed in her fragrance.

"Mr. Statler, Mr. Statler."

A woman of faultless complexion and engaging countenance leaned in close and spoke his name gently but persistently.

"I beg your pardon, Mr. Statler. But you asked to be awakened at five. I apologize for interrupting your sleep," she said. Her name tag bore the name Gaida Rameya, and she most decidedly was not Gudrun Cassandra Wince, and a new pang of grief enveloped him.

He nearly cried out in agony but caught himself and said, "Thank you, ma'am. I appreciate it."

Clayton Hughes Statler reclined in a big armchair in his private, first-class suite aboard an Emirates A380 aircraft bound for Dubai. His suite was equipped with a sliding glass door, a private minibar and an on-demand touch-screen television.

"May I bring refreshments, Mr. Statler?" Ms. Rameya asked sweetly.

"Do you have a menu?"

"Yes, sir, but I am pleased to say we will be delighted to prepare anything—anything at all—that you wish for your meal. We offer all varieties of beer, liquor and wine. And, as you may know, high tea and hors d'oeuvres are always available at the onboard lounges. I will escort you to one of the lounges if you wish."

Clayton stretched and realized he had slept nine full hours, nearly the entire amount of time he'd been aboard this five-star hotel in the sky.

"Ma'am, I'd like to wash up first if you will direct me to the washroom."

"Certainly, sir," she said. "As a first-class passenger, you are entitled to use one of two onboard shower spas so that you may arrive at your destination entirely refreshed."

"Oh, well, I . . . uh, forgot my toiletry case."

"That is not a problem, Mr. Statler," Ms. Rameya said. "I will bring you a complimentary shower kit. It will have everything you need."

"Why, thank you," Clayton said. "And, ma'am?"

"Yes?"

"I'd like a three-egg omelet with a T-bone steak and an order of fried potatoes for breakfast. With orange juice and coffee, if you don't mind."

"Certainly, sir. How would you like your steak cooked?"

He told her how Gladys broiled steaks at the Mug. She smiled and said, "Yes, sir. Of course. Shall I serve your meal in about twenty minutes?"

"Make that thirty minutes if you don't mind. And, oh, just one more thing," he said.

"Yes, sir?"

"Can I exchange dollars for dirhams onboard?"

Edith Fay sat motionless, aware of every breath she drew, aware of Ted Cavotte's patient presence, aware of the shift in her identity that had just occurred.

The bell of Glory Hallelujah Church tolled ten times, and she tried to push her thoughts to the day's duties. The Girls had to prepare for their work Tuesday at Saint John's Church.

"Edith Fay, are you all right?"

"Oh, excuse me, Ted. Yes, I'm fine."

"I take it you are surprised both by the terms of Gudrun's will and by the revelations of her letter," the attorney said.

"To say the least," she said with a wry expression.

"How can I help?"

"I am concerned about carrying out . . . my sister's wishes regarding her funeral. It will not be a conventional one, in accordance with her directions."

"May I suggest that you consult with your own pastor, the good Reverend Scovill, in that regard?"

Edith Fay looked stricken. "Oh my. I don't know why I didn't think of that. Yes. I will talk with the pastor. She will understand. Yes, that's what I'll do."

Edith Fay sat still, contemplating another family funeral. Doors opened and closed and people spoke elsewhere in the attorney's office suite. The smell of coffee wafted into the room, reminding Edith Fay of her responsibilities.

"Ted, I want to know if either my mother or father is living. Can you assist me?"

"With your permission, I will employ a . . . reliable and discreet investigator to find out. I take it you want to know . . . either way?"

"Yes, Ted. If they are deceased, I would like to know when that happened and where they might be buried. And, naturally, if they are alive . . ."

"I understand," Ted said.

The intercom on Ted's desk buzzed. "Excuse me," he said to Edith Fay. "Yes, Pansy?" A disembodied voice said, "Ted, Carolina Milnes is here."

"Tell her I'll be right out," Ted said to the air.

Edith Fay collected her handbag and documents and said, "I am quite grateful for your time today, Ted. I have only one more question for now, though I am aware it will sound crass. . . ."

"I assure you, Edith Fay," Ted said, "that it's imperative you be informed fully about the extent of Gudrun's estate."

Ted Cavotte pushed a typed list across the desk to Edith Fay.

There is nothing permanent except change. *Proverb*

CHAPTER TWENTY-NINE

While Buddy Lee Delbert and Patty Leta Keys were checking in at a Motel 6 on the east side of Columbus, Ohio, Patty's dad was placing a missing-persons report with the Skyler County sheriff.

Sheriff Skiles was on a conference call with FBI Special Agent Miles McCullough and State Police Captain Andy Brewster. But he heard the hubbub in the outer office and put the call on hold to go and calm Granville Keys.

Dooley walked Granville, one of his high school classmates, to the break room. "Gran, I'm pretty sure Patty's with Buddy Lee Delbert."

"Why would she be with him?"

"Oh boy," Dooley said, lowering his voice. "I'm not a hundred percent sure, Gran, but I have reason to think Buddy Lee took off overnight too, and I know he's been sweet on Patty Leta for a while."

"I had no idea," said Granville, who had been a single father since the death of Patty Leta's mother when his daughter was only nine years old.

"I could be wrong," the sheriff said, "but we can look for her if you want us to."

Granville Keys ran a sporting goods store and was missing a lot of business on this Saturday morning in June. He said, "Gimme a minute, Doo."

Granville punched numbers on his phone and soon said, "Look, Geneva, I already asked you this once today, but I'm asking you again now that I know she done run off with Buddy Lee. . . . No, there's no use denying it. . . . No, I'm not gonna turn you in to anybody. . . . No, I'm not gonna go get her. She's an adult after all. . . . All right then. Columbus, you say? . . . All right, thanks, Geneva. You're a good friend to my girl. . . . Yeah, just ask her to call me when you hear from her, okay?"

Dooley, who had meanwhile been responding to text messages, including one from Edith Fay, looked up as Granville clicked off.

"That about does it," Granville said. "My girl's gone off with one o' the dopiest guys in the county. Reckon I can't do a thing about it now. She's twenty-two, ya know."

"You sure, Granville? One of the boys can go after her, make it look like we thought she was kidnapped or such."

"Nah, her ma'd want her to make up her own mind about this kinda stuff," Granville said dejectedly. "I'll leave now. Thanks for your help, Doo."

Dooley watched his classmate walk out, shoulders slumped and hands in his pockets. But the sheriff could not linger over the departure of Buddy Lee and Patty Leta. They'd be back.

Dooley finished up with Andy and Miles and shouted a few instructions to deputies before fetching Gudrun's purse from the evidence locker where he'd registered it as soon as Laverna and William Wharton had left the station.

He put on plastic gloves and covered his desk with a clean sheet of brown paper ripped off a big roll. He took each item out of the purse separately and described it on a dated and initialed notebook page.

Twenty minutes later, lined up on the brown paper, lay a makeup compact with a worn hinge; three tubes of lipstick; a partly used package of tissues; a coin purse containing $3.77 in coins; a billfold containing $56 in tens, fives and ones; a small spiral notebook; six paper clips; five letters with a rubber band around them; two fountain pens and one gel pen; six aspirins, thirteen small green capsules and nineteen purple capsules; a checkbook; a date book; a plastic bag holding grocery coupons; one comb; and a key ring with twelve keys and seven store loyalty tags attached.

Dooley read the letters, all of which had been written by parents concerned about their children's grades at Biddlebourne High School.

He went through the carbon copies in Gudrun's checkbook. The only notable fact to emerge was that Miss Gudrun Wince had spent more money on clothes and restaurant meals than all other expenses combined.

"Lucy Jane!" he yelled.

"What?"

"Call up the clinic and tell 'em I got things I want x-rayed."

"We were wrong."

Hazel Simons could scarcely believe her ears. Thelma Blivins had never admitted an error. About anything when she was running Blivins Stone Works or about anything when she wasn't.

"What about?" Hazel asked.

"About Jass. He didn't do it," she announced.

"Didn't kill Gudrun or didn't mess around with her?"

"Well, there ain't no doubt he was messin' around with her. But he didn't kill her. Guess who did!"

Hazel gave the question her most intense thought.

But Thelma could not bear the wait. "Laverna Wharton did it!" she nearly screamed.

"Holy moly, Thelma. Why in the world would she go and do that? She's a businesswoman. Sure, her business is in her basement, but I heard she's makin' over twenty thousand a year with that consultin' stuff."

"Be that as it may," Thelma counseled, "I have it from a vurry direct source that Laverna went to the sheriff with her husband and confessed and the sheriff let her go home on her own recognition and she ain't allowed to leave her house now till the deputies come and get her."

Hazel didn't know much about the workings of the law, but she was an avid viewer of numerous televised police dramas. So, with much authority and even a little disdain, she said, "That don't make sense, Thelma, him lettin' her go like that. If she done it, he'd have arrested her and put her behind bars, and her husband woulda had to go and put up her bail."

Thelma took this resistance in stride. "Oh, no. He let her go on account o' her mother, who was best friends with his mother way back, oh, to the fifties. Couldn't arrest his mother's best friend's daughter, ya know."

"Hmph. I don't believe that either. But did you find out why Gudrun done gave her money and stuff to Edith Fay Smith?"

"I got some ideas on that," Thelma said mysteriously.

"Like what?"

"I don't know whether I should mention them or not."

"Come on, Honey. You know you're my best friend. If you can't tell me, who can you tell?"

Thelma Blivins, for reasons she neither understood nor wished to understand, had fewer friends than she thought she deserved. The people at the beauty shop, the grocery, even in her own neighborhood had all gone their separate ways—away from Thelma. Indeed, Hazel Simons was at the top of Thelma's very short friends list.

Thelma lowered her voice to give her views the proper import. "I heard from Hannarae Tallman that her girl Kagen—she's the one with that big mop o' ginger-colored hair, the second youngest one—got a summer job cleanin' up over at Ted Cavotte's office. . . ."

Hazel, duly impressed, said, "Oh my. That's an important job."

"Sure is. Kagen told her mama, and her mama told me, well, this is a secret so you can't tell anyone. You have to promise."

"I promise," Hazel said with bated breath.

"Kagen said she saw a paper that made out like Gudrun was Edith Fay's real mother. Whaddaya think of that?"

"Oh my! Is the Tallman girl sure?"

"Told her mama the paper got left in the copying machine by mistake, so she just put it on the secretary's desk but got a little look at it first. Sure did look like it."

"I'm shocked," Hazel admitted.

"Me too."

"But you know what? That's about the only thing that could explain Gudrun doin' a crazy thing like givin' her money to Edith Fay," Hazel said. "I never thought she liked Edith Fay."

"Oh, you're right," Thelma agreed. "I was at Ladies Aid one time when Gudrun come right out and called Edith Fay a liar. At Ladies Aid! Right there in the church!"

"Oowee. I didn't see this comin'. I reckon Edith Fay's all shook up."

Thelma concurred, adding, "I wonder what she's gonna do with all that money."

"Edith Fay's already rich. I know that because I heard she gives six thousand dollars a year to the church. Now she's just gonna be richer," Hazel said.

"I always wondered 'bout Edith Fay. Doesn't look a thing like Malcolm or Julia. Doesn't act like them either, with all her highfalutin' schoolin' and everything. Didn't do her a bit o' good. Now all she does is cook over to the church," said Thelma.

"But I gotta admit she's a fine cook," Hazel allowed. "You ever have any o' that lasagna she makes with sausage and fresh tomatoes from her garden? Best I ever ate."

"Tsk, she still didn't need to go to school up north to learn how to make lasagna," Thelma said.

Dooley saw the pain behind Edith Fay's eyes and stepped inside the door to embrace her and murmur into her ear, "I came as soon as I heard."

"Thank you." She straightened, nearly as tall as the sheriff, and dabbed her eyes with a wadded blue handkerchief.

"It's hard enough to lose a family member. I know how that it is. But I can't imagine what it's like when you didn't even know Gudrun was your birth mother," Dooley said.

Edith Fay's mouth dropped open and her eyes rounded like double *O*'s.

"What?!"

"Oh, Edith Fay, I'm sorry. I shouldn't have mentioned it."

Her shoulders drooped. "Dooley, I gather the gossip chain has been at work again," she said. "Gudrun was not my mother. She was my sister."

Dooley felt as if he'd been struck. He could hear the grandfather clock ticking in the hall and smell fresh-baked bread. "Forgive me, Edith Fay. When Arnie Coker told me about that letter she wrote to you, I wrongly assumed he knew what he was talking about."

"It's all right, Dooley. Either way, it's a shock, and I've only begun to deal with it," she said, motioning Dooley toward the kitchen.

Dooley pulled a chair out for Edith Fay and stood behind her with his hands on her shoulders. He held his tongue.

After a moment, Edith Fay said, "The worst of it is that I harbored hard feelings toward Gudrun.

She will never know that I . . . forgave her for those things she said and did. They came out of her pain and sorrow."

As her tears flowed, Dooley felt the trembling of her body and the heat of her skin.

"You have no reason to feel guilty, Edith Fay," he said. "You never treated Gudrun the way she treated you. You accepted her hurtful words and actions without retaliating. You allowed her to try out for the Girls when you must have known she'd try to cheat and that she'd be awful to deal with."

Edith Fay wore a faraway expression. Her cell phone beeped but she ignored it. "I . . . I always wanted a sister," she said, then added slowly, "My Girls have been trying to solve Gudrun's murder, but one by one they've been calling to say they're stumped."

"I'm as stumped as they are," Dooley admitted. "But Edith Fay, this has all been hard on you. Will you promise me that you'll give yourself time to mourn?"

"Yes. In good time." Edith Fay fiddled with the knives and forks on the table. "Thank you, Dooley. I'll be all right."

"How about a cup of tea?"

"I'd appreciate it," she said. "Do you know where the teabags are?" She smiled wanly when he said, "Sure do."

Edith Fay had laid out two place settings with sandwiches of new brown bread, a hearty green salad and a plate of banana bread flecked with black walnuts collected from the ancient tree on the south side of the Smith farm.

"I'm sorry. You're expecting company," he said as he filled a pot with water.

"I hoped you would come for supper," she said. "I forgot to mention it when I texted. That was good timing, Sheriff."

He took Edith Fay's tea to the table and poured coffee for himself. As they ate, Edith Fay told Dooley the real story of her birth and adoption and of Gudrun's life and its many disappointments.

"That explains a lot of things I've been hearing about," Dooley said. "Gudrun was a woman of many, uh, moods. Edith Fay, would you mind if I look at that letter she wrote you? I know it's personal, but . . ."

Edith Fay put down her fork and gazed intently at Dooley. "I trust you," she said finally. She reached into her apron pocket and withdrew a piece of paper.

Dooley was moved by Edith Fay's trust. In his law enforcement career he'd learned to trust some of his colleagues occasionally but to trust none of them unconditionally. In his world, trust offered too hastily led to bungled investigations, obstructive gossip and jammed-up justice.

While Dooley read Gudrun's letter, Edith Fay cleared the table and served ice cream and the banana bread.

"I haven't had black walnuts in banana bread since my Great-Aunt Barbara made it when I was a kid," Dooley said. "This is delicious."

"Thank you. It's my mother's recipe. No, I mean my adoptive mother's."

"I understand," he said.

She laid her spoon on the placemat. "I take comfort that, toward the end, Gudrun seems to have forgiven me for growing up differently from her."

"Yes, she wrote that she did not blame you for anything. Maybe your kindness to her through the years—without even knowing she was your sister—finally touched her."

"Maybe," Edith Fay said.

A thump on the front porch indicated the daily newspaper had arrived.

"Well, let's see what Wilford Nicklin has to say today about the investigation," Edith Fay said as she rose from the table.

CHAPTER THIRTY

Three Flee Biddlebourne After Church Slaying
Probe Continues in Stabbing of High School Principal
by Wilford Nicklin
Sentinel Staff Writer
Saturday, June 16, 2012

Biddlebourne Mayor Jasper E. "Jass" Pinbiddie is among three city residents with potential ties to Thursday's fatal stabbing of Biddlebourne High School Principal Gudrun C. Wince who have since disappeared, according to reports.

Miss Wince was an entrant in a cook-off at Glory Hallelujah Church, an interdenominational community church in Biddlebourne, when she was stabbed by an unknown perpetrator and found sprawled on the floor of the church kitchen by cook-off assistant Buddy Lee Delbert. She was 61.

Also missing as of midnight Friday were Delbert, 27, and Barry Dale Green, an employee of Pinbiddie at Biddlebourne Feed & Grain.

Meanwhile, a source said a Biddlebourne businesswoman, Laverna I. Wharton, had been questioned in the slaying. Speaking anonymously because he is not an authorized spokesperson, the source said Wharton turned over evidence in the case while being questioned by Skyler County Sheriff Dooley Skiles and was then permitted to leave in the custody of her husband, Biddlebourne attorney William Wharton. The Whartons reside at 309 Muzzy Rd., Biddlebourne.

Pinbiddie, 55, of 200 Bailey St., is the subject of an interstate manhunt led by Skiles in connection with the slaying.

The sheriff declined comment on the hunt for Pinbiddie, who has been mayor of Biddlebourne the last eleven years. But the anonymous source confirmed that the West Virginia State Police and the FBI are cooperating in the search.

Sources also reported that Sheriff Skiles has identified Pinbiddie only as a person of interest in the Wince case. Other, unconfirmed reports surfaced late Friday that Pinbiddie had been seen in Cleveland, Ohio. No details were available.

Mayor Pinbiddie was a known confidant of Miss Wince and, upon arriving at the scene shortly after her body was discovered, expressed deep personal anguish over her death. A sedative was administered to Pinbiddie at the scene by Dr. Cecil Weber of Biddlebourne, who declined comment.

At the time of the slaying, Pinbiddie was meeting with constituents in his office at the City Building, according to members of his staff.

Pinbiddie reportedly has not been seen in Biddlebourne since he was accompanied from the church to his home Thursday afternoon by Weber.

Pinbiddie's home, a three-story structure in the historic original plot divided in the early 1800s by settlers of what was then Skyler County, Virginia, has been unoccupied since shortly after he left the scene of the slaying, according to numerous neighbors questioned by the *Sentinel*.

Pinbiddie's business, Biddlebourne Feed & Grain, was closed Friday, and store associate Green was said by some neighbors to have left for vacation with his mother, Ida Jean Green, of Biddlebourne.

Other neighbors of the Greens, however, noted that household goods filled Green's vehicle, a black Toyota 4Runner, when he and Mrs. Green drove out of town and that furniture was tied to the roof of the car.

Members of Pinbiddie's staff at the Biddlebourne City Building were unavailable for comment. His office secretary, Marthleen Lewis, did not return phone calls.

Skiles reportedly questioned Delbert in his office. An anonymous source said Delbert gave the sheriff a signed statement. The contents of the statement were not made public, and Delbert returned home after the interview.

Neighbors of Delbert, however, said they were questioned by deputies early Saturday about the young man's whereabouts. They said he had not returned home as usual Friday night and that they had not seen him taking his routine walk Saturday morning. One neighbor said he'd seen Delbert leave his premises Friday evening with a woman in a car. Delbert does not own a vehicle, according to neighbors.

Skyler County Chief Deputy Sheriff Stan Neiswonder confirmed that the murder weapon has not been found despite a thorough search of the entire Glory Hallelujah Church complex by sheriff's deputies. Miss Wince's body, originally transported to the Skyler County medical examiner's office, was later taken to the

Charleston headquarters of the West Virginia state medical examiner, which specializes in criminal investigations. An autopsy will be conducted by the state medical examiner to determine the official cause of death.

Miss Wince was pronounced dead at the church Thursday at 12:40 p.m. by Weber. Members of the Glory Girls service group and eight other cook-off contestants present in the church kitchen were among those initially questioned by deputies and released.

The cook-off was to have been the final elimination event for membership in the service group and will be rescheduled, according to spokeswoman Ella Mae Pugh.

Bertram Kimble, operator of the Kimble Funeral Home in Biddlebourne, said funeral arrangements for Miss Wince are pending.

"They say so" is half a lie. *Proverb*

CHAPTER THIRTY-ONE

"I'm sick of this," Dooley told Edith Fay as he folded the newspaper and tossed it into a trash basket.

"What are you sick of?"

"All those unnamed sources and anonymous informants. They compromise my investigation by giving away information too soon or providing false information. They're like snakes hidin' in the bushes."

Edith Fay's phone buzzed. "I'm sorry, Dooley. I have to take this."

She held a tense, brief conversation with Ella Mae Pugh. When she clicked off her expression was grim.

"What's wrong?" he asked.

Edith Fay turned her head upward toward the white light streaming through the skylights. She set her jaw and spoke stiffly. "I'll tell you in a minute," she said, "but first tell me whether you know who the anonymous informants are."

Dooley made a decision. It was a subjective choice but also a logical one.

"I believe there are several informants," he said. "At least one of them is in my department, and I think it's Arnie Coker."

"Really?" Edith Fay exclaimed. "I thought he was one of your most trusted deputies."

"He was . . . until he started working on the side for the mayor. Standing security for him when he went to Charleston and Washington for political meetings. I guess they got thick as thieves during those trips."

"Um-hm. I've heard some rumblings along those lines," she said. "But who else do you suspect?"

Dooley got up to help himself to more coffee and banana bread.

"That bunch of guys who hang out at the Legion, you know who I mean?"

"Rymer Neff, Harley Baker and Bucky Feinmeister?" she said.

Dooley nodded. "Arnie's their ringleader. They all have too little to do and too much to say about everything. They repeat whatever they hear from Arnie to whoever they can get to listen."

"Bucky did some work in my kitchen, and he told his buddies all about it, including what I paid him," Edith Fay remarked. "People came up to me at the Value Mart, at the drugstore, even at church to tell me Bucky had shown them pictures of my entire home. I found it awkward. . . ."

"I see your point," Dooley said.

"Thelma Blivins and Hazel Simons are also culprits when it comes to spreading misinformation," Edith Fay volunteered. "Thelma consistently plies me for news. I don't give her much because she twists what she hears and makes up what she doesn't."

"Gossip is a disease around here," Dooley said.

"I wish we could do more to prevent it," Edith Fay said.

The big hall clock bonged. Dooley stared at his cup. Edith Fay mused on the life of Gudrun Wince, her sister, who had forgiven her and whom she had forgiven. Wind stirred the pawpaw and sourwood trees, and wood frogs rasped in the summer pond.

"Dooley, I have an idea about dealing with the gossips and blabbermouths," Edith Fay said.

"And catching Gudrun's killer at the same time?" he asked with a grin.

"First, let it be stated for the record that today's proceeding is highly extraordinary in that today's date is *Saturday*, June 16, 2012, and that this hearing has been scheduled at the express request of suspended employee Emerson Fellows Duty."

Unit supervisor Blaize Luzader sat at the head of the conference table in a new set of hot pink workout clothes and a bad mood.

She had agreed to Emerson's early morning entreaty for an immediate hearing, not because she sympathized with the little cheat, but rather because she wanted to get him out of her department as soon as possible and no higher-ups were available on a Saturday to witness her connection with Emerson Duty.

Also present were Emerson's dowdy wife, whose name Blaize had already forgotten despite having written it in her notes; office clerk Aveline Marsh, who had been roundly admonished by Blaize not to lose, misspell, misplace or for heaven's sake shred her report of the meeting; and Doctor Cecil Weber, who sat calmly with knees crossed and a cell phone grasped in his left hand.

"Mr. Duty has asked to make a statement," Blaize continued. "The time is 11:06 a.m. Everybody present except Dr. Cecil Weber has been asked to turn off their cell phones."

Blaize Luzader eased the zipper of her sweat top down a couple inches, then picked up a pen sprouting a purple flower and held it over a form containing many empty boxes and lines. Aveline Marsh had a death grip on a steno pad and a new package of pencils. Emerson and Eleanor held hands. Doc Weber held silence.

Emerson Fellows Duty cleared his throat. Cleared it again.

Blaize Luzader would have tapped her long fingernails on the tabletop if the recorder hadn't been on.

"I, um, wish to say that I am guilty of all the offenses that . . . my supervisor . . . accused me of on . . . what was the date? . . . on June 14, 2012."

"Let the record show," Blaize interrupted, "that the offenses at issue are failure to notify the operator of an inspected establishment of alleged violations in a timely manner, failure to give the operator of said inspected establishment the required seven days in which to answer and/or remedy alleged violations, and closure of an inspected establishment without the consultation and agreement of the unit supervisor. Is that correct, Mr. Duty?"

"Yes."

"Go on, Mr. Duty," Blaize said.

Emerson squeezed Eleanor's hand and stammered, "Um, um, well I want to say what happened that made me do it."

For forty-five minutes, Emerson Duty outlined the contacts he'd had with Biddlebourne Mayor Jass Pinbiddie, their lengthy negotiations over Jass' payment for Emerson's "services," Jass' instructions on how and when to conduct the spurious inspection, and the aftermath in which Emerson had been unable to get in touch with Jass.

At several points in his confession Emerson called on Doc Weber to display or repeat text conversations from the phone the physician had confiscated the day before.

"How much did Mayor Pinbiddie pay you for improperly inspecting the kitchen of the Glory Hallelujah Church in Biddlebourne?" Blaize asked.

"He paid me one thousand dollars, Ms. Luzader."

"Did you find any actual health code violations in the church kitchen?"

"Yes, there were violations, but all of them pertained to the unfortunate death of a woman there earlier in the day."

Blaize licked her lips and put down her pen. "Did your inspection reveal any violations of health code involving the storage, preparation or serving of food outside the area contaminated by the . . . dead body?"

"No, ma'am," Emerson said. "On the contrary, I found the refrigerators and freezers, stoves, small appliances, cabinets, serving ware, cleaning equipment, floors and all surfaces in dry, clean, temperature-controlled condition."

"Were there any signs of insect or animal infestation?"

"None, ma'am."

Blaize restacked the documents she had carried into the hearing. "Let the record reflect that the violations previously reported at the premises of the Glory Hallelujah Church in Biddlebourne, Skyler County, West Virginia, on June 14, 2012, are hereby rescinded and removed from the file of the establishment, and that the operators of the food service operation may resume said operation. The notice of violation posted at the establishment is to be removed by a representative of the Skyler County Department of Public Health on this day, June 16, 2012, and a summary of today's hearing is to be sent to the Glory Hallelujah Church, the West Virginia Department of Public Health and the Skyler County Sheriff's Department."

Relief spread through the conference room like the summer smell of alfalfa in the south forty.

Doc Weber handed Emerson's phone to Blaize Luzader. Aveline Marsh ventured a small smile.

"What will happen to me?" Emerson asked.

"I regret, Emerson, that it is my duty to terminate your employment by the Skyler County Department of Public Health. You have the right of appeal."

"Will I have to go to jail?" he asked.

"I don't know. I will have Aveline transcribe the texts on your telephone as possible evidence that you were coerced into the actions you took, but I cannot say what the courts will do."

Cecil Weber finally spoke. "If it matters, Ms. Luzader, the church does not plan to sue Mr. Duty."

Emerson and Eleanor turned to the doctor. "Thank you," they said in unison.

The Community Health and Recreation Subcommittee of the Glory Girls service organization of Glory Hallelujah Church, Biddlebourne, West Virginia, shall develop, organize and provide events, programs, projects and facilities supporting the physical health and enjoyment of Biddlebourne residents of all ages. *Glory Girls Book of Bylaws,* adopted May 1959

CHAPTER THIRTY-TWO

And just so, on a Saturday evening two days after the dastardly death of Gudrun Wince in a church kitchen, the sheriff of Skyler County and the president of the Glory Girls service organization of Glory Hallelujah Church joined hands—figuratively and actually—to figure out who had done it.

Now two notebooks rested alongside the coffee pot, teakettle and cups. Dooley's notebook was small, to fit his shirt pocket, and fat, bristling with notes, numbers, conjectures, opinions, clippings and evidence receipts.

Edith Fay's notebook was the same size as her favorite cookbook, six by nine inches, and divided by tabs. Pockets in the front and back held summaries of her thoughts on Gudrun's slaying, the kitchen sketch drawn by the Glory Girls Friday afternoon, and another sketch drawn by Edith Fay in the sleepless early hours of Friday night.

They sipped their beverages for a minute. Edith Fay said a prayer under her breath, but Dooley heard her mumbling and closed his eyes too.

Fortified, they smiled, took each other's notebooks and began reading. The owls that lived in Edith Fay's barn called soulful notes, the Taggarts' dog next door barked at a loose chicken, farm machinery clacked in the bottoms, and Dooley and Edith Fay's phones emitted sundry dings and buzzes.

Dooley closed Edith Fay's notebook first and checked his text messages. Edith Fay soon finished her own reading, went to a hall closet and returned with a handful of markers and a lined easel tablet three feet high by two feet wide.

"The Sunday school teachers draw cartoon characters on these for Bible stories," Edith Fay said, "but I use them to plan big dinners."

Dooley picked up the biggest black marker. "And today we'll use 'em to solve a murder."

"What's first?" Edith Fay asked.

"First," he replied, "we list who *didn't* do it."

The sheriff scribbled *no* at the top of a big page and said, "People who were in the kitchen Thursday morning but had no motive or opportunity to kill her. Go."

"The photographer, Winona Wilcox," she said.

"Charlie Simons, church custodian," he said.

"The church secretary, Belle Watkins."

"The four guys who delivered food."

Edith Fay observed, "It feels good to start with eight definite *didn't-do-it*s."

"Next part's harder," the sheriff said.

Ida Jean Green insisted they celebrate with a fancy dinner.

So she put on the flowered polyester dress she'd worn to the funeral of her husband Arthur, who was her third husband and Barry Dale's dad.

Barry Dale had only his work clothes, which consisted of worn jeans and T-shirts. At Ida Jean's insistence they had stopped at Walmart and bought him a new T-shirt for this occasion.

Sitting in a red plastic booth at a suburban Lexington Ponderosa, they waited for the waitress to bring them their entrees, sirloin tips with noodles for the mother, lobster and steak with fries for the son.

Ida Jean adjusted her sleeves and smiled at the other diners. But Barry Dale stared without interest at the greasy condiment bottles on the table.

"What are you thinking, Sonny?" she asked.

"Nothin,' Mom," he said. "Nothin' 'cept that surprise you been talkin' about. I been a-worryin' about it."

"Everything's gonna be all right," she said. "I can tell you now. I just figgered we'd make it a special night for both of us."

Barry Dale had taken care of his mother since Arthur Green's untimely death at age forty-six. Barry Dale was only sixteen when his dad died of a pulmonary embolism that took their small family by ugly surprise.

The teenage Barry Dale had quit Biddlebourne High School and gone to work for Jass Pinbiddie two weeks after his father's burial. Jass had taken advantage of Barry Dale's grief, and his lack of education, and his financial need every day since then.

But now Barry Dale would start over. He'd saved as much as he could from the wages paid by his penny-pinching employer, and he'd even multiplied his savings with a few conservative investments.

His plan was to settle his mother and himself in a comfortable apartment—one without a huge yard that demanded constant mowing or snow removal—and earn a GED before going to business college. Ida Jean could get a part-time job to help out.

Then, after he earned a two-year business certificate, he would open his own business and put to use all he had quietly learned at Biddlebourne Feed & Grain.

He had been planning this move for years and was secretly pleased when Jass Pinbiddie's disappearance gave him the chance, and the wherewithal, to step up the schedule.

All that could be ruined in the next few minutes.

"Okay, Mom, I'm ready."

"Well, as you know, Mr. Houston and me's been seein' each other quite a while now."

"Ye . . . ss," Barry Dale conceded.

Uel Houston, a retired farmer, came to the Greens' home every Sunday afternoon and ate dinner with Ida Jean. They talked about the weather, commodity prices and the health of calves born to the neighbors' cows.

After dinner, Ida Jean and Uel washed and dried the dishes until Barry Dale came home from Jass Pinbiddie's feed store. The three of them watched television while Barry Dale sat in the overstuffed chair with his dinner tray on his knees. Uel stayed until eight o'clock exactly, then walked home. This routine had been followed every Sunday for no fewer than five years.

Ida Jean's face flushed and she stopped speaking.

"Go ahead, Mom. It's okay."

"Me and Mr. Houston been talkin' 'bout maybe gettin' married. But I'd want your blessin' to do it."

The waitress dropped off their dinner plates and left without a backward glance. Ida Jean slid Barry Dale's plate to him before taking her own. They got busy with the seasonings and sauces and a long silence.

Barry Dale's throat was too constricted for him to eat. But he managed to say, in a muffled croak, "Mom, if you and Uel been talkin' about gettin' married, why'd you come with me?"

"I told Mr. Houston I was gonna leave with you. I know you asked me not to tell anyone, but I had to tell him so's he'd know not to come over Sunday afternoon. When I told him, he said he wanted me to stay and marry him."

"What did you answer him, Mom?"

"I told him you needed me to get settled in your new place, but I'd come back and be his wife if it was okay with you."

Barry Dale blew out a long breath.

"You're not eating, Sonny. Is something wrong with your food?"

"No, Mom. It's fine."

"Mr. Houston and me figured we could live in his house. It's his free and clear. He has his government pension, and I got mine. We won't need much. We'll get by just fine. We talked it over, and we want you to come and live with us too."

Barry Dale's brain was spinning. He had no intention of returning to Biddlebourne, not with $80,000 of Jass Pinbiddie's *store cash* in his possession. He figured that either Jass had killed Miss Wince, in which case Jass would never return to Biddlebourne, or that Jass had gone somewhere to soothe his sorrow over losing Miss Wince, in which case Jass would eventually go back to Biddlebourne, find the money missing and know who took it.

That was why Barry Dale Green wanted to put as many miles as possible between himself and Biddlebourne, West Virginia.

But Barry Dale Green also loved his mother, who had sacrificed a great deal for him and who had her own second chance at happiness now.

Hear all parties. *Proverb*

CHAPTER THIRTY-THREE

Who else didn't do it?" The sheriff stabbed the marker on the big tablet while he numbered a few lines.

"Jass didn't do it," declared Edith Fay.

"Why not?"

"When she was killed, he was in the city building arguing with my pastor about meal taxes. That's one reason."

"He coulda paid someone. We need more."

"I have more," she said. "Very simply, Jass Pinbiddie and Gudrun Wince were in love."

"Are you sure?"

"Dooley, I've been over to the high school dozens of times to work out service projects with Gudrun. Whether we were talking, visiting classrooms or interviewing volunteers, she received and made a constant stream of cell phone calls. They were . . . intimate and personal, and she addressed her caller as J.P. Besides, we all saw how Jass behaved at the church when he realized she was gone."

"Then why did he leave town?" Dooley quizzed Edith Fay.

"He left town because he's afraid he'll be linked to the illegal diamond business through the investigation of Gudrun's murder," she said. "He's probably guilty of a lot that's criminal around here, but not of murder."

Dooley stroked *J A S S* into the *no* category and added, "Plus, I think Doc Weber's right that Jass and Gudrun were in cahoots in the diamond business. They needed each other, that is, unless he wanted to cut her out. But, nah, there woulda been a dozen less messier ways to do it than a stabbin' in a church."

"That's a big one out of the picture," Edith Fay said. "Who's next?"

"Laverna Wharton."

"Did she really come to your office this morning?" Edith Fay asked.

"She brought in Gudrun's purse," he said, "but she wouldn't tell me how she got it." The sheriff shook his head.

"I can tell you why she wanted it—and give you my guess as to how she got it," Edith Fay said.

Dooley listened closely as Edith Fay recounted Laverna's unexpected visit, her presentation of the unusual chicken casserole, and the Girls' suspicions that Laverna had illicitly obtained the recipes of the late high school teacher Theodocia Price.

"I spoke with Laverna at length after the other Glory Girls left," Edith Fay explained. "I asked how she got the chicken recipe, but she wouldn't tell me."

"You sure that recipe used to belong to Theodocia Price?" the sheriff asked.

"Without question."

"Hmm." Dooley rubbed his chin. "All she confessed to this morning was having Gudrun's purse."

"Dooley, was there a recipe box in it?" she asked.

"No, just the usual woman's stuff."

"Hmm." Edith Fay fetched a bowl and a basket of fresh green beans from the counter, returned to the table and began snapping the beans. Dooley stared out a window. The hall clock ticked and the bean pods cracked.

"Dooley, I interviewed Buddy Lee yesterday after you did," Edith Fay blurted. "That's what led to my speculation on how Laverna got Gudrun's purse."

Dooley rubbed his brow. "Sounds like you've been doing your own investigatin'," he said in a flat tone.

"I must apologize, Dooley," she said. "I felt responsible because we Girls allowed Buddy Lee to participate in the cook-off. The consequences for the church would be . . . extensive if Buddy Lee committed a murder while on the church payroll. I desperately needed to clarify that question."

"What did you conclude?" Dooley asked.

"Buddy Lee told me that he went to Value Mart to buy butter for Gudrun—and that he dropped Gudrun's purse into a recycling cart behind the store after his purchase."

The sheriff slapped his holster and said, "I knew I shoulda checked the outside tapes as well as the inside tapes from the store. Dad blast it all!"

Edith Fay continued, "I asked Buddy Lee how he got the purse out of the church, and he said he just put it in that backpack he carries around everywhere. He said it was easy because Gudrun had her purse under the counter and Mary Ellen Brinkman had instructed him to pull the biggest cook pots from the lower cabinets for the contestants to use."

"This was right after the contest started?" Dooley interrupted to ask.

"Yes. Buddy Lee said Laverna had paid him $100 to get Gudrun's recipe box, and Laverna told him it would be in Gudrun's purse."

"Wait a minute," Dooley said. "Didn't Gudrun need the recipe box to cook her entry?"

"Of all the cooks I've ever known, Gudrun was the least likely to follow a recipe. She had no concept, no concept at all, how to prepare food. Didn't know a whisk from a grater."

Dooley was scratching his chin and tapping his left foot. "Makes no sense, Edith Fay. How did she hope to make food for the contest if she couldn't even read a recipe and didn't know one tool from the other?"

"You ever hear of YouTube, Dooley?" Edith Fay asked. "Look here."

Edith Fay took her expensive phone from her apron pocket and entered a search phrase that produced a clip of a famous TV chef making dim sum.

"I gotta pay more attention to technology," Dooley confessed. "I had no idea this kinda stuff is online. Shoot, I could even learn to cook," he said, laughing.

"I can think of a better way for you to learn to cook," Edith Fay said with a smile. "Anyway, Buddy Lee could hardly believe his good luck when he spotted Gudrun's purse—with the recipe box in it—where she had placed it for safekeeping in that bottom cabinet.

"He said nobody was looking at him. Each cook was checking her stove, her ingredients, her utensils. He just popped the purse into his backpack and planned to carry it out of the church after the contest.

"But when Gudrun asked him to go to the Value Mart, he took advantage of it by dropping the purse into the bin behind the market. He used that pay phone in front of Elderdon's Pharmacy to call Laverna and let her know where it was."

"That little devil," Dooley commented. "Gave me nine pages o' notes on what happened at the cook-off. Left out everything you just told me, of course. He's smarter 'n I thought."

"Most everybody thinks that," Edith Fay noted. "Buddy Lee's learned to use it."

"So . . . then . . . you think the purse-nappin' had nothing to do with the murder," Dooley observed.

"Yes, and not just because Buddy Lee had no motive to kill Gudrun, but also because Laverna's motive was something else.

"Laverna wants to be a Glory Girl in the worst way," Edith Fay went on. "She made a production of her 40th birthday, and I think the main reason was to announce she was age-eligible for the Girls."

"Pardon me, but you ladies have more rules than the state legislature," Dooley said. "I don't know how you keep 'em all straight."

"There are probably fewer than you think," she said with a chuckle. "And we keep them straight with good records, for your information."

"I am advised," Dooley said. "But go on."

"As I've said, Laverna yesterday showed me a recipe that certainly came from Theodocia Price. Theodocia had kept that recipe as a kind of joke—an inside joke. When Theodocia died, Gudrun took her recipes from her classroom. Just went in and took everything out of her desk without asking the family or anyone else that I know of."

"You saw that happen?" Dooley interjected.

"No, but two students saw it happen, and I believed them when they told me."

Dooley scratched his jaw. "I gotta say I don't exactly see how that exonerates Laverna."

"Laverna has her heart and soul set on becoming a Glory Girl. She might lie and cheat to make that happen and hope not to be found out, but committing murder would of course put her out of the running for good. She just would not risk that."

Dooley took a deep breath. "Edith Fay, if she would lie and cheat, I'm not so sure she wouldn't kill."

"All right," Edith Fay said slowly. "I know something else that I will trust you not to repeat," she said. "It's not directly related to the case."

"All right, I promise," Dooley said reluctantly. "What is it?"

"Laverna wants a child desperately. Probably more desperately than she wants to be a Glory Girl. Ending life is so opposed to her personal views that she could not live with herself as a mother if she did such a thing."

"I thought there was a rule that a Glory Girl can't have children," he interjected.

"The rule is that a Glory Girl may not have children in her care at home, but Laverna wants to make her mark as a Glory Girl before a baby comes."

"And that's why she was willing to turn in the purse this morning," Dooley said. "She already had what she wanted from it—the recipes. But that doesn't clear Laverna either."

"There's one last thing," she said.

He gazed steadily at her, waiting.

"When I talked with Laverna yesterday about the recipes, she was sneezing all the while. But then I asked her if she killed Gudrun. I asked her that outright. And she stopped sneezing. She said that, no, she had not killed Gudrun, and she seemed shocked and offended that I'd asked. That's her tell, Dooley. Laverna has always sneezed when she's nervous. I noticed it the first time when she applied for the open Glory Girls spot last year. She sneezed like she'd sniffed black pepper for lunch. I've seen her do it three or four other times since then."

Dooley seemed to be mulling what she said.

"I've thought all along there were two crimes: the murder of Gudrun and the theft of her purse and recipe box," Edith Fay supplied.

"Okay," Dooley said as he slowly marked *L a v e r n a* on the *no* list. "There's only one more so-called likely suspect."

"Buddy Lee," she said.

"My gut tells me no," Dooley said. "I've known the kid all his life and haven't seen anything even close to this outta him. I guess there's a long shot someone paid him to do it, but he's such a screw-up that no one in their right mind would hire him as a hit man."

Edith Fay added a thought. "I regret it, but the Girls won't even hire him again to lift stew pots."

"By the way, don't be surprised if you hear through the grapevine that Buddy Lee has also left town," the sheriff said nonchalantly as he put the young man's name on the *no* page.

"Really? I would think that sheds a different light on what we just decided about him," Edith Fay said, pointing to the *no* page.

Dooley grinned. "I think he and Patty Leta Keys spent the night together somewhere."

"Oh, my. I'm surprised."

Dooley eyed Edith Fay but said nothing. He flipped the page, picked up his notebook and proceeded to write under *maybe*:

Glory Girls—Edith Fay Smith, Lloyda Ruth Dent, Shari Odell Ankrum, Mary Ellen Brinkman, Ella Mae Pugh, Zula Ruby Hissom, Alwildia Louise Doak, Ula Maude Ferrebee, Fonda Renee Postlethwaite, Bida June Pyles and Jo Claire Carsey.

Cook-off contestants—Eulalah Bee Pritchard, Marcella Ivy Weekley, Roma June Riggle, Penny Kay Gorby, Imogene Dess Dotson, Ivajean Hardman, Emmy Rae Newsome and Daisy Anson Duff.

Edith Fay could not help noticing that her name was at the top of the list.

The Housing Subcommittee of the Glory Girls service organization of Glory Hallelujah Church, Biddlebourne, West Virginia, shall assist Biddlebourne residents ages eighteen (18) years and better in obtaining and maintaining housing in Skyler County. *Glory Girls Book of Bylaws,* adopted May 1959

SUNDAY, JUNE 17

CHAPTER THIRTY-FOUR

Saturday's expected rain waited until Sunday morning— Sunday morning at the exact moment the congregation of Glory Hallelujah Church said "Amen" and quick-stepped out of Saint John's Church to head for the Mug's lunch buffet.

The sky over Biddlebourne spit raindrops as big and sharp as frozen peas. A rare east wind swirled the peas around buildings and trees as if to make soup. Lightning jabbed the horizon, and thunder boomed and echoed off the mountains.

Soaked to their skins, those who hungered for meatloaf and fried chicken piled into their minivans and pickup trucks while the Glory Hallelujah pastor stepped down from her borrowed pulpit, choir members stacked their borrowed hymnals, and two of the Glory Girls huddled in a borrowed classroom.

"Are you sure?" Edith Fay asked. A thunderclap split the air, sharp and short, and she shuddered.

"I wish I weren't," said Ella Mae Pugh. "I've checked the charts three times. She's the only one who had the opportunity to do it."

Edith Fay replayed the routine in her mind. The assignment of contestants to cooking stations. The instructions given orally and in writing. The timepieces of contestants synchronized to the clock in the kitchen. The inspection of contestants' purses and totes for electronics, forbidden ingredients or other contraband.

A pain spiraled from the middle of Edith's back to her neck. She rotated her head to ease the pressure and said, "Go through it one more time, please."

"I want the garage cleaned out today," Bertha Baker announced at lunch. "Your tools are all over the place, and I can barely get my car inside. It's gonna be a mess after this storm and you'll need to get the car into the garage to wax it again."

Harley Baker, who had planned to spend the afternoon at Creed Fedderman's house watching sports reruns and helping solve Gudrun Wince's murder, groaned.

Much to his surprise and chagrin, Bertha heard him.

It was not the response she sought.

So Harley got on the horn to Creed. "Nah, no hope o' comin' over today," he said. "Bertha's got a bee the size of a baseball in her bonnet."

"Just as well," Creed Fedderman said. "Rymer's missus got him paintin' that fruit cellar o' hers. And, oh yeah, ya know that stone wall out front o' Bucky's house holdin' up his wife's rosebushes? Well, the storm started undoin' the wall and she won't leave off him till he fixes it up."

"In the rain?"

"Said he'd rather be standin' outside in a hailstorm than sittin' in the house with her right now," Creed reported.

"Maybe we ticked off the girls with our little adventure the other night," Harley surmised.

"Looks like it. Listen, I gotta go. Zelma wants to use the phone. Says it's urgent."

Harley Baker clicked off and sent a text message to Arnie Coker, who always had an idea how to avoid an irksome chore.

But Arnie did not text back. As it happened, Deputy Coker was driving to Charleston, where on orders of Sheriff Dooley Skiles he was to personally observe and report on the state medical examiner's examination of Gudrun Wince's body. And Sheriff Skiles did not permit his deputies to use private cell phones while driving county vehicles.

"And then Mayor Pinbiddie gave me the money, and I left Biddlebourne," Emerson Duty said.

Sheriff Skiles, with whom Emerson had just enjoyed a free and delicious meal of pork chops and gravy over real mashed potatoes, nodded. "Was that the only such transaction you ever had with Mayor Pinbiddie?"

"It was the only transaction that actually happened. He called me once before and asked me to do something similar at a

Republican fundraiser, but me, I don't get into politics. I am, I mean I was a government employee."

Astounded at Emerson Duty's belated display of uprightness, Dooley stuffed a spoonful of potatoes into his gob and managed not to smile.

"All right, then, Emerson. I have . . . looks like . . . about three pages of notes here. That oughtta do it."

"Sheriff?"

"Yeah? Ya got somethin' else?"

"I just need to know if we've got a deal. I turned all my evidence over to you like I said I would. Will you hold up your end of it?"

"Mr. Duty, I have every intention of keeping my word."

Laverna Inys Wharton retched and heaved.

No remnant of her breakfast, lunch or dinner remained in her body.

No movement of her body felt normal.

No thought in her head seemed sane.

But today she was the happiest woman in the world, and William the happiest man. They were lying on the bed in their underwear.

"When do you think it will be?" he asked.

"About the end of January," she said, laughing despite the wave of nausea that started in her midsection and rose without mercy to her throat.

"May I get you something, maybe some toast?" William asked.

"Oh, no. The smells. The sounds. I want nothing to do with food—nothing at all."

It was easier to break into Biddlebourne Feed & Grain the second time.

But Barry Dale Green took his mother home first. Ida Jean Green was now entertaining her fiancé, Uel Houston, with carefully edited stories of the whirlwind trip she and Barry Dale had just completed.

After Ida Jean had run into the house with a garbage bag over her head, Barry Dale had approached his neighbor Howdy Fitchell, who was sitting on his screened porch with a six-pack of Coors and his girlfriend. They caught up on various bits of news, including the fact that Jass Pinbiddie hadn't showed up for Saturday night poker.

"Ask me, old Jass done it and ain't never gonna come back," Howdy said with a burp for his buddy and a wink for his girl.

"Well, I gotta git all that stuff in," Barry Dale said as he turned to leave.

Howdy and the other neighbors who watched Barry Dale unload numerous household goods from his vehicle clucked in respect for his efforts to prevent home theft and in pity for his having to do the job in pounding rain and sloppy mud.

The neighbor on the other side, however, tossed the Saturday edition of the Skyler County *Sentinel* onto Barry Dale's broken sidewalk. The Sunday edition had not yet appeared, its delivery having been delayed by the relentless thunderstorm.

Barry Dale had sat in his 4Runner reading the latest on Jass Pinbiddie. So now, filled with a volatile mix of fatigue and fury, Barry Dale parked the vehicle in front of Biddlebourne Feed & Grain. In broad daylight obscured only by thick thunderclouds, he used his key to open the front door of Jass Pinbiddie's store, walked to the closet that held Jass Pinbiddie's safe and put back Jass Pinbiddie's $80,000.

Barry Dale had worked out the scenarios in his head while driving home from Lexington. If a deputy or a nosey townie came while he was in the store, he'd say he was checking the place for his absent boss. If somebody asked why he had the safe open, he'd say he was checking the drawer change for Monday's customers.

However, nobody nosey or otherwise showed up. He was slightly disappointed.

So Barry Dale locked up the store and went to the Value Mart. He hit the front door ten minutes before closing time and bought the grocery items on the list provided by Ida Jean, plus a case of Cherry Coke, half a dozen packages of Oreos and two dozen Heat and Eat Turkey n' Trimmins meals.

Barry Dale stashed his personal groceries under a blanket in the passenger seat of his vehicle and took the other items home to Ida Jean. When he arrived he found his mother and Uel Houston smooching on the couch, a spectacle that sent him to his room without dinner.

In his bedroom, Barry Dale opened the newspaper provided by his neighbor and turned to the job ads.

When he went to the kitchen around eleven to get a glass of milk and a sandwich, Barry Dale found a note on the table from Ida Jean.

"Sonny, I know you done it for me. You gave me another chance at happiness. Uel says he's awful glad we come back. I'm going home with Uel tonight. We'll be over tomorrow to pick up my clothes. You are a good son. Love, Mom."

Barry Dale folded the note and put it in the pocket of his pajamas before drinking his milk and eating his sandwich.

"The law is an ass." *Comment familiarized by Charles Dickens*

CHAPTER THIRTY-FIVE

On Sunday afternoon at 3:45 in the back room of the sheriff's station, the capture and prosecution of Jasper Eugene "Jass" Pinbiddie changed jurisdictions.

Sixteen Chinese takeout boxes, hand-delivered by Li Chu himself on promise of a $100 tip, sat empty on top of a chair appropriated from the duty room. Because this room was a cheap add-on that grew hot in summer and cold in winter, it was the one place at the station where deputies did not gather to shoot the bull.

Skyler County Sheriff Dooley Skiles, who had limited his lunch intake, pushed a boxful of financial documents along the streaked linoleum to Miles McCullough.

"All yours," he said.

FBI Special Agent McCullough grinned and started picking through the papers. "Oh, boy," he said. "Oh, boy. This is terrific."

"What's in there?" Andy Brewster asked between mouthfuls of shrimp fried rice.

Dooley said, "Printouts from Pinbiddie's computer, ledgers that he kept at his home and at his business, and seven or eight notebooks—you know, the kind kids use in school—filled with diagrams and lists and names."

"The mother lode," Andy said.

"That's not all I'm turnin' over today," the sheriff said. "Look at this."

Dooley took a large manila envelope from a box of evidence marked "Pinbiddie" and removed two items from it.

"You got x-rays of his teeth? To ID him? Whoa, that's brilliant," said Andy.

"Ha! That's not a bad idea," Dooley allowed, "but these here are x-rays of capsules I found in the purse belonging to Gudrun Wince, our murder victim. Here. Look for yourselves."

Agent McCullough whistled in awe. "Whoa! Are those rough diamonds?"

"Sure look like it to me," the sheriff confirmed. "I gotta keep the purse and its contents in evidence for my case, but these will help your case against Pinbiddie. I got my own set."

"Sheriff Skiles, you're gonna get a commendation from the Department of Justice. I just don't know when."

"Does that mean you and your boys haven't tracked Pinbiddie down yet?" asked Andy.

The agent shook his head. "Got him as far as the Ontario airport. I got people tryin' to figure out what he did then. These papers oughta help."

"All kindsa places would welcome an American with money to burn," Andy observed.

"Yeah, and would flip a finger at American efforts to bring him back," Dooley said.

"There are some special weapons we can bring to bear in the case," Miles said.

"Such as?" Dooley asked.

The FBI agent leaned back and stretched his arms. "Such as the United States Department of State, which has a special office that deals with conflict diamonds. They'll plug us into people and places most likely to shelter Pinbiddie."

All was quiet for a while as Dooley responded to text messages and Andy and Miles worked on their meals.

"Wait a minute," Andy said when he'd eaten the food on his plate and ascertained that none was left in the boxes.

"What?" Miles asked.

Andy turned to the sheriff and said, "You givin' the feebs, sorry Miles, this material. Does that mean Jass is out as a suspect in your murder investigation?"

Dooley's face relaxed into a wide smile and he laughed.

"Sure does."

The green plates, picturing an old grist mill, had been formed and fired at the Scio Pottery Company in Ohio before World War II and given to Julia Burdette Stealey upon her marriage to Malcolm Smith.

The china glowed on Edith Fay's cream linen tablecloth, the one on which her late grandmother had hidden her initials after buying the fabric from McCrory's in Wheeling, stamping it with the blue outline of three hundred flowers and leaves, and hand-embroidering those florals in red, orange, yellow, purple and green thread.

This was only the second time Edith Fay had used her mother's favorite dishes, the first being the luncheon at which she had hosted two of her Wellesley College sorority sisters who dropped by to give her a certificate proclaiming her to be an Alumna of Distinction.

Two circumstances prompted today's celebration.

The first was the liberation of the Glory Hallelujah Church premises from law enforcement occupation. Sheriff Skiles had telephoned the news to Pastor Scovill around noon, and members of the Glory Girls ad hoc cleaning team had hastened forthwith to the church complex.

The second happy circumstance was that Dooley was coming to dinner.

Not a snack. Not a sandwich and slaw. Not leftovers. No. A real dinner of corn and scallion salad, grilled flank steak, cinnamon-roasted sweet potatoes, summer squash gratin with salsa Verde and Gruyere cheese and, for dessert, a fresh cherry tart.

Dooley arrived with a bouquet of cooking herbs, a jug of homemade sweet tea and a small box of Godiva chocolates, each item dampened a bit by rain. Edith Fay gave him a hug and a smile.

"I didn't have time to change out of my uniform," he said as he laid his gun and holster on the hall table.

"Doesn't matter a bit," Edith Fay said. "Dinner's all ready."

Dooley stopped short at the kitchen door. "What a great-lookin' spread," he said. "Thank you, Edith Fay."

"You're welcome, Dooley. Those are Mother's dishes," she explained.

"Currier and Ives?" he asked.

"Yes! How did you know?"

Dooley blushed. "Aw, Grandma Kearns had some like that."

Needing to change the subject, he said, "Edith Fay, do you have a nickname?"

"Not really, though Dad called me Edie Fay sometimes. Why?"

"Can I call you Edie Fay too? I know we haven't talked about . . . things yet, but I'd count it a privilege to . . . uh . . ."

"To court me?"

Edith Fay put down a dish of butter and walked to Dooley. She kissed his cheek and lingered near his ear to whisper, "You may call me Edie Fay . . . privately."

Dooley's pulse quickened. His ragged breathing gave him away, but he didn't care. He bent his head slightly and touched her lips with his own. He kissed her passionately, and she responded passionately.

After a moment, she pulled away and said, "Everything's getting cool."

Dooley laughed and said, "Not everything, Edie Fay."

They took their time with the meal, savoring the marinated steak, toasting with the sweet tea and closing their eyes with the sweet pleasure of the flaky-crusted tart.

Dooley got up and started putting the dishes into the dishwasher.

"Oh, I should have mentioned it, Dooley," Edith Fay said. "I wash Mother's dishes by hand. Just stack them on the sink, please. I'll do them later."

"No, ma'am," Dooley said. He turned on the tap and looked under the sink for dish detergent.

"Dooley," Edith Fay protested.

"I insist," he said. To prove it, he took Edith Fay's denim everyday apron from a hook next to the back door and tied it over his uniform. "Sit right there," he commanded as he splashed silverware into the water.

He whistled a tune as he washed the utensils until Edith Fay spoke. "Dooley, there are some things that perhaps I should have told you about earlier," she said.

He turned and smiled. "What things?"

She hesitated.

The sheriff laid the dish sponge on the sink and went to sit next to Edith Fay. "What's got your tongue, Edie Fay?" He held her warm hands in his soapy ones.

"Oh, my goodness. Well, nothing's to be gained by putting it off," she said, swallowing hard. She bent to a tote bag on the floor and took out the sketch of the kitchen drawn by the Girls, notes of her conversations with Ella Mae Pugh, and a Saturday edition of the Skyler County *Sentinel*.

"Dooley, as you know, I've been . . . taking my own . . . look into Gudrun's death. I think I know who did it."

The Education Subcommittee of the Glory Girls service organization of Glory Hallelujah Church, Biddlebourne, West Virginia, shall provide textbooks and other school supplies to qualified students enrolled in Biddlebourne public schools, and scholarships to qualified Biddlebourne adult students enrolled in college or trade school. *Glory Girls Book of Bylaws,* adopted May 1959

THURSDAY, JUNE 21

CHAPTER THIRTY-SIX

The people of Biddlebourne laid Gudrun Wince to rest.

They opened the gymnasium of Biddlebourne High School for the occasion, and members of the Future Teachers of America Club escorted 1,791 attendees to their seats, by actual count of the club's recording secretary.

The Rev. Annie Ido Scovill, Gudrun's longtime pastor, gave a very fine talk about Gudrun's dedication to the children of the community, an attitude mirroring that of Jesus Christ himself.

Everybody said *amen* when she stepped down from the podium.

Mayor Pro-Tem Ernie Blankenship gave a very long talk about projects he had worked on with Gudrun, projects he was sorry he had not worked on with Gudrun, and projects he might lead in the future that would surely do Gudrun proud if she were alive to see them.

Everybody said *hallelujah* when he stepped down from the podium.

The funeral committee, formed of persons unable to come up with workable excuses from the duty, severally recited writings by famed educators, fittingly including Dr. Diane L. Reinhard, the first woman to serve as acting president of West Virginia University.

Everyone clapped when the funeral committee stepped down.

Edith Fay Smith, leader of a local women's group, gave a very brief talk on Gudrun's community service through Glory

Hallelujah Church. Nobody applauded those comments, but the people rose from their seats as one when Edith Fay announced the establishment of the Gudrun C. Wince Memorial Trust to pay for the four-year college education of any qualified resident of Biddlebourne.

The parents and grandparents, bankers and lawyers, accountants and merchants, teachers and pastors, doctors and dentists, builders and plumbers roared with approval. Janessa and Jeremy Graber, parents of seven, jitterbugged in the aisle until a future teacher admonished them. The president of the Biddlebourne Chamber of Commerce, Abe Montrose, who had not organized the grand opening of a new store in eight years, stood and wept.

Edith Fay spoke once more. "Also, friends, in honor of our benefactress Gudrun Cassandra Wince, a bronze likeness of her will be erected in the town square next to the veterans' memorial and the recently authorized monument to the town's . . um . . sanitation engineers."

Her final comment quieted the people, but after a moment they all shrugged and filed out of the gymnasium while Mary Ellen Brinkman sang, "School days, school days, dear old Golden Rule days. . . ."

It was the best funeral lunch anyone in Biddlebourne could remember.

Not just because the sky hung blue and nearly cloudless over Hearth House.

Or because a sweet west wind blew among the mourners.

Or because Rowdy Gibson and the Poorhouse Gang played banjos and fiddles on the lawn while the diners sat in the shade of the pavilion.

Or because they feasted on barbecued beef ribs, pulled pork and fried chicken.

Or even because the menu featured Gudrun Wince's suddenly famous Mammy's Marvelous Biscuit Casserole, in a version discreetly adapted by Zula Ruby Hissom and containing broccoli because, as it turned out, that was Gudrun's favorite vegetable.

No. The highlight of the day happened around three in the afternoon, when the guests were thinking how good a nap would feel and the only people on their feet were the eleven Glory Girls, several dozen members of the Ladies Aid Society, the husbands or boyfriends of those women, and church custodian Charlie Simons.

Two sheriff's cruisers stopped at the curb next to the pavilion. Sheriff Dooley Skiles, four deputies and Corndog the Coonhound got out and walked to the spot where two Girls were bristle-brushing burnt stuff off the griddles.

The women looked up in surprise. "You boys are a little late for lunch," said Shari Odell Ankrum. "But we can rustle you up something. You need it in boxes?"

But Dooley did not reply. With his deputies in a tight line on either side of him, he walked over to a Glory Girl who had her hands in a bucket of water that smelled of ammonia.

"Alwildia Louise Doak, I'm placing you under arrest for the murder of Gudrun Cassandra Wince. You have the right to remain silent. Anything you say can and will be used against you in a court of law. You have the right to an attorney. If you cannot afford an attorney, one will be provided for you. Do you understand the rights I have just read to you?"

Atremble, Alwildia Louise lowered her head and whispered, "Yes."

She held out her hands, and Chief Deputy Stan Neiswonder obliged her by clicking a set of handcuffs to her wrists.

Dooley continued, "With these rights in mind, do you wish to speak to me?"

"No."

The hush that had fallen over Hearth House turned into a gentle rush of air as diners and workers breathed out. By coincidence, a single gossamer cloud floated past the sun and shifted the shadows around Glory Hallelujah Church and Biddlebourne, West Virginia.

The Poorhouse Gang put down their banjos and bows. The Girls with the bristle brushes bowed their heads. Tears brimmed from the eyes of Alwildia's best friend, Bida June Pyles.

Edith Fay walked quietly to Dooley and said, "May I say something to Alwildia?"

"Make it brief, Edie Fay," he murmured.

Edith Fay pressed a handkerchief into Alwildia's hand and said, "We'll get you a lawyer."

CHAPTER THIRTY-SEVEN

Church Worker Charged in Wince Slaying
'She was going to ruin it all,' Suspect Claims
by Wilford Nicklin
Sentinel Staff Writer
Friday, June 22, 2012

Skyler County Sheriff Dooley Skiles yesterday arrested a longtime church volunteer in the stabbing death of Biddlebourne High School Principal Gudrun C. Wince, whose bloody body was discovered June 14 during a cooking competition at Glory Hallelujah Church.

Alwildia Louise Doak, a member of the widely known Glory Girls service group at Glory Hallelujah Church, was arrested Thursday afternoon in Hearth House, the church's picnic pavilion, at a lunch after the funeral of Miss Wince.

Doak, 47, a resident of West Street in Biddlebourne, was arraigned later Thursday before Circuit Court Judge Timothy W. Lincoln, who set bond at $300,000. Doak remained in the Skyler County Jail this morning.

In an exclusive interview with the *Sentinel*, Doak admitted stabbing Miss Wince with a knife around 12:30 p.m. during an elimination cook-off for membership in the Glory Girls. Eight other contestants also competed.

Questioned about her motive for the slaying, Doak told the *Sentinel* that she feared Miss Wince's involvement in certain activities, all unrelated to the work of the Glory Girls, would hinder the group's mission of providing support and assistance across a broad range of community issues. .

"She (Wince) was up to no good," Doak said. "She had no business even trying out for the Glory Girls. But she done passed all the preliminaries, so we had to let her do the cook-off."

The cook-off follows strict rules, according to Glory Girls spokeswoman Ella Mae Pugh, because the group acquires its mission funding from private and public meals served at the sprawling church complex on Bailey Street.

"She was going to ruin it all," Doak said. "The Glory Girls stand for good, not for evil."

Bainton Boyles, a criminal defense attorney from Pittsburgh, arrived during Doak's interview and advised his client to comment no further.

Skiles said a 7-inch Wusthof fish fillet knife was seized from Doak's residence Thursday morning, but he would not say whether it was the suspected murder weapon. (See story and photo on page 3.)

Biddlebourne Mayor Jasper E. "Jass" Pinbiddie, who witnesses said went to the church soon after the discovery of Miss Wince's body and expressed anguish over her death, reportedly left town the same day.

Though Pinbiddie was initially sought as a person of interest in the slaying, Skiles said Thursday night that a "sufficiency of evidence" showed Doak to be the sole perpetrator.

However, sources close to the Wince investigation, speaking on condition of anonymity, said Pinbiddie had been named in another, wider investigation unrelated to the Biddlebourne slaying. (See story and photo on page 3.)

Buddy Lee Delbert, 27, of Biddlebourne, who assisted contestants during the cook-off, returned from what he called a "mini-vacation" early this week and denied he had been a suspect in the slaying. "All I done was find the body," he said at the home of his wife, the former Patty Leta Keys. "I wrote out everything that happened on paper and gave it to Doo (Sheriff Skiles). Well, I did leave town when maybe he didn't want me to, but me and Patty Leta didn't want to be bothered on our honeymoon."

Skiles declined further comment on details of the slaying, saying only that they would come out in the trial.

Pinbiddie's commercial property, Biddlebourne Feed & Grain, was closed for four days after Miss Wince's death but reopened Tuesday under management of longtime store employee Barry Dale Green, who told the *Sentinel* that he took over its operation through a previous arrangement with Pinbiddie.

Miss Wince, a fixture in Skyler County education, began as a teacher of business education at Biddlebourne High School in 1989 and was named principal in 2001. School graduation rates climbed and truancy rates dropped during her tenure, according to Sloan McKenzie of the Skyler County Board of Education, who noted, "We've lost a fine educator in Gudrun Wince."

Nearly 2,000 mourners attended her funeral Thursday morning at Biddlebourne High School. Edith Fay Smith, administrator and heir of Miss Wince's reportedly large estate, announced formation of the Gudrun C. Wince Memorial Trust to provide college funding for Biddlebourne students. (See story and picture on page 3.)

Mayor Pro-Tem Ernie Blankenship reported that designs are being considered for a statue to be erected in the Biddlebourne town square in memory of Miss Wince. (See full obituary on page 3.)

Murder is always a mistake—one should never do anything one
cannot talk about after dinner. *Oscar Wilde*

CHAPTER THIRTY-EIGHT

Hearth House reflected a new calm after the sheriff and his
posse left with Alwildia Louise Doak and a bagful of beef bones
for Corndog.

The Ladies Aid Society and their significant others, along with
the Glory Girls, sat at the long picnic tables with their feet up on
the benches.

They had already prayed together for Alwildia and her family
and called Bainton Boyles, who had represented Mary Ellen
Brinkman's distant cousin Leroy Brinkman on car-theft charges
and specialized in defendants who had done what they were
accused of but otherwise had led lawful lives.

"We need to get ready for the next cook-off," said Lloyda Ruth
Dent.

"And for *Home Cookin'* magazine," added Ula Maude
Ferrebee.

"Well, first we must bring Family Ministry Day home and do
the Asher wedding reception," said Jo Claire Carsey.

The Girls nodded because they were too tired to speak and
because they, and the Ladies Aid Society and everybody else in
Biddlebourne, wanted at that moment to hear about only one topic.

The moment had come, and Edith Fay was ready.

"Here's what happened," she began. The women settled in and
drank their leftover lemonade.

"As you all know, Buddy Lee was helping the cook-off
contestants with heavier tasks. After they arrived at their assigned
cooking stations, he took out the big pots from the lower cabinets.
Gudrun had placed her purse under the counter, and Buddy took
that opportunity to steal her purse, which contained her recipes. He
wanted the purse because Laverna Inys Wharton had bribed him to
get Gudrun's recipes, which, as many of you have suspected,
Gudrun stole from Theodocia Price at the high school. During the
contest, Gudrun cheated by muting her cell phone and using it to

access a YouTube cooking video. There's no use pretending Gudrun could cook worth a darn. She knew she couldn't win without giving herself an edge, whether or not it fell within our rules. When Gudrun had mixed her entry and was ready to bake it, she didn't have enough butter to grease the dish and dot the top of the casserole. So she asked Buddy Lee to go to the Value Mart and buy it. She told Buddy Lee to hurry because she still needed an hour to bake her casserole. Buddy told me later that he became frightened when Gudrun asked him to run the store errand because he had taken her purse from the cabinet by then. But he was relieved when Gudrun took out a money clip—from her bra, he told me—and gave him the money. At that point, Alwildia Louise spilled sugar near another cooking station to create a diversion. You will remember that we allowed the contestants to take a comfort break while Buddy Lee swept up the sugar and mopped the floor. The eight other contestants did leave the kitchen for a break, but Gudrun stayed, though we are not sure why. At any rate, we believe that Alwildia and Gudrun were alone in the kitchen after Buddy Lee cleaned up the spill and went to Value Mart. That was when Alwildia . . . attacked Gudrun."

Edith Fay gave the women an opportunity to absorb the information. Eulalah Bee Pritchard started to ask a question but thought better of it.

Edith Fay continued, "The rest is what you witnessed when Buddy Lee came back from the market and found Gudrun on the floor."

Eulalah Bee could contain herself no longer. "Edith Fay, I heard that Buddy Lee gave the purse to Laverna Wharton. Did he give it to her at the Value Mart? Because of the recipe box? I know Gudrun carried that recipe box around in her purse. I saw it for myself."

Charlie Simons was washing the concrete floor at the opposite end of the pavilion, and his mop made swish-slap sounds. The town church bells rang five o'clock. The women waited for Edith Fay's answer.

"There is a connection between Buddy Lee and Laverna and Gudrun's recipes, but it really has nothing to do with Gudrun's death," Edith Fay said. "The sheriff asked me not to elaborate about it, so I won't. It will help tremendously if all of us refrain from speculating on that aspect."

"How did Gudrun sneak a phone into the contest?" Opal Burch asked.

"She carried it in her bra," Edith Fay said. "She had the phone on one, um, side and her money on the other."

The women stifled stray giggles while Edith Fay went on, "The sheriff reports that her cell phone was found in a canister of flour."

"The big question in my mind is what Alwildia hoped to gain by killing Gudrun," Mary Ellen mused.

Edith Fay looked to Ella Mae Pugh, who picked up the report. "We must be careful not to speculate among ourselves on matters that could compromise the case. I will say, though, that Alwildia took advantage of her position as a cook-off organizer."

"And Alwildia Louise helped guard the crime scene after Buddy Lee came upon the body. Oh, my goodness. Who knows what she did while she was standing over there," Zula Ruby exclaimed.

Patience, time and money accommodate all things. *Proverb*

CHAPTER THIRTY-NINE

And so life changed—just a little—in Biddlebourne and environs because of Gudrun Wince.

The Glory Girls, thanking God thoroughly for looking after the people of Biddlebourne and Skyler County, invested a hefty portion of Gudrun Wince's estate in high-yield certificates of deposit to support scholarships and other community betterment.

Marthleen Lewis swore she saw Jass Pinbiddie tagged in a Facebook picture that disappeared from the site the next day.

Arnie Coker was placed on permanent patrol duty and had to haul in speeders eight hours a day in the outer reaches of the county.

Laverna Inys Wharton testified on her own behalf and, being eight months pregnant, received a suspended sentence and a sturdy fine for organizing the theft of Gudrun Wince's purse. William Wharton paid her fine in cash and then took her to Pittsburgh to shop for a crib.

Buddy Lee Delbert went to work at Biddlebourne Feed & Grain as Barry Dale Green's right-hand man and did a fine job of it.

Patty Leta Keys Delbert broke in a new principal at Biddlebourne High School with no muss or fuss and was promoted to secretary of the school board.

Theodocia Price's recipe box and its original contents were presented to Theodocia's granddaughter Nancy Decker, a computer analyst in Steubenville, Ohio.

The Glory Girls commissioned a portrait of Gudrun Wince and installed it in the museum at Biddlebourne's original high school, which was the first county high school built in West Virginia.

Pearl Gay Osbourn got herself a pit bull named Oscar that barked every time a Hoot 'n' Scoot customer drove up and sat on her lap the rest of the time.

Eleanor Duty began cooking for her husband the way she had when they were honeymooners.

Bertram Kimble had advertising posters made from the picture taken of himself with several hundred of Gudrun Wince's friends at her funeral.

Dooley Skiles started attending worship with Edith Fay at Glory Hallelujah Church, where they were seen holding hands. Afterward, they picked up Corndog the Coonhound at Dooley's house and ate lunch at her house.

Winona Wilcox received an Associated Press award for her *Sentinel* photo of Sheriff Skiles with the long, skinny knife allegedly used by Alwildia Louise Doak to kill Gudrun Cassandra Wince.

Attorney Ted Cavotte discovered that Felkin Wince and Archer Buckingham had died, she in 1972 and he in 1981. But Ted also located their graves, which Edith Fay, Dooley and Corndog visited regularly.

And, oh yes, the backroom boys went fishing.

THE END

ABOUT THE AUTHOR

Appalachian author Susan Spencer-Smith draws on her experience as pastor and journalist to write fiction and nonfiction. Susan wrote and edited at the *Weirton Daily Times* and *Wheeling News-Register* in her native West Virginia and at daily newspapers in Milwaukee, Philadelphia and Dayton. She answered God's call to pulpit ministry at age 40, earned a master of divinity degree at United Theological Seminary, Dayton, and served 16 years as a United Methodist pastor. She lives and writes in Weirton, West Virginia, with help from her husband, Grant Beamer, and Thud the Cat.

Susan's inspirational cozy mysteries come to life in Biddlebourne, the literary double of Middlebourne, West Virginia. Middlebourne is pure Hoopie. What's Hoopie? Hoopie is a special place along the Upper Ohio River Valley claimed by feisty Scots-Irish settlers. And it's a special people marked by hard work, firm opinions and staunch loyalties.

The author, who was born in Sistersville, West Virginia, and whose forebears lived and worked in Middlebourne and surrounding Tyler County, invites readers to pull up a chair to a corner of Appalachia where corn grows tall in the bottoms, muskies run thick in the creek, and locals do things their own way.

www.ingramcontent.com/pod-product-compliance
Lightning Source LLC
Chambersburg PA
CBHW020314260626
47156CB00004B/1219